MINE TO KEEP

SAFE HARBOR SERIES

JEN TALTY

JUPITER PRESS

PRAISE FOR JEN TALTY

"Deadly Secrets is the best of romance and suspense in one hot read!" *NYT Bestselling Author Jennifer Probst*

"A charming setting and a steamy couple heat up the pages in a suspenseful story I couldn't put down!" *NY Times and USA today Bestselling Author Donna Grant*

"Jen Talty's books will grab your attention and pull you into a world of relatable characters, strong personalities, humor, and believable storylines. You'll laugh, you'll cry, and you'll rush to get the next book she releases!" Natalie Ann USA Today Bestselling Author

"I positively loved *In Two Weeks*, and highly recommend it. The writing is wonderful, the story is fantastic, and the characters will keep you coming back for more. I can't wait to get my hands on future installments of the NYS Troopers series." *Long and Short Reviews*

"*In Two Weeks* hooks the reader from page one. This is a fast paced story where the development of the romance grabs you emotionally and the suspense keeps you sitting on the edge of your chair. Great characters, great writing, and a believable plot that can be a warning to all of us." *Desiree Holt, USA Today Bestseller*

"*Dark Water* delivers an engaging portrait of wounded hearts as the memorable characters take you on a healing journey of love. A mysterious death brings danger and intrigue into the drama, while sultry passions brew into a believable plot that melts the reader's heart. Jen Talty pens an entertaining romance that grips the heart as the colorful and dangerous story unfolds into a chilling ending." *Night Owl Reviews*

"This is not the typical love story, nor is it the typical mystery. The characters are well rounded and interesting." *You Gotta Read Reviews*

"*Murder in Paradise Bay* is a fast-paced romantic thriller with plenty of twists and turns to keep you guessing until the end. You won't want to miss this one..." *USA Today bestselling author Janice Maynard*

MINE TO KEEP

A SAFE HARBOR NOVEL

USA Today Bestseller
JEN TALTY

BOOK DESCRIPTION

All Brynleigh "Bryn" Tinsley wanted was to find a safe harbor and put the past behind her so she could raise her little girl in a peaceful, loving environment. Now, three identities later and two thousand miles away, she finds herself in the small, seaside town of Lighthouse Cove, Florida.

The last thing she needs is a pesky firefighter who keeps showing up at every turn, doing his best to become her handyman—and more.

But when her daughter's life is on the line, she'll do whatever it takes to protect her from the hell that is her past.

Jamison Kirby can understand not wanting to speak to your family. He's barely spoken to his mother or brothers in almost two years—much to his father's dismay. So, he doesn't think much of Bryn not wanting anything to do with her daughter's extended family. However, he does take being lied to personally. So, when he finds out that Bryn isn't even her real name, he goes digging into her past. And doesn't like what he finds.

Worse, he pokes a hornet's nest, putting Bryn and her daughter in the line of fire, and forcing Jamison to do the one thing he swore he'd never do.

Call his cop mother and brothers for help.

A NOTE FROM JEN TALTY

Welcome to Lighthouse Cove and the *SAFE HARBOR* series. This series will be all about finding our place in the world. Not just where we belong and who we belong with but searching for the one place we can feel at peace. A connection. Some people come to Lighthouse Cove to relax. To get away from the hustle and bustle of the outside world. However, everyone can agree they stay because the small seaside town gave them the safe harbor their souls craved and the love their hearts desired.

This is Jamison Kirby and Brynleigh's story. Jamison is a local firefighter who is struggling with his identity and Brynleigh is running from a past that will soon catch up to them both. Grab a glass of vino, kick back, relax, and find safe harbor in this romantic story of finding true love when you least expect it.

For Jon Kaplan. And for his beautiful wife, Liz.
Thanks for lending me a few names and ideas!

1

$\mathcal{B}$rynleigh Tinsley rested her hands on her round belly and inhaled sharply. The warm, salty air tickled her nose. She stared at the small, two-bedroom cottage as butterflies filled her gut. After six months of hiding out in one musty hotel after another in the middle of nowhere, she finally felt safe enough to begin her new life.

She smiled. This was it. Her safe harbor.

A place she could call home.

At least, for now.

She glanced over her shoulder. Across the street, a man about her age mowed his front lawn. Two doors down, a young woman planted flowers with her children. Another family rode their bikes down the street.

No one here wanted to hurt her or take away her child.

She glanced down at the life growing inside her body. "We're going to be fine," she whispered.

Living in a place like Lighthouse Cove in south Florida had been something she'd fantasized about for years. It didn't have to be Florida, or the ocean. Just a place where the sun shone, and she could see and hear water on a daily basis. Her late husband had hated tropical weather. Loathed anything this close to sea level. He much preferred the mountains and the snow. He used to say that if he weren't working to stay warm, it wasn't worth it.

Well, her husband wasn't here anymore to tell her what to do, and his family was out of her life.

For good.

That thought was still surreal.

She blew out a puff of air. No way would she shed another tear. Nor would she live in fear. Not anymore. This was her time.

She patted her belly.

"Let's get unpacked."

Not that she had a lot of things. Three suitcases and a duffle bag, to be exact. She'd done her best to save as much money as she could over the last few years of her marriage. Actually, it was more like stealing from the grocery allowance and hiding it where her husband wouldn't look. And it wasn't much. Barely enough to live off. But it was a start.

She lifted her big bag and set it on the sidewalk. The area was even cuter than the pictures she'd seen online. From where she stood, she could look down the street and see the center of town, along with the small harbor that opened into the intracoastal, and the inlet that gave way to the ocean. The scene was right out of a movie set. She loved the little anchors on all the streetlights and how people strolled through town wearing bathing suits and flip-flops. It had a chill vibe. Exactly what she and the baby needed after the year she'd been through.

A cold shiver crawled across her skin. She glanced up and down the street. Gripping her suitcase, she scurried up the sidewalk. The feeling of a million needles prickling her back reminded her that she could change her name and her hair color, but the possibility that Mark and Barb Perish would find her was always there. And if that were to ever happen, Bryn knew the consequences would be worse than death.

The landlord had texted her the code to the keypad and told her to call his buddy who lived a few blocks away on the water if she had any problems at all. Some firefighter, who moonlighted as a handy-man. Chip had said the guy's name was Jamison and that he could handle any problems she might have.

Well, she didn't plan on having any issues. If she did, she'd figure it out. Wasn't that what do-it-yourself videos were for? She couldn't afford to get too close to anyone or rely on someone other than herself. It was a small price to pay to keep her and the baby safe.

The second she stepped into the cottage, she sneezed.

Not once.

Not twice.

But three times.

Blinking, she saw dust particles dancing in the sunlight beaming through the windows. When Chip said that he'd reduce her first month's rent if she cleaned, he'd assured her that the place wasn't in bad shape, and he'd given it a thorough cleaning after the last tenants left.

But that had been two months ago, which meant this place had been sitting empty for that long, collecting cobwebs and all sorts of tiny particles that were now floating around and making her skin itch.

She turned in a circle, scanning the small family room. A picture of a sea turtle rested on the floor next to a dark blue sofa in desperate need of a cover. A matching, oversized chair and ottoman sat in the corner. A television took up space over a working fireplace—and a thick layer of dust coated everything.

It could be worse.

Quickly, she checked the two bedrooms and the one shared bathroom, thankful that the landlord had kept his promise and put a brand-new crib in the smaller room. Only it wasn't assembled. Well, she still had a few weeks to go, and it couldn't be that hard to put together.

She'd wanted to be independent, and this was her

chance to learn how to fend for herself for the first time in her life.

The kitchen had all new appliances and opened into a small, fenced-in yard. To her surprise, she found a swing set, and it looked new.

It would be a while before she'd be using that, but it was a nice touch. She'd have to thank Chip with her famous home-baked bread and a bottle of inexpensive wine.

Now, all she needed was some groceries and cleaning supplies.

Because what she found in the utility closet wouldn't work. She only used organic products because of the baby, and she doubted if that vacuum cleaner had any suction action whatsoever.

Mentally, she did a quick calculation of her funds. She needed to be careful. She only had six weeks before the baby was due. She'd done extensive research on creating an online store for her one-of-a-kind jewelry that she'd started making. However, it wouldn't generate the income she needed to support herself and her child. Not right away. She needed to get a job. Unfortunately, that would be tricky because she couldn't afford daycare.

Her belly bounced as her baby kicked and stretched. She took that as a sign that it was time to head into town.

She stepped out onto the sidewalk and glanced at the sky. The sun beat down on her face, warming her skin. She'd moved from one dingy hotel to the next, each time using a different identity. The idea was to make sure she had no ties to her old life. To erase any kind of paper trail that could lead her in-laws to her or her baby. No one from her past could know where she was. The world she'd come from needed to believe that she'd died.

Tears burned her eyes.

Her late husband and his family had taken almost everything from her, but she'd protect her child. She wouldn't let them destroy an innocent baby like they'd shattered her universe.

Pulling her cell from her bag, she found an all-purpose discount store about ten miles out of town. She'd be able to get everything she needed there, or at least enough to get her through for a few days until she got settled.

As she slipped into the driver's seat, her stomach tightened. She ran her hands over her hard-as-a-rock belly and breathed. This had happened once or twice before. The first time, she'd panicked.

False labor, her previous doctor had called it and then warned her that it could continue happening right up to the last month. He'd assured her that she shouldn't worry, though.

That was another thing. She didn't have a doctor here, and she would have to find one. Fast.

As well as a pediatrician.

The pain in her belly eased, and she let out a long

sigh. It was nothing. She had plenty of time to prepare for the birth of her precious little gift.

She pulled out and made a right as her GPS indicated. No sooner had she sped up than her stomach tightened again. This time, it took her breath away. She blinked, doing her best to focus on the road as she held the steering wheel in a death grip. It lasted all of maybe a minute.

But, damn, it hurt.

The baby kicked and punched as if he or she felt the intensity of it, too.

She laughed. "Did that bother you, little one?" She reached for the knob on the radio just as another —dare she even think it?—contraction hit. This time, she latched onto the wheel as she leaned forward and panted.

The light ahead at the intersection turned red. It took all her energy to lift her leg and hit the brakes. The fierce pain centered in her midsection was all she could focus on.

And it was like nothing she'd ever experienced before.

The light changed to green, but the agony didn't ease. Warmth settled between her legs and grew. She glanced down and gasped.

"No. No. This can't be happening. It's too soon."

A horn honked in the background. Someone shouted for her to move her vehicle. Tires screeched as a car sped past her, but she couldn't find it in her to do anything but rub her belly as the pain slowly eased.

Inhaling sharply through her nose, she dropped her head back and exhaled.

Tap. Tap.

She jumped.

The car lurched forward a tad. Quickly, she put the vehicle in park and rolled down the window.

"Ma'am. Are you okay?" a gentleman with kind, light-blue eyes that reminded her of the ocean asked.

She opened her mouth, but instead of answering him, she groaned and rubbed her stomach. Staring into his pools of comfort, she took a deep breath and blew it out in short pants. The sudden urge to push tore through her body. She felt her face heating.

"Don't push," the man said as he opened the door.

More honking echoed in her ears.

People shouted for her to move out of the way, but all she could think about was how much pressure she felt and that this baby was coming now, whether she wanted it to or not.

The man put his cell to his ear. "This is firefighter Jamison Kirby. I need an ambulance at the corner of Wilton and Sea Side. I've got a woman, early thirties, in labor."

"It's too soon," she managed.

"How far along are you?"

"Thirty-four weeks," she managed between pants,

trying desperately not to push as the contraction subsided.

"She's six weeks early, so we might need a NICU transport," he said in a calm voice. Too calm. He was so even-tempered she wanted to kick him. "I don't know. I haven't gotten that far," he continued. He reached in front of her and set the cell on the dash. "I need to get you in the back seat."

She nodded.

"What's your name?" he asked.

"Brynleigh, but everyone calls me Bryn." She had no idea why she went through that lengthy explanation when this was only the second time she'd even said that name aloud.

"Nice to meet you. I'm Jamison," he said. "I'm a local firefighter, and this isn't the first time I've delivered a baby."

"I'm not having—oh, shit." She fell into the back seat and found there was no controlling her urge to push.

He tore off his shirt. "I know this is hard, but you can't be doing that yet." He lifted her shirt and rolled down her maternity slacks before placing his T-shirt over her belly.

"I can't stop," she managed as she gritted her teeth.

"I can see that. I can also see your baby's head."

Panic squeezed her heart. "I can't do this on the side of the road."

"That's good because you're not on the side, your smack dab in the middle of it. And it's happening right now whether you like it or not, so I'm going to need you to listen to me and do what I say." He caught her gaze. "Bryn. Give me a big push with your next contraction. Okay?"

Hot tears burned a path down her cheeks. She'd known that starting over would be hard. And while she wasn't technically on the run, if she hadn't disappeared, she never would have gotten out from under her late husband's family's thumb.

But she'd never expected to be giving birth, six weeks early, with a stranger delivering, in the middle of town with people standing around and watching, pointing their fingers, holding their cell phones up, snapping pictures for their social media posts. That could destroy everything she'd worked so hard to protect.

However, she couldn't be concerned with any of that now as pain like she'd never experienced before took over her mind and body. She bore down and did her best not to scream a million obscenities.

"That's it, Bryn. Keep pushing. You've got this."

She wanted to tell the handsome firefighter to fuck off. But she didn't have the ability to do anything but push.

And push.

"I need you to stop pushing. Now."

The uncontrollable urge had been like nothing

she'd ever experienced. Had he not tapped on her window earlier, she probably would have been giving birth right through the seam of her pants.

"I can't." She reached between her legs and felt what she thought might be the baby's head.

He pushed her hand away. "Whatever you do. Don't push. Not until I tell you." Jamison took something from his pocket. His arm jerked in a swift motion. "Okay. I need one last push. Now. Bryn. Push now."

She did as he requested and felt her baby leave her body. She exhaled and tried to sit up. "What are you doing?" She stared in horror as Jamison placed the baby on his lap and covered the baby's mouth with his before aligning his fingers with the center of the baby's chest and pushing up and down methodically.

He repeated this action.

"What's wrong with my baby?" she screamed.

Jamison said nothing as he continued breathing oxygen into her baby's lungs before rubbing the center of her body.

Her.

Bryn's eyes filled with more tears.

She had a little girl.

The baby's arms and legs jerked. A sudden cough and cry filled the air. A collective gasp and cheers echoed in the background.

"That's it." Jamison smiled. "You gave your

mommy and me a bit of a scare." He placed her daughter on Bryn's stomach. "She looks big for being born six weeks early. I think she's going to be fine. The ambulance is only a block away. Can I call someone for you?"

She hugged her little girl. Her sweet baby. "No."

"What about your husband?"

"There's no husband. No boyfriend. No father." She rested her hand on her sweet girl's stomach, making sure it rose and fell with breath. She kissed her daughter's head. She smelled like sunshine and sea salt with a hint of caramel. "It's just me and now Zadie."

"That's interesting. Is it a family name?"

She glanced up, but Jamison had taken a step back as a couple of paramedics raced to her side.

As more strangers began examining her and the baby, she searched for the one who had saved her child's life.

But he was no longer anywhere to be found.

Jamison Kirby took the clean shirt his father handed him and tugged it over his head, taking a moment to catch his breath. "Thanks for coming." The crowd had dissipated, and the ambulance had pulled away, carrying mother and child toward the hospital.

"No worries. My office is two blocks up. You're

just lucky I happen to live above where I work."
Dalton Kirby pointed toward the car that Bryn had
given birth in. "If she has no one to call, what are you
going to do with that?"

"I told Bryn I'd have it detailed and leave it at her
place. She literally just moved to town today. She's the
one renting Chip's cottage." Jamison leaned against
his Jeep and adjusted his baseball cap. His heart still
beat wildly and a bit out of control. During his seventeen years as a firefighter, he'd helped deliver two
babies, but they'd been considered easy births in the
sense that the umbilical cord hadn't been wrapped
tightly around the baby's neck, nor did the children
have to be resuscitated.

In all of Jamison's career, he'd never been so terrified as he had been the moment he'd seen the cord
choking the poor child. He'd done his best to remain
calm. The last thing he'd wanted to do was panic
Bryn, but he'd known he had when he started
the CPR.

"I'm glad he was finally able to find someone. I
know it has been hard on him financially to carry his
mom's place."

Jamison nodded. Chip had been incredibly close
to his mother and letting go of her things had become
increasingly difficult. Selling her home was the one
thing that Chip just couldn't do. He believed that if
he did, he'd lose his mother forever. It was a sentiment
that Jamison wished he shared.

"Speaking of mothers. Have you spoken to yours lately?" His father gestured toward his police officer brother, Nathan, who happened to work for their mother, the current Chief of Police.

"Nope. And we're not having this conversation."

"It's been two years since——"

"You finally divorced her," Jamison said. He was tired of the same old argument. "You couldn't forgive her, so why should I?"

"For the record, I left your mother before everything went down. And that's not the only reason we divorced, and you know it. Our relationship was a rollercoaster ride from the get-go, and let's not forget that we married because she was pregnant. That's not necessarily the best reason. Sometimes, I think we kept getting pregnant, thinking it was the only way we would stay married. And we both loved the idea of a big family. But the point is, Steve was only the icing on the cake."

"Are you kidding?" Jamison struggled to understand why his father had stayed with his mom after she'd slept with another man, which had then resulted in a child.

And then, his father had raised that child as his.

Of course, Jamison shouldn't question that decision since he *was* that kid, and he loved the man he called Dad more than he could ever express in words. He was grateful for his father's decision and, most days, wished he'd never been informed of Steve's sperm donation.

Jamison wondered if Steve had only decided to come back into the picture because his wife decided to leave his sorry ass after all the years of the guy pining after the woman who'd chosen to stay with her family instead of running away with him.

"Come on, Dad. You left Mom because she never got over Steve. When he came back to town, it ended your marriage."

"That's not entirely true." His father ran a hand across his unshaven face. "Your mom and I have always struggled, and we were in a bad place when she and Steve had their affair. I left her before that happened, not the other way around."

"Why do you always make excuses for her?"

"I'm not," his father said. "When we got back together, she had no idea that she was pregnant. When we found out, we decided that I was the father, and I was okay with that. I loved her and wanted my family back."

Jamison was the youngest child of six boys, and until a couple of years ago, he'd thought that he was a Kirby. He'd had no idea that his entire existence had been a sham.

"I missed your brothers, and then you came along, and…God, you were such a cute little bugger," his father continued.

Jamison had heard this story so many times over

the last two years, he could mouth the exact words that would tumble from his father's lips.

His mother's exact language would be slightly different, but he could repeat that verbatim, as well.

"She lied to me for my entire life," Jamison said.

"So did I, and you've forgiven me."

"That's different."

"I don't see how," his father said, holding up his hand. "And if you're going to start in on why she and I finally called it quits around the time that Steve came back to town, I had already moved out a few months before. However, I will admit that his return was the final blow. But he's not the only reason. If you think back to your childhood, you'll likely remember that your mom and I had a pretty crappy marriage. As much as we loved each other, we couldn't live together. How or why we stayed all those years after you boys grew up, I don't know. Maybe it's because we were afraid to be alone. Steve made it easy for your mom to make that decision, and it was a relief for me."

"Steve was in Lighthouse Cove for a year before he decided to fuck with our family and had to know if I was his biologically or not. And now they both want me to have open communication. That's never going to happen." It twisted Jamison's gut that his mother even thought it was okay to encourage Steve to text and call. Jamison would never be a part of Steve's life.

He'd had thirty-seven years to get to know Jamison and had done nothing.

No. Jamison was not Steve's son. It didn't matter that the biology was there. Not one bit. Dalton Kirby was his father. He was the man who'd raised him. Who loved him unconditionally. Dalton deserved Jamison's respect. His loyalty. And his love.

"I can't say that I was thrilled he did that, but deep down, your mother and I knew he was your father, even before you were born," his dad said. "I don't like Steve, but he's not going anywhere, and I want you to have a relationship with your brothers and your mom, and that includes Steve's children. Those are your brothers and sisters, too."

Jamison had met Steve's four children a couple of times. They were nice enough, and they struggled with the entire idea, as well. But they were more concerned that Jamison would come in and take their money.

Jamison could care less about that.

"How you deal with Steve's kids is between you and them, but I hope you open your heart to getting to know them. They are *your* flesh and blood." His father tapped his chest. "It hurts *my* heart that you barely talk to your brothers and that you haven't really spoken to your mom since you found out. I blame myself for that. I could have handled the situation differently." His father inched closer, resting a firm hand on Jamison's shoulder. "Nathan is on his way over. Be kind. Your brothers don't deserve your wrath. They didn't do anything wrong."

"They think I should get to know Steve, and not just because of the biology. Because Mom is dating him."

"If you're doing this because of me, then stop. I'm not the least bit intimidated by you having any kind of relationship with Steve. I know the kind of bond we have, and no one can take that from us. No one." His father pulled him in for a manly hug. "I love you, son."

"I love you, too, Dad."

"I'll take your Jeep back to your place," his father said. "You did a good thing today." He patted Jamison on the back. "I'll see you for dinner tonight?"

Jamison handed his father the keys to his SUV. "Of course." He stepped back and watched as his dad had a short conversation with Nathan. He should make a beeline for Bryn's small sedan, but if he did that, he'd never hear the end of it at his dad's place, and tonight was all about meeting his father's new girlfriend, Lanie. Though Jamison had recently learned that his father had been secretly dating Lanie on and off for the last year. The only reason they'd kept it under wraps was that Lanie wasn't sure she was ready after her own divorce, and she lived an hour north.

However, she planned to move to Lighthouse Cove and in with Jamison's dad at some point.

It was something that Jamison had mixed emotions about. He wanted his dad to be happy, and he knew that would never be with his mother. But he wasn't ready for either of them to move on in such a permanent way.

"Hey, Jamison," Nathan said as he strolled across the sidewalk.

Everyone in Jamison's family had ties to law enforcement, except for him and Miles, who was a mechanic—though being a firefighter did put Jamison in the first-responder category. His brother, Rhett, was a private investigator. That said, his defense attorney father used Rhett often, as did Jamison's oldest brother, Seth, who was also an attorney, though he worked in corporate law.

"I'm in a bit of a hurry. What's up?" Jamison exhaled through his nose. The only time he saw his brothers these days was at his father's house or if he bumped into them in town. Otherwise, he avoided them simply because they didn't see any problem accepting Steve into their lives.

They didn't understand why even going for coffee would bother Jamison or make him feel uncomfortable.

"Pretty amazing what you did today," Nathan said.

"Just doing my job."

Nathan laughed. "You were off duty, and you're not a doctor."

Jamison shrugged. Every time he saw one of his brothers, they always tried to shoot the shit like nothing had changed.

When *everything* was different.

At least it was for Jamison.

His entire identity had shifted. Even though he tried to pretend that it hadn't and that he'd forever be a Kirby when his biology said he was a Jayne, his world had changed. His heart ached, and his mind constantly churned all the things about him that were different from his brothers and his dad. Those thoughts haunted him daily.

"You would have done the same thing in my shoes." Jamison didn't feel like a hero, and he didn't want to be labeled as one, especially by any of his brothers. Granted, he put his life on the line every time he ran into a burning building. What he did was dangerous. He understood that the good citizens of Lighthouse Cove needed heroes, and they needed their first responders to be exactly that.

But he was human. Flesh and blood like everyone else.

"I can't say I've ever delivered a baby, much less revived one," Nathan said, glancing around. "Have you talked to Mom lately?"

For fuck's sake. Leave it to Nathan to have a shitty segue into that topic.

"This isn't the time or place to get into it," Jamison said.

"It never is." Nathan glanced around before locking gazes. "Mom would be mad if she knew that I said anything, but she's going through something, and I think you should know."

Jamison rubbed the back of his neck. His mom had been dealing with shit for his entire life. He understood that her job was stressful and that it had caused many of the problems in her marriage to his dad. It was one of the reasons he'd chosen being a firefighter over being a cop.

But that was no excuse for ending up in another man's arms.

And his choice of careers hadn't helped his love life any.

"If Mom wants me to know what's going on, she knows how to get ahold of me."

"That's really fucking funny," Nathan said with a sarcastic tone. "You don't answer her calls, and the last time she showed up at your house, you left by boat so you didn't have to talk to her."

"I had to get to work."

"You can't get to the fire station by water."

"I don't like it when people come to my home unannounced." Jamison had had about enough of this conversation. "Get to the point. I have things to do."

"Mom hasn't said anything to anyone except Nancy and me, and that's only because Nancy was getting a mammogram the same day." Nathan ran a hand across his neatly buzzed head.

"Isn't Nancy kind of young to be having those?"

Nathan and his wife had a couple of young kids, and Jamison had to admit he missed all his nieces and nephews. They were the only reason he went to family gatherings, but he never stayed long because if he did, he always ended up in a fight—if not with his mother than with one of his brothers—and that was never fun.

"She had a scare."

"Is everything okay?" Contrary to popular belief, just because Jamison was pissed off at his brothers for expecting him to forgive their mother and accept Steve, he still loved and cared for them and their families. Just as he loved and cared about his mom.

Nathan nodded. "She has to have a biopsy."

"Shit," Jamison mumbled. He might have issues with his mother, but he didn't wish cancer on anyone. "When is it happening?"

"Next week sometime. And Dad doesn't know, so don't tell him."

"Why are you informing me?" Jamison didn't really need to ask the question. Nathan meant well. All his brothers did, and if they didn't all constantly push Steve in Jamison's face, he'd still be hanging with his bros down at the Crab Shack every Friday night. "If Mom doesn't want people knowing her business, I'm sure that includes me."

"I thought maybe you'd cut her some slack the next time you ran into her. Or perhaps find it in your heart to forgive her."

"Does that forgiveness include bringing Steve into my life?" Jamison pointed the key fob toward Bryn's car and aggressively pressed the button.

"He's in Mom's life whether we like it or not."

Jamison laughed. "Are you trying to say that you don't like Steve or some shit?" When it had come out that Steve was Jamison's biological father, all the brothers had been blindsided. They'd all felt betrayed. For the first month or two, they'd been on Jamison's side. But, slowly, his brothers had started accepting Steve, especially when it became apparent that he and their mom were back together in a romantic way, and that wouldn't change.

His brothers were okay with it because it'd appeared to happen after their parents had divorced —as if that made the entire fucked-up situation okay. It also hadn't happened to them. No one understood what Jamison had to live with or how it affected him psychologically—something he still saw a therapist about.

"I don't dislike him." Nathan planted his hands on his hips and glanced around, letting out a long sigh. "He cares about Mom. He's not a bad person, and I'm not willing to cut her out of my life. Partly because of my kids and—"

"You don't have to explain yourself to me."

Jamison had heard it all before, and he honestly understood where Nathan and his brothers were coming from, especially where the grandkids were considered. If he were in their shoes, he might feel the same way. However, their biology hadn't changed in a flash. Their entire identity—who they thought they were—hadn't become something different overnight.

And the bigger issue for Jamison had always been the fact that no one seemed to care how it affected him on any level. They believed it didn't change anything when it changed *everything*.

"Can you just be kind to Mom and maybe come to Nancy's birthday party this Saturday? I know my family would love to see you, and if you could be kind to Mom, it might calm her down a bit before she goes in for the biopsy on Tuesday. She's pretty nervous about it."

Jamison imagined she would be. "I'll be at Nancy's party. And I'll be on my best behavior. But I'm not ever going to accept Steve into my life. That is something this family needs to accept if they want me to keep coming around."

2

*B*ryn picked up her cell. The battery power was at fifteen percent, and she had no way of charging it. She pulled up the internet and googled a few key phrases about a woman giving birth in the middle of the street in Lighthouse Cove.

A few tweets and Instagram posts popped up, mostly about the man who'd delivered Zadie but it had little about her, which calmed her nerves some. She stared out the window, concentrating all her energy on her daughter. This had to be the longest six hours of her entire life. When they told her that her baby appeared to be strong and healthy, despite being born six weeks early and having had the cord wrapped around her neck, the idea that she had to spend any time in the NICU made Bryn want to crawl right out of her skin.

She set her phone onto the bed and let out a long sigh.

The nurses had taken her down there twice. They'd told her that Zadie weighed in at five pounds three ounces and was eighteen inches long. They considered that to be big for a little one born that early. The doctor had also told her that her daughter's lungs were healthy, and that he saw no reason that Zadie would have to stay in the hospital more than maybe two days—three, tops.

"Here she is," a nurse said as she pushed open the door and rolled in a bassinet with a sleeping Zadie swaddled safely inside. "She's doing great. I wouldn't be surprised if she woke soon looking for her mama. Will you be nursing?"

"I've tried a couple of times. The first time it didn't work so well. The second time, we did pretty good."

"It takes a bit of practice for both baby and Mom." The nurse patted Zadie's belly. "Hit the call button if you need anything."

"Thanks." Bryn hadn't even had a chance to unpack. The crib hadn't been set up—not that she would be using that anytime soon. However, she hadn't even shopped for a car seat. How the hell was she supposed to get her baby home? Heck, she didn't even have bottles or diapers at the house. She dropped her head back and squeezed her eyes closed.

A tear burned a path down her cheek. She

blinked, reaching her hand into the crib to rest it on her baby.

Her precious Zadie.

Knock. Knock.

Zadie startled. Her little body twitched. Her eyelids lifted but quickly closed as she turned her head and settled back into her deep sleep.

Another tap at the door made Bryn swallow her breath. "Who's there?" Bryn called. Her heartbeat sped up. Normally, the doctors knocked but then waltzed right through the door.

"It's Jamison. May I come in?" He stuck his head inside her room.

"Oh. Sure." She sat up in her hospital bed and smoothed down her hair. Never in a million years had she expected to get company. However, she *had* planned on finding Jamison and personally thanking him for what he'd done. She knew that she'd never be able to repay him for saving her baby, but he deserved the gesture, nonetheless.

"How are you feeling?" Jamison held a bouquet in one hand and a teddy bear in the other. He set the vase on the windowsill and stood awkwardly at the foot of her bed. "How's Zadie?"

"We're both doing great. Thanks for asking. And thanks for coming. I was going to try to reach out to you so I could thank you properly. I don't want to even think about what might have happened to me or my little girl had you not stopped."

"I'm glad you're okay." Jamison shifted, squeezing the teddy bear. "I wanted to check in and make sure there weren't any complications. And to let you know I had your car cleaned and dropped it off at your place."

"What do I owe you for that?" No way would she become beholden to anyone for anything. Not even a Good Samaritan.

Jamison glanced down at the stuffed animal before setting it at her feet. "Nothing. Really. Consider it a welcome-to-the-neighborhood gift." He caught her gaze. "You mentioned you had no one to call, and I couldn't help but notice that you had a suitcase and a couple of boxes in your car. Chip, your landlord, who is also a close personal friend, confirmed that you literally moved in today."

"I wouldn't say I moved in," Bryn admitted. Why she felt compelled to tell this stranger anything baffled her. Perhaps it was because he'd delivered her baby. They'd certainly shared an intimate moment. Or maybe it was because she'd spent months not talking with anyone while zigzagging her way across the country, doing her best to disappear from the face of the Earth. "I made a deal with Chip that I'd do the cleaning. I just hadn't expected it to be so dusty. And I'm a little weird about my cleaning products, so I was on my way to the store to get some when I went into labor." She spoke so fast, she became winded by the time she finished her statement.

Jamison smiled. It was kind and sweet and it made his blue eyes sparkle like a million stars in the sky. "Chip loves making deals. And he hates cleaning."

"That's obvious, though the place was in good shape. Just dusty."

"I'm sure. That was his mother's place. She passed away a little over a year ago, but he can't bring himself to sell the place, so he's been renting it." Jamison made himself comfortable in the big, ugly chair next to Zadie. He crossed his legs before taking off his baseball cap. He rested that on his knee and fiddled with the bill.

"I'm sorry to hear that."

"She was a good woman. Everyone loved her," Jamison said. "So, I'm sorry to keep bugging you about this, but you don't have any family or friends here who can help you unpack and clean and get ready for Zadie's homecoming. And you're going to need a ride. This place won't discharge you without an exit plan."

She fought the tears. No way would she cry in front of Jamison. Not about this. She couldn't allow him to see the most vulnerable parts of her life. It was bad enough that she owed him everything. "I'm going to look into one of those medical cabs."

"It's a small town," he said. "I'm not sure one will come out here. And if they do, it's going to cost a small fortune. Besides, it's not necessary. I'm happy to help out."

Being reliant on a man was the last thing Bryn wanted or needed. Her chest tightened. "That won't be necessary."

"But someone needs to drive you home, and I'm offering."

"This is a new beginning for me and Zadie." Time to lay on the thick lies she'd been practicing for the last few months. "You see, my husband passed away right after I found out I was pregnant."

"Wow. That's heavy. I'm so sorry for your loss. But all the more reason to let someone give you a hand."

God. She hated that. She wasn't fucking sorry at all. Not one bit. The bastard *deserved* to die for what he'd done.

"Thank you." She managed the standard response. "However, I'm working on being self-reliant."

"I'm all for that," he said. "Do you have any family who can help you?"

"My parents died a long time ago." She ran her hand over Zadie's bald head. Lying about her family made her stomach cramp. Her mother might be dead, but her father and sister were alive and well and must still be mourning her disappearance and subsequent death.

But it had been the only way to get out from under Mark and Barb Perish's control.

The only way to save Zadie from a life of pure misery.

"That's rough," Jamison said. "What about siblings or your husband's family?"

One of the things her old friend Hatti had taught her was that too much death wasn't believable.

"I have one sister, but we haven't spoken to each other in years. And I'm good with that. She's a self-absorbed bitch." Bryn swallowed her horrible lie about her sister. She might have called her older sister conceited and annoying when they were kids, but if Bryn needed something, she knew she could always count on Anna. "My husband's father died when he was a kid, and he didn't have a good relationship with his mother, so she and I don't speak. I'm okay with that, too."

"That really sucks, but I get it," Jamison said as if he actually understood and didn't judge. Not many people would be okay with the way she'd laid that out, but part of her reasoning had been to keep people at arm's length. Still, she couldn't come off as too cold and uncaring because she needed to find part-time work.

"Honestly, I've tried with my mother-in-law, but she always manages to make it awkward and uncomfortable." Maybe she was opening herself too much to Jamison. But they had shared one of the most intimate moments any two people could.

The birth of a person.

"I'm sorry. I don't know why I'm telling you all of this."

"It's okay. I'm glad you did," Jamison said. "Where's your phone?"

She pointed to the tray next to the bed. "But it's going to die soon, and I don't have a charger."

"I can get you one, no problem." He stood and strolled to the other side of the bed. "Let me give you my number. Call me when you know when they're releasing you, and I'll pick you up and bring you home."

"You've done too much already." How many times did she need to tell him no before he got the hint?

"I don't mind." When he smiled, it created a few deep-set wrinkles around his eyes and showed he'd lived some. "I'll get someone in your place to clean it."

"No," she said sternly. "I can take care of myself."

"I'm sure you can." He crinkled his forehead. "But my sister-in-law told me that one of the nicest things anyone ever did for her when she had her kids was to have someone take care of all the cooking and cleaning while all she did was rest and care for the little ones." He pointed toward Zadie. "She looks all cute and innocent now, but in a day or two, she's going to be keeping you up all night. Why not let me do a few little things now while I've got the time?"

"For starters, I need specific organic products. I'm particular that way."

"Give me a list, and I'll make sure that whoever

cleans follows your instructions to the letter. Or, I'll do it myself." He smiled as if he'd won the lottery.

"Oh, no. I can't let you do that. It's too much." Her voice cracked. She cleared her throat annoyed that so much emotion had bubbled to the surface.

He placed his hand over hers and squeezed. "Do you have anyone else to help you do this stuff? Because if you do, I'll back away slowly and let them take over."

She swallowed the thick lump that had formed in the back of her throat. Honestly, she didn't want to answer that, but if she lied, he'd know it, and there was no point. "What if you're working or something? You said you were a firefighter."

"I am. I have this entire week off." He chuckled. "Though not by choice."

"That sounds interesting and kind of scary at the same time."

"I was injured on the job." He rubbed his shoulder. "I've been in physical therapy for the last two weeks, though I've finally been cleared to go back to work next week."

"I'm glad you're okay."

"It wasn't anything. Just dislocated this sucker." He held her cell in his hands. "So, care to unlock this for me so I can give you my contact information and I can get yours?"

"For all I know, you could be a firefighter by day and a serial killer by night."

He laughed. "I'll just give you my phone number, and you can ask the nurses and doctors about me." He waved her cell under her nose.

Quickly, she unlocked it and handed it back. "Fair enough."

Zadie let out a killer scream.

"I'd better leave you two ladies alone. I'll make sure you get a phone charger before the end of the day. You've got my number. Call me if there's anything else you need. I really don't mind." He curled his fingers around her forearm and squeezed. "Take care of yourself, Bryn."

"Thanks for everything. I'll never be able to—"

"That cry is repayment enough." He smiled before turning on his heels and disappearing out into the hallway.

Bryn reached into the bassinet and lifted her daughter into her arms. "I want to believe that's the kind of man you should find when you grow up, but your father destroyed my faith in all men."

Jamison sat in his father's backyard and rubbed his sore shoulder. He'd gone right from the hospital to physical therapy, where a girl who didn't look as if she were older than twenty tortured him for over an hour. She'd at least given him the thumbs-up to go back to work.

That was all he cared about.

That and making sure Bryn and Zadie came home to a nice, clean house and had everything they needed. Bryn's story broke his heart, and it gave him something else to focus on other than his problems— which, right now, seemed like nothing compared to what had happened to Bryn. She was a brave woman to move to a new town and start her life over from scratch, alone.

"What has you so deep in thought?" Seth asked. He handed Jamison a fresh beer before settling into the chair across the table. Seth was Jamison's eldest brother and a lawyer—a profession he shared with their father. He was married to Farrah, and they had three beautiful children. Jeremy and Kyle were twelve and nine. And Ally was five. The boys were currently out on a fishing boat with friends and their parents, while Ally was with her grandmother, giving her parents a night alone.

Jamison regretted that his niece and nephews weren't present, but he understood that tonight was about Lanie, and he wanted to get to know the woman who had his father's heart. If the youngsters were around, all his attention would be focused on them, not his dad and Lanie.

Though he didn't want to spend much alone time with any of his brothers. He wasn't ready to open himself and let them in just yet.

"I was thinking about Bryn and her baby,"

Jamison said truthfully. He could carry on a conversation, as long as he kept it about anything but their mother and Steve.

"You made the evening news," Seth said. "Though there wasn't much about Bryn, nor were there any pictures of her and the baby."

"She didn't want to be interviewed, and she didn't want to have her image or her baby's plastered all over the place. I can't blame her. That's not how I'd want the first few photographs of my child shared." Not that he would ever have any. He tapped the center of his chest. His life hadn't quite turned out as he'd planned; however, that didn't mean he couldn't find happiness.

"You have a valid point." Seth tilted his beer, raising it in the air as if toasting. His brothers all seemed to be backing off a little and respecting Jamison's wishes.

That was progress, and Jamison had to give them credit for trying. In return, he could honor the promise he'd made to his dad and do the same.

"I certainly would have wanted some privacy for my wife if that had been any of my kids. However, Bryn's family has to be grateful for what you did." Seth had been the first to ask Jamison to accept Steve into his life. To forgive their parents for their actions and let it all go. Seth had told Jamison that it wasn't worth being upset over.

That had hurt Jamison's heart and soul. He'd

hoped that at least one of his brothers would understand his need to take a step back and process how it'd changed the way Jamison felt about himself and his identity.

But, instead, Seth and the rest of his family only wanted to put the past in a bubble and move forward.

It wasn't that simple.

"It's not that big of a deal, and we don't need to keep talking about it." Jamison wasn't about to tell anyone Bryn's business. It wasn't his story to tell. Besides, he did what anyone in his family would have done if they had been driving by—including Seth. He might not be a cop or a firefighter, but he would have done whatever he could to help Bryn and her daughter.

Not because he had to but because he was human, and it was the right thing to do.

"I know you're being all humble and shit, but, seriously, what you did was nothing short of a miracle," Seth said.

"No. It wasn't. And this conversation stops here." Jamison hadn't meant for his tone to come out so harsh. It was hard to be with Seth and not remember the last time they'd been in the same space.

Seth had mentioned something about Jamison acting like a child, and Jamison had asked Seth what he'd do if *he'd* found out that one of his kids wasn't his. Seth didn't take too kindly to that thought but reminded Jamison that while the truth may have come out, nothing else had changed. His mother still loved him just the same, and so did his father and the rest of the family.

The only thing that was different was that Jamison had someone new in his life to get to know, and that wasn't necessarily a bad thing.

Jamison didn't like hearing that, so he'd stormed off.

A childish move. However, all Jamison wanted was to be acknowledged. To be heard. He wanted his family to recognize his feelings instead of expecting him to blindingly move forward.

Seth held up his hands. "Okay, fine."

"I'm sorry," Jamison said, not wanting this dinner to blow up before it started. He not only owed it to his dad to be on his best behavior; he also owed it to himself. Things could not continue this way. Not with his brothers. "It's been a long day. I don't mean to take out my exhaustion on you."

"Enough said." Seth crossed his legs and leaned back. "So, what do you think of Lanie?"

Jamison appreciated that Seth could change the subject without missing a beat. "This is only like the third time I've been around her, and the first time I'm spending any real time with her. I haven't had a chance to form an opinion, but she seems nice, and Dad is happier than I've ever seen him." What mattered to Jamison was his father's happiness, and based on what Jamison had seen so far, his dad was downright giddy.

"Farrah likes her."

"That's always a good test." Jamison smiled. For the first time in a long while, he felt like his old self around his family. "As I recall, Farrah used to like me more than she liked you."

"Oh, no you don't." Seth shook his head vehemently. "Just because my wife went out with you on one date before she and I got together doesn't mean she had any real feelings for you. As a matter of fact, if memory serves, she asked you to take her home before the date really got off the ground because she thought you were me."

Jamison laughed. Hard. It was a full-out belly laugh. "That's a true statement." It felt good to joke around with his family like old times, but he wasn't about to get too comfortable. The second he did, the topic of his mother and Steve was bound to come up, and then things would get ugly.

They always did.

"Don't get up," Farrah said as she stepped through the sliding glass doors, holding a tray of cheese and crackers. "I wouldn't want either of you boys to hurt yourselves."

"Is that a passive-aggressive way of asking me to help?" Seth set his beer on the table and stood. "What else needs to be brought out?"

"There's a platter of shrimp cocktail." Farrah

glanced over her shoulder. "And all the meat that needs to be grilled."

"What can I do to help?" Jamison asked.

"Sit there and look cute because you do that better than my husband." Farrah plopped down in one of the seats.

"Are you kidding me?" Seth curled his fingers through Farrah's hair and tugged. "I'm so much better-looking than him." He planted a kiss on Farrah's lips.

"And a better kisser." Farrah winked. "Now, go help your dad. It's both your turns to do everything. The last time Lanie and I got stuck cooking while the two of you yahoos watched the game."

Jamison took a swig of his beer. He decided that it was best to stay out of this one.

"That's right." Lanie appeared on the patio, holding a bottle of wine and a couple of glasses.

His father stood at her side with two more glasses, setting them on the table. "Seth and I will take care of dinner while you all get to know one another."

Jamison wanted to remind his father that he'd known Farrah since they were in middle school but decided that wouldn't be a good idea since the entire idea behind this evening was for him to spend time with Lanie. Perhaps Farrah would be a good buffer in case Jamison decided to go off the rails.

That was always a possibility.

"I'm happy to sit on the sidelines for this one."

Jamison took the wine bottle and the corkscrew. "Is everyone switching to red for dinner?"

"Hell, yes," his dad said. "My steak demands it."

"Since when do you give a shit about what wine goes with a good steak?" Jamison asked.

"Since he started dating me," Lanie said proudly. "The first time we went out, I was mortified that he was drinking a white and ordered a porterhouse steak. How embarrassing."

"Then I guess we're going to toast to a good woman." Jamison hoped that wasn't too weird to say, but by the smile on his father's face, it wasn't at all.

"So, tell me how it feels to be a local hero." Lanie eased herself into one of the patio chairs and tucked her short, silver hair behind her ears. Even though she'd let her hair go natural, Jamison couldn't believe that she was in her mid-fifties. She had the body of a thirty-year-old, and her skin was flawless. Even her gray hair didn't give away her age.

Her blue eyes sparkled like the stars in the night sky, and she had a smile that could knock the socks off any man.

She looped her arm over the back of her chair. She had a relaxed way about her that Jamison had to admire, especially when he'd been so damn cold every other time he'd been around her—even though he had no reason to be. She had nothing to do with why he was so angry with his family.

"I don't mean to be rude, but I'm not a hero. Not

41

by any stretch of the imagination," Jamison said softly. "And I'd prefer not to speak of it anymore." Though it wasn't just because he was tired of being asked about the day's events. Every time someone brought it up, he saw Zadie with the cord around her neck, her little body turning blue, and the terror filled his mind all over again. He didn't want to relive that anymore.

"Oh, but you are," Lanie said with confidence. "I completely understand your humility and the fact that you don't want to draw attention to yourself, but put yourself in that young woman's shoes or those of her family. Or think if that were Farrah or Nancy and you were any of your buddies. You'd be grateful for their efforts."

He had to admit that she had a point. But that didn't make him a hero.

And it didn't change the horrifying realization that Zadie could have died. If she had, then what would be calling him? Because it certainly wouldn't be a hero.

"That doesn't make me a hero. It makes me an off-duty firefighter doing his job." Jamison uncorked the bottle of wine and left it on the table to breathe while he took a long draw from his beer. There was nothing he hated more than being the center of attention.

Lanie nodded. "If that makes you sleep better at night, I'll give it to you." She took the wine and poured herself a glass. She waved the bottle in front of Jamison and Farrah.

Jamison shook his head. While he enjoyed wine a lot, he wanted to finish his beer first.

Farrah nodded, pushing her glass toward Lanie. "I'll never turn down a good vino."

Lanie took a long sip of her wine and leaned forward. "You know I have two kids of my own, right?"

"Yes," Jamison said. "And my father told me you have a grandchild on the way."

"I do," Lanie said with a beaming smile. "My eldest, Janet, is due in two months. However, Janet was born much like Zadie."

Jamison arched a brow. "Really?" he said.

"My ex and I were on vacation when I went into labor, five weeks early. We were driving on the interstate when my water broke. A police officer delivered Janet at a truck stop. Everything was fine until it wasn't. My daughter was okay, but I nearly bled to death. I'm sitting here today thanks to that officer. He'd tell you that he's no hero, too, but in my eyes, my daughter's, and even my asshole ex-husband's, he's the most amazing man who ever walked this Earth because of what he did that day. Perhaps you believe you were just doing your job, but not everyone can do what you do." Lanie reached across the table and took Jamison's hand. "I get being humble. I understand not wanting everyone to make a big deal of things. But understand that to those you rescue, and to those who witness it, it's a fucking huge deal. Just roll with the compliments. We appreciate you."

No matter how hard Jamison wanted to argue with Lanie, he couldn't. He nodded and smiled. "Thank you," he whispered. "I look forward to meeting your kids."

"Good. They will be at Nancy's birthday party." Lanie pushed the wine bottle in Jamison's direction.

He took it and poured himself a hearty glass. "I'm going to need this after that declaration."

"I thought so."

"This is a lot for me," Jamison admitted.

"I know," Lanie said. "I don't want to bombard you with my family. However, I love your father. He makes me happy."

"That's obvious." Farrah stood. "I'm going to see if those two clowns need my help."

Before Jamison could protest, Farrah was halfway across the yard, and he was left alone with his father's girlfriend.

"I don't believe she was supposed to leave us unattended," Jamison said.

"Your father was more worried about you and Seth than the two of us, but that seemed to go okay."

"So far." Jamison felt at ease with Lanie, a sensation he welcomed, especially when he was in any of his brothers' presence. "The night *is* still young. One of us could stay something that will piss the other off."

"I heard you had a dry sense of humor."

Jamison sipped his wine, swallowing his normal go-to response, which would have been: *I get that from my dad.* But he often didn't know *what* he got from being raised by Dalton Kirby or what he got from having Steve Jayne as his biological father.

"You're not alone," Lanie said. "Some go their entire lives believing one thing about their identity, only to find out something entirely different."

He narrowed his eyes and opened his mouth; however, not a single word tumbled from his lips. He hadn't said that out loud, had he? He cleared his throat. "Excuse me?"

"Did your dad tell you where we met?"

Jamison shook his head.

"I run a support group for family members dealing with an identity crisis."

"Oh, shit," Jamison mumbled. "My dad tried to get me to go to those meetings. I guess I never put it together that you were the woman running it."

Lanie smiled and nodded, much like his therapist did, the one who'd told him that a support group might do him a world of good. But no fucking way was he driving an hour to go and sit, hold hands, and commiserate with a bunch of strangers. It felt weird. It was hard enough to bare his soul to a certified counselor. "The group helped your dad understand what you were going through better. Your anger."

Jamison searched his brain for any memories of

conversations he'd had with his dad about that support group, but he came up with very little because he always tuned him out. Jamison didn't want to hear it. He wanted to hold onto his rage. His hurt. His pain —for as long as he could. It allowed him to feel. Otherwise, he went numb, and that scared him more than anything.

"My dad's been there for me, so thanks for helping him."

"I've been chatting a little with your brothers. Mostly Seth and Miles. I hope that's okay."

"I can't stop you," he said. "But I don't want to be part of any intervention or group-therapy session."

She leaned back, taking her wine glass with her and swirling it gently. "I would never do that. Dalton is my boyfriend now. I'm going to be moving here, and I can't be involved with any of you in that way. But I want to tell you one more thing about myself because I think it's important for you to know."

"All right."

"I was kidnapped when I was two years old." Lanie raised her hand, shushing Jamison. "I didn't know this until my mother, the woman who kidnapped me, was on her deathbed. I was forty-three years old at the time, and she decided to grow a conscience and tell me that she had taken me from a playground. That I wasn't Lanie Fitzpatrick, but that my real name was Tonya Longworth. I thought maybe my mom had lost it in her last days, but a few weeks after she died, I just couldn't let it rest. I had to check into things. Sure enough, I *was* a missing kid. Another mother was out there. One who had mourned me for decades."

"Jesus, that's horrible," Jamison mumbled.

"For the Longworths, yes, it was. But for me, the truth was even worse. I didn't want to know them. I sure as hell didn't want them in my life or upsetting my family. My father, who is technically my stepfather since he married my mom when I was ten, though I call him *Dad*, was devastated. He had no idea, and all the finger-pointing and accusations that came with the truth nearly killed him and the love he had for my mom, who, in my eyes, had been the best mother ever. She'd loved me. Gave me everything. I didn't see a kidnapper or a criminal. A wanted woman. All I saw was my mom." A single tear rolled down Lanie's cheek. She wiped it away. "And she's *still* my mom."

"What about the Longworths? Where do they fit in? Or do they?"

"Oh. They do now. But it took some time for me to get there. Just like this is all taking you some time." She set her glass down and reached across the table. "Just remember that no matter what mistakes people make—and, trust me, they make some big ones while you pay the price—don't let it fester. Nothing here can't be forgiven, and all these relationships can be mended."

3

"Come on little one. You've got this." Bryn had decided to sit in the lounge chair in her hospital room instead of the uncomfortable bed. Her thought process had been that she'd be more comfortable in a fully upright position for breastfeeding and that Zadie would latch on better.

Not.

Zadie smooshed her face against Bryn's breast, her mouth open, grabbing everything but the nipple until she finally found the sweet spot.

Bryn groaned. The nurse had warned her that it would start to hurt and would continue for a good two weeks before it subsided.

Oh, the joys of motherhood.

She smiled. She was a mom. Her precious little girl was here and they were both alive thanks to Jamison. "I wonder if he has a girlfriend or something. I could make him a necklace to give her." She closed her eyes and pulled up a memory of Jamison standing at the foot of her bed. He had such kind, warm eyes, and a sweet, inviting smile.

If only she were any other woman at any other time in her life.

Knock. Knock.

"Brynleigh Tinsley?" a woman asked as she entered the room. She looked vaguely familiar, but Bryn couldn't place her.

"Yes."

"Hi." The woman stood in the middle of the room and smiled. "My name is Suzie Walton. I'm with Channel Four News, and I was wondering—"

"I'm sorry. No." Bryn quickly covered Zadie with the blanket as her pulse soared. Her heart dropped like a brick to the pit of her stomach. "I won't be doing any interviews with anyone. Please, leave."

"But the entire town would like to—"

"She said no." Jamison strolled into the hospital room. "And she asked you to leave. Don't make me call security, Suzie. Because you know I will."

Suzie narrowed her eyes. "Nice to see you, too."

Jamison held the door open. "Take care."

The reporter turned on her heels and stormed off.

"Thank you. Again." Bryn lifted the blanket and checked on Zadie, who was blissfully unaware of what had been going on.

"Suzie's always looking for a story. She was at my

door before I even poured my morning coffee." Jamison sat on the edge of the bed. He set a bag down on the tray, and she noticed the amazing aroma before it registered. Meat. Cheese. Something fried. It was incredible. "You were right to say no to her. She's a gossip and tends to twist things. And, she lies. I bet she told you she was with the local news."

Bryn nodded. "Well, she's not. She does some YouTube and podcast thing. Sadly, she has a ton of followers and gets a lot of attention, but I'd steer clear of her. However, if you do want to tell your story, I know a guy who will do it right."

"I prefer to stay out of the spotlight. I hate social media and all that stuff."

"I'm with you on that," Jamison said. "You never texted me your contact information."

"My phone died."

"I figured. That's why I brought this." He held up a cord. "Where is it?"

She pointed to the tray next to the bed.

"How was your first night as a mom?" Jamison asked as he plugged in her cell.

"Pretty uneventful, which I guess is good." She resented Jamison showing up and helping her with her cell, but whatever was in that bag smelled so freaking good she was salivating. The hospital food had left her feeling less than full. "I do appreciate you coming back with the cord, and I'm hoping that whatever is in that food bag is to share. However, as I told you yesterday, this is a fresh start for me. One of independence. One where I take care of myself." Now, she was talking too much. She bit down on her lower lip.

"For the record, I have a mandatory work meeting in the hospital in forty minutes. Figured I'd stop by, charge your phone, and make sure I have your discharge information because, seriously, they won't let you out without a ride home. So I told them I'm that guy." He pulled the tray to the foot of the bed and lowered it as he took out two Styrofoam containers.

She adjusted herself and rested Zadie over her shoulder, giving her a good pat on the back. "If I agree to you bringing me home, will you promise to back off?"

He opened the boxes, and the aroma hit her nostrils like a rocket ship punching through the atmosphere.

Fried, crispy onions.

Greasy meat.

Melting cheese.

She scooted to the edge of the chair and went to stand but groaned instead.

"May I help you?" He held out his arms. "I can put her in the bassinet. You can trust me. I'm really good with babies."

"I know. You saved her life." Bryn handed her precious Zadie to Jamison. "I don't mean to sound ungrateful."

"You don't." Jamison lifted an onion ring and plopped it into his mouth.

She followed suit. It had to be the best thing she'd eaten in months.

"I guess I feel a little responsible for you and Zadie, considering what happened. I only want to make sure you're both okay. That's all. So, yes. I can back off once you're tucked safe and sound in your home." He picked up a pickle and waved it in the air.

Jamison was like no one Bryn knew back in her old circles. Her late husband and his family wouldn't dare eat anything with their fingers. Not even fried chicken. God forbid.

"Speaking of which, Chip and I are going to make sure it's all ready for you and Zadie to come home tonight because the nurse told me that she believes they are letting you out tomorrow."

"As long as everything stays the same, that's what they told me, as well." She took the fork and knife and cut the cheeseburger in half. "Are you sure you don't mind bringing me home?"

"Not at all. Now, eat. You're not going to find a better burger than that one."

"It smells freaking awesome." She took a bite and immediately closed her eyes and moaned. She'd been living on fast food for months. This tasted like the finest sirloin burger money could buy. "I've died and gone to hamburger Heaven."

"If you'd like, I can put together a list of restaurants, stores, and anything else you might want or need and leave it at the house."

"Chip said he had a book for me somewhere."

"I'll check on that for you tonight."

She glanced over her burger. "I appreciate it. But, really, you've done enough, and I like to explore."

"Am I really coming on that strong?"

"Like a category-five hurricane."

He laughed. "It's all Zadie's fault." He glanced over his shoulder. "She's kind of stolen my heart. Seriously, though. I understand. And I hear you."

"Thank you." For now, Bryn would enjoy the food. Tomorrow, once she was home, she'd be able to lose herself in her work and, hopefully, the sexy firefighter would stop coming around. Because not only was he way too helpful, he was incredibly easy on the eyes.

And that was a distraction she didn't need.

She couldn't afford to let her guard down. Just because the world thought she was dead, didn't mean someone like Suzie Walton couldn't accidentally resurrect her.

Jamison cracked open a second beer and handed it to Chip before settling down in one of the Adirondack chairs he'd purchased for Bryn. He knew it went beyond the scope of being neighborly. However, she needed something for her backyard. She needed a lot of things. He didn't want to overwhelm her, but he'd likely insult her by just doing it. He didn't know her tastes, and he should have learned from his ex-wife that buying things for the house without a woman's approval wasn't the smartest thing in the world.

"I'll reimburse you for these," Chip said as he settled into the other chair. He wiggled as if testing out the sturdiness.

"It's not a big deal." Jamison knew that Chip was strapped for cash and should probably sell the house, but he couldn't bring himself to do it. Not only had it been his childhood home, but his mom had grown up here, as well. Two generations. If it were up to Chip, he and his family would live here, but his wife thought it was too small—which it was, but they could expand if they wanted to and without too much work. When Chip found out that his new tenant was single and pregnant, he'd made some minor adjustments, like buying a crib and lowering the rent. But he could have had the place cleaned instead of negotiating it into the reduction of the monthly payment. But that was Chip. He had a soft heart, but he was cheap as hell.

His wife was probably steaming mad over the entire thing. She constantly threatened to put the place on the market while he was sleeping, but she'd never do it. Deep down, she understood that it might take a year or two before Chip could let the house go.

"I get the impression that Bryn, your tenant, doesn't have a lot of money to buy the extra things she needs." Jamison leaned back, crossed his ankles, and looked at the evening sun. No matter how hard he tried, he couldn't get Bryn out of his head. He'd delivered two babies. One when he was only twenty-two years old, and a pregnant woman had gotten trapped in an elevator. When they finally got it open, the baby's head was already crowning.

It had been a profound moment in Jamison's life, and he'd never forget it, but the woman hadn't stuck in his mind the way Bryn did now. Something about her tugged at his heartstrings. It wasn't her sad story, though that twisted his gut. He couldn't imagine what it would be like to have to raise a baby alone.

It was more than that. Maybe it was her fierce need to do things her own way. That was something he could relate to.

"Yeah. I figured that out. I wish I could do more to help. I've already reduced her rent to the point where I'm only paying my bills on this place."

"I bet that pissed Erica off."

"You have no idea. I think I'll be sleeping on the sofa for a few nights until she cools off." Chip raised his beer. "I can't pay you for any of the work you're doing today and can only reimburse you for a few things you purchased."

"I don't expect you to, and I'm sure Erica understands."

"I'm sure she does, too. She's just tired of me holding onto the past."

"You'll get there when you're ready."

"You've had one too many therapy sessions."

Jamison didn't tell many people his personal business, but Chip knew enough. However, he didn't want to talk about it. "What do you know about Bryn?"

"Not much. She paid both first and last plus security deposit. All her paperwork was in perfect order, and you know me, I'm a sucker for someone in need. And you, my friend, don't know how to say no or stop doing things for people, like buying all this stuff." He waved his hand around at the patio furniture.

His standard response would normally be: *It's in my DNA.* But that wasn't something he could say anymore so he sipped his beverage instead.

Jamison could tell that Bryn was a proud woman and she wouldn't let him do all this for nothing. That was something he could understand. But he wasn't sure he could take a single penny from Chip or her. He'd have to find something to barter.

"You're never going to make being a part-time handyman pay off if you don't start taking money for your work, or at the very least, let me pay for some of the materials."

"Trust me. I'll get this business off the ground and make it profitable. And I'll take some pictures of what we're doing here today and tomorrow to put on my website."

Chip tossed his head back and laughed. "Because you actually set one up and know so much about computers."

"I will eventually." Jamison had started doing side jobs when he got married. A firefighter's salary wasn't anything to brag about, and his ex-wife had a taste for the finer things in life. He had loved her, though, and had wanted her to have some of those things, so he was willing to take on extra work to make his wife happy. But nothing he did was ever good enough.

Now, he could certainly live on his income, but he preferred to be busy, and this gave him something to occupy both his mind and body. Not to mention, it would keep him out of trouble. "I need more work than I'm getting from word of mouth."

"I'm always recommending you."

"I appreciate that." Out of the corner of his eye, he saw his mother's police SUV turn the corner. Inwardly, he groaned. In the last two years, he'd thought about moving several times. He'd even gone so far as to reach out to a few fire chiefs in other towns. But he couldn't bring himself to leave his hometown. He'd always thought that he'd raise his family in Lighthouse Cove.

Of course, that dream had left the building when Cheryl, his ex-wife, decided that he wasn't a good enough provider. That what he did would never be the right profession. When she found out that Steve was his biological father, she'd wanted Jamison to ask him for a job.

Never going to happen.

It had been a year since his divorce, and while he'd dated, he hadn't found anyone that he was willing to risk having his heart ripped to shreds for again.

That thought brought him right back to Bryn for some reason.

She had a certain strength that he admired. A fierce, independent streak. But behind that was a vulnerability that he couldn't ignore. He'd felt the loneliness that seeped from deep within her soul. And he could tell that she wanted to hide the pain that'd brought her to this seaside town. Whatever it was, though, she wanted to bury it and then forget it.

Only, of all people, he understood that wasn't possible. When he'd first found out about Steve, Jamison had taken all his vacation time and left for six weeks. He hadn't told anyone where he was going, except his ex-wife. He'd begged her to come with him. To help him through his difficult time, but she'd chosen to stay at home.

And get to know Steve.

That didn't help.

Jamison didn't call home or answer his cell. He'd spent nearly the entire time on a friend's boat, fishing in the Bahamas.

And drinking.

And thinking.

Cheryl had been livid, but for all the wrong reasons. She'd thought that Jamison was being unreasonable. That he should be bonding with his new father.

No fucking way.

Of course, Jamison had suspected that the affair had begun about the same time. Not that it was his fault, but he certainly hadn't helped his marriage any by telling his wife that if she chose not to come and be by his side, she could kiss his ass. She'd hung up. Eventually, he'd felt bad and tried to make amends. He'd wanted his wife by his side as he tried to sort out the fact that he had two sisters and two more brothers, and that his mother had been in love with someone other than her husband for as long as he'd been alive.

It had been a lot to take in.

But Cheryl wouldn't leave, And when they spoke on the phone, because she was the only one he answered his cell for, she always seemed to take Steve's and his mother's sides.

Never her husband's side.

That had been a different kind of betrayal.

The sound of a door shutting caught his attention. He closed his eyes for a brief moment. "How does my mother know I'm here?"

"I didn't tell her." Chip stood. "Do you want another beer?"

"If I have to deal with her, I'm going to need that and maybe a shot of something a little stronger."

Chip laughed. "I might have brought over something a little stronger." He ducked into the kitchen just as Jamison's mother walked around the side yard and entered the patio through the back gate.

Growing up as the son of the Chief of Police had been interesting, to say the least. It was never fun getting caught doing typical teenage shit, and he often had to be the voice of reason only because his mother would have personally put him in handcuffs.

And she would have enjoyed it.

Jamison inhaled sharply. He covered his forehead and squinted. "Hello, Mother," he said. "What are you doing here?"

"Looking for you. I've tried calling and texting, but you haven't responded. Like usual." She folded her arms across her chest and leaned against the fence. She wore a pair of dark slacks and a golf-type shirt with the Chief of Police logo on the upper right side. Her gun was secured to her hip like it had been for as long as he could remember. "I heard what you did yesterday. That young mother and baby are very lucky from what I understand."

"It was nothing." The last thing Jamison needed was his mom making him out to be some hero when she, herself, had done some pretty heroic things throughout her career, especially when he knew that she was only using this particular incident to strike up conversation. All she wanted was to mend fences and have him accept her boyfriend into his life.

He wasn't ready.

And he might never be.

"You saved a life."

He rubbed the back of his neck. Every time he thought about Zadie, he remembered how utterly terrified he'd been that she wouldn't make it, and how scared Bryn had looked the second he'd started CPR. That first cough that'd led to a cry had been music to his ears. "What do you want, Mom?" He thought about bringing up the biopsy that Nathan had told him about, but he didn't want to get his brother into trouble. Besides, if his mom wanted him to know, she'd tell him. Actually, he was surprised that she wasn't using it to gain sympathy.

"It's really good to see you, too, son."

It was hard to miss the sarcasm in his mother's tone.

"This isn't my home, so you've gone out of your way to find me. Is something wrong? Is someone sick?" Hopefully, by putting it out there, if his mother's health was why she'd come by, that would be the segue she needed.

"No." His mom let out a long breath. "Everyone is fine. I wanted to talk to you about Nancy's birthday party. If you're not there, all your nieces and nephews will be upset. And if their grammy isn't there, they won't be happy either."

"Have I ever missed a family event because you were there?" He went to every single one and did so with a smile on his face. He didn't always stay long, though. That depended on his mother and if she expected him to carry on any kind of conversation.

"No. But I've never brought Steve before. Your father's bringing Lanie, and this party will be huge. Oh. And Cheryl's coming, as well."

Fucking wonderful. But if Jamison dared to miss Nancy's big fortieth, he'd never hear the end of it. Besides, he was trying to repair his relationships with his brothers. So far, it hadn't been going all that well, and Jamison wasn't sure if it was because they were so accepting of their mother and her boyfriend or if Jamison was intolerant of it.

Perhaps it was something else altogether.

Then there was the issue of his ex-wife and her relationship with his mother. It didn't make sense.

Or maybe it did. Perhaps Cheryl and his mom had bonded over cheating on their husbands.

Shit. He doubted that was true, but his mom sure did want him to get back together with his ex, and that was never going to happen.

Not in this lifetime.

"I can't control who you date or who is invited to a party that isn't mine." Jamison swallowed. He had no intention of disappointing his sister-in-law or any of his nieces and nephews. They were all innocent in this family feud. And if Jamison were being completely honest with himself, he wanted all his brothers in his life. The last two years without them had been harsh.

His father was right. It was time to fix those relationships. It wouldn't be easy, and all five of his siblings would have to at least try to understand his point of view when it came to Steve. After the other night with Seth, that was looking like more than a possibility.

But he couldn't forgive his mother. Not until she stopped forcing Steve and his four kids down his throat. His siblings needed to accept that, as well. Their situation with Steve was much different than Jamison's, and they needed to stop pretending that it wasn't.

"Does that mean you'll be there even if I bring Steve?"

"Yes," Jamison said, wishing Chip would hurry the fuck up with that damn beer.

"And what about if any of his kids are there? They are your half-siblings."

"Thanks for the reminder that my other brothers, you remember, the ones you *birthed*, are only actually my half-brothers," he said sarcastically.

"They are all your family. That will never change," she said. "Do I have your word you'll be there."

"I said I'm coming. I won't back out."

"You have no idea how much that warms my

heart. Steve will be so happy. He wants to get to know—"

"You can stop right there." Jamison leaned forward and caught his mother's gaze. "I'm not going to spend time with that man, so don't you dare ask me to, or put me in a situation that will force me to."

"That *man* is your biological father."

A deep growl filled Jamison's throat. He stood and turned his back on his mother.

She placed her hand on his shoulder.

He shrugged it off and spun on his heel. "Don't you ever call him that. I have a father. You know, the man you cheated on."

"I understand that this has been hard for you, but it's not like I'm asking you to go and change your name or forget who raised you."

"Well, thank God for small fucking favors," Jamison mumbled. Too often, when he got into these conversions with his mother, he felt like a small child having a temper tantrum. The problem was that it wasn't only the fact that his mother had had an affair that'd resulted in a child. Him. Or that she and his father had lied about it until two years ago.

It was that Steve had suspected that he was Jamison's father and had done nothing until he came to town and decided that he was still in love with Jamison's mom.

"Don't be like that," his mom said. "I don't think it's too much to ask that you show some kindness to

Steve." She swiped at her eyes before the tears that had welled in them could escape. "Hell, I wouldn't mind it if you could be a little nicer to me." She shook her head. "You forgave your father for lying, but you can't find it in your heart to even try with me, and I don't get why you stay so pissed off at your brothers."

Jamison had different reasons for each of his siblings, but mostly it had to do with how he felt as if he'd somehow become an outsider in his own family. Not one of them understood how he saw the differences between himself and them all of a sudden instead of the similarities.

And it became worse when they pointed out how much Jamison looked like Steve. Or that he had the same hair color.

Or how he had some of the same mannerisms.

That was the last thing Jamison needed.

"I'm trying, Jamison." His mother lifted her palms to the sky and then let them fall to her thighs. "I gave you space when all this came out because I thought you needed some time to digest, but the longer we go on like this, the harder it gets to talk about anything."

"It all comes down to one thing, Mom. I'm not interested in knowing your boyfriend. I don't want to have any kind of casual conversation with him or sit at a table and break bread. I will tolerate being in the same space at family gatherings hosted by my brothers, but I won't shoot the shit with him or engage at any level. So, if you have any expectation of that happening, you're only going to be disappointed."

His mother pursed her lips. "What about our relationship? How are we to ever repair it if—?"

"Get rid of Steve. That would be a good start."

"That's not fair." His mother planted her hands on her hips. "When you married Cheryl, we accepted her into the family."

Jamison laughed. "Are you fucking kidding me? That isn't even close to the same thing. And you still favor her over me half the time."

"Because I'm not sure you should have divorced her so quickly. You didn't even go to therapy when there was so much going on in your life. You basically cut Cheryl out and—"

"And what, Mom? Because if that next statement isn't that she cheated on me and destroyed our marriage, I've got nothing left to say."

"You're behaving like a spoiled child."

"Perhaps I am." Actually, he knew that was how he was acting. And, frankly, he didn't give a rat's ass. Every single time this came up, he felt like the rug had been pulled out from under him and was remined how his entire world had changed in a flash.

"Your father doesn't have a problem with you and Steve—"

"This isn't about Dad," Jamison said. "This is about you and what you and Steve did to me and how it changed my life. You didn't think about my feelings

—or Dad's—when you did that DNA test. It was all about Steve."

"It was about finally telling the truth." His mother sniffled. "Steve came back because the guilt of leaving you had been eating him alive for years. You don't know what it's like to let another man raise your child."

"Really? Then why did he wait a full year after moving back to Lighthouse Cove to tell me that he was my father?"

"It's complicated. He left. He got married and had a family. He couldn't just leave. Just like I couldn't. "

"A bunch of excuses." Jamison's stomach turned over. This was the part of the conversation when he generally lost his shit. Tonight, he would bite his tongue. He'd made a promise to his father, and now to Lanie, that he'd do better. "I don't want to fight. But I also don't want to talk about it constantly."

"If we don't, then how do we get past it?"

"You all made the choice to make me a Kirby. And, to be honest, I'm happy as a pig in shit that you did. I'm proud to be Dalton Kirby's son. I want to keep it that way." The worst day of Jamison's life had been when everyone in Lighthouse Cove had found out that he wasn't a Kirby by blood. "I don't think we have anything else left to discuss."

"You're breaking my heart."

"You broke mine two years ago when you showed

up at my door with Steve and told me that he was my father," he said.

His mother turned and slipped through the fence. She didn't glance over her shoulder once before disappearing around the corner.

A few minutes later, the sound of a car engine tickled his ears.

Jamison stomped though the door into the kitchen where he found Chip leaning against the counter with two shots lined up next to a couple of open beers. "You could have come out and saved me."

"Fuck, no," Chip said. "I know better than to do that with your mother, especially when she's carrying a loaded weapon." He handed Jamison a shot. "Bottoms up."

Jamison clanked the glass on the granite top before downing the liquid. It burned for a few seconds before warming his gut. "Let's go paint a baby girl's room and put together some furniture." He would make sure that Bryn and her precious daughter, Zadie, had more than they needed when they came home.

4

*B*ryn's heart pounded so fast she could barely catch her breath. In her previous life, she'd had all the comforts money could buy. When she'd first met Timothy, he'd been super charming and showered her in lavish gifts, constantly surprising her with romantic weekend getaways. They would board a private jet and head off to Paris or the Greek islands for three or four days and think nothing of it.

The first year of their relationship seemed unreal. Looking back, there had been signs of what was to come, but she'd completely ignored them. She hadn't wanted to believe that her perfect future husband wasn't so perfect.

But she'd found out three days after they returned from their honeymoon exactly what type of man she'd married, and no amount of pretending could change what went on behind closed doors.

She stole a quick glance at Jamison. He had short, dark hair with piercing blue eyes that she found herself swimming in every time she looked into them as if they were a pool.

"Are you okay?" Jamison asked. "You're being really quiet."

"As opposed to what? Because you barely know me." She chuckled as he rolled his Jeep to a stop in front of a red light.

"I guess I'm not used to women who don't talk a lot. My mom can be quite the chatterbox, and my two sisters-in-law certainly know how to dominate a conversation."

She studied the street signs and any major landmarks, trying to get her bearings. She'd only been in town for three days, and she hadn't a clue as to where she was. Of course, she'd spent that entire time in the hospital.

"Now I know where you get it from."

He laughed.

She shouldn't have teased him. It could give him the wrong idea, and the last thing she needed was him thinking that she liked him or something.

"I do get picked on at the station occasionally for talking too much. I often turn the television on just because I don't like silence. I think it's because I'm the youngest of a bunch of loud-mouthed boys."

She yawned.

"Am I boring you?"

"I'm sorry. I'm tired and don't know where I am."

"I was kidding."

The Jeep jerked forward when the light turned green.

Jamison turned left on May Circle. That felt vaguely familiar, but she didn't recognize anything about the street.

"I keep forgetting you only spent about five minutes here before you gave birth to that cutie back there." He glanced over his shoulder and smiled. "When you're feeling up to it, why don't you let me show you around? Lighthouse Cove is small and pretty much everything you need is right within the town limits, but there are some things you might need that are twenty to thirty minutes away, like some of the big-box stores."

"I can't let you do that. You've done too much for me as it is. I'm sure you've got better things to do." The last thing she needed was to become dependent on Jamison. Or to owe him any more than she already did. "Do you have a girlfriend?"

He did a double-take. "I do not. Why do you ask?"

"I make jewelry. I thought maybe I could give you a few special pieces to pay you back for all you've done."

"My sister-in-law is turning forty this weekend,

and I do need to get her a gift. But I would insist on paying for it."

"Absolutely, not," Bryn said with some enthusiasm. "I won't take your money, and it would be an honor for me to make her something."

"I can't let you give me something you're selling."

"Oh. Yes, you can." She nodded wildly. This could be her first big break. If Jamison knew people in this town, and that was the impression she got, he could send people in her direction. "Especially when you can tell people about my business. You'd be doing me a favor."

He turned onto the main drag. Finally, a road she recognized.

"I haven't gotten my website up and running yet, and I plan on selling on Etsy and some other places. Now that I'm home, I should be able to get something simple done by this weekend. I doubt I'll be able to get cards with my URL and contact information printed by the party, but I do have a website name. They could google it. I'm sure I'll have it done by next week, but if you could tell people about my jewelry, and if you find something you like for your sister-in-law, that would be amazing."

"I'm happy to help spread the word about your business," he said. "Who's doing your site?" He pulled into the back driveway and parked behind her vehicle, which he'd parked under the carport. "If you don't mind me asking."

"I am. It's not that hard. It's a template. All I have to do is populate it with my product."

"I'm an idiot when it comes to stuff like that." He shut off the engine. "I do a side handyman gig and keep meaning to set up a place where people can find me online, but I don't know shit about doing things like that."

"It's super easy. The only negative is that it's time-consuming."

He laughed. "I don't have the patience. I just need to hire someone to do it for me. Interested?"

"Are you serious?"

"Very."

Zadie stirred, making screeching noises, which meant she'd be at a full scream in about ten minutes. The nurses had all told her that she needed to let Zadie wake up and cry some before feeding her; otherwise, she'd simply go back to sleep. "I'd feel weird taking your money, considering all that you've done for me, especially when I bet I can do your website in an afternoon."

"I'm happy to barter," he said. "A piece of jewelry for the website."

"You've done so much more."

"Okay," he said with a chuckle. "My niece will be having a birthday in about three weeks. She's turning six. Maybe you could find me some appropriate earnings since she does have her ears pierced. That's two pieces for a website."

"Sounds fair, except what about all this other stuff?" She twisted and pointed to the car seat, which held her precious baby. "You wouldn't let me give you anything for that. And you mentioned that you and Chip put together my crib. Which I appreciate, but I have to tell you that I feel weird about you being in my home and putting away my stuff." Bryn had wanted to keep a picture of her sister, but Hatti had talked her out of it, reminding her that if she had a single picture or kept any items from her past, even something obscure, it could be a clue that brought her past into her present.

And that wouldn't be good.

Bryn couldn't afford to have her ex-in-laws anywhere near Zadie. They would do whatever it took to take her daughter away from her. So, Bryn wasn't afraid that Jamison would have found something while he was in her home. That wasn't the point.

She just didn't want anyone in her space. Timothy didn't allow her any privacy, and having someone poking around her stuff made her break out in hives.

"I didn't mean to offend you. I was only trying to be neighborly and help. You didn't have a few things, and they were absolutely necessary. If you need to pay me back for the car seat and stuff, you can. I'm okay with that."

"Thank you." Now, all she had to do was figure out how she would manage it. She'd blown through much of her savings, and rent was due soon.

"But don't feel like you have to pay all at once," he said as if he'd read her mind. "Also, I bought a few things I didn't tell you about." He held up his hand as he scooted from behind the steering wheel and slipped from the driver's seat. "Some of it Chip needed to do for this place, and he's going to pay me for it."

She let out a long breath. Before her mother died, she always used to tell Bryn to never look a gift horse in the mouth. That there was nothing worse than insulting someone who went out of their way with a kind gesture. Her mom then asked Bryn to put herself in the other person's shoes.

If it had been Bryn who'd done all this for a friend, and it had been genuine, she'd be upset if someone weren't appreciative.

Jamison opened the passenger door and took her hand. "For the rest, I have all the receipts so you can exchange anything you don't like. And I get that you want to pay for your own things. I do. But you didn't even have a baby shower or anything. My two sisters-in-law had those, and they got a ton of stuff. Consider this that."

"But you're one person, and please don't think this rude, but I don't want to feel like I constantly owe you something."

"Just the website. That's all I want in return. And maybe a few pieces of jewelry." He winked before pulling the car seat out of the vehicle.

"I could have gotten that." She tilted her head and glared. "I gave birth. I didn't break my arms."

"You should be taking it easy for the next few weeks. And since you live alone, you can let me carry this inside for you. Besides, I was raised to be a gentleman."

A year ago, she would have thought chivalry had died. She strolled toward the front door, biting her tongue. Jamison wasn't Timothy. And just because he was being nice and a bit over-the-top didn't mean he would turn into a controlling, manipulative asshole. Especially because she wasn't going to let him worm his way into her life. She was a totally different person than she was ten years ago.

"Let me get that," he said.

Her pulse raced as she stepped through the threshold. Holding her breath, she covered her mouth. Tears burned the corners of her eyes. Everything looked different.

It wasn't just clean. There was a white cover over the sofa, and a new rocking chair in the corner with a blanket tossed over the back. He'd hung a picture over the couch and a television above the fireplace.

And the best part was, there wasn't a speck of dust anywhere.

"I didn't unpack your suitcases. I thought that might be weird." Jamison set the car seat on the coffee table.

"Because the rest of this is all completely normal."

He seemed to ignore her sarcasm. "They are on your mattress in the bigger bedroom. I did, however, put away the few things I bought for Zadie. Though, I suspect you're going to need a lot more."

Zadie fussed. Her legs wiggled, and she stretched out her arms.

Bryn rocked the seat back and forth as she contained her frustration by taking one cleansing breath through her nose. Anger was not the appropriate response in this situation. "While I appreciate all of this, I really do, you can't keep randomly doing things for me without my knowledge or without asking."

"I know," he said. "I never would have gone this far if you had family or friends here. But you don't, and you needed the bare necessities." He raised his hand when she opened her mouth to protest. "You have my word that this is the end of it."

"Thank you." She bent over and unbuckled Zadie, lifting her into her arms, cradling her against her chest and taking a deep breath of new-baby smell. It was a hundred percent better than new-car smell— one of the only things she'd learned to appreciate when married to Timothy.

Back then, becoming a mother had been all Bryn wanted, but she'd put it on pause after the first time Timothy had put hands on her. Lucky for her, he had wanted to wait a couple of years. She'd thought maybe the stress of joining the family business had gotten the best of her new husband, but she'd soon learned that Timothy had a temper, and the longer they stayed married, the worse it got.

Jamison smiled like a giant kid. "However, you do need to go and see Zadie's room. And before you go and get mad at me, most of it was Chip's idea, and he footed the bill for it. He also left you a note."

"He mentioned something about the baby and a housewarming gift." She pressed her cheek against Zadie's forehead. She wasn't used to this kind of generosity. Not unless it was attached to a condition that came in the form of a bruise. Her husband might have lavished her with expensive presents. However, everything he'd ever given her was either out of guilt for something he'd done or as a way to control her. And it'd worked. For years.

"Chip can be a little bit on the cheap side, but he wanted to do something nice when he heard about what'd happened."

She followed Jamison down the short hallway, which had a fresh coat of paint. She gasped the second she stepped into Zadie's room, which now had decals of all the Disney princesses plastered across the walls. Her crib had been set up by the window, and matching princess sheets covered the mattress. On the other wall was a brand-new changing station, and across from that, a dresser.

Everything she and her daughter could possibly need was in this room.

Tears filled her eyes. "I can't accept all of this."

"Yes, you can." He looped his arm around her shoulders and gave her a firm squeeze. "Every fresh start in life deserves new, fun things."

"You don't understand what it's like to be alone," she managed between sniffles. Thus far, she'd told him as little as possible about her past, but she had mentioned her sister and how hard it was not to have her in her life. That was a true statement. When her best friend Hatti had suggested that Bryn not only disappear but also find a way to fake her death, Bryn had thought she was nuts. But Hatti had been right when she mentioned that it wouldn't be a good idea to have the world turning over every rock searching for a missing person. Especially because the Perish family had unlimited funds, and if they knew about the baby or had any inclination that Bryn was still alive, they wouldn't stop until they found her.

It was best if everyone believed that Brenda Thompson Perish had died the same way her husband had—in a tragic car crash.

"I have no one. And while when it comes to my mother-in-law and sister, that's by choice. I'm starting my life over and—"

"You don't have to explain anything to me." He smiled as if he totally understood, which made her a little uneasy. How could he have any understanding of her situation. "My entire family lives close by, but I'm not on good speaking terms with most of them."

He gave her shoulder a friendly squeeze, the gesture there and gone so fast she almost missed it. "Are you hungry? Like I said, I only got you the basics, but I can order you a nice burger and fries or maybe a fish fry from the restaurant in town."

"Are you talking that same burger you brought me yesterday." Her stomach growled. "Would you like to stay for lunch?"

"A man's got to eat," he said with that huge grin of his that reminded her that she was, indeed, a woman.

She bounced up and down while Zadie's faint cries turned louder and louder.

"Sounds like someone else is hungry," he said. "How about I order our food. Is there a place you're going to set up your jewelry-making shop? Will you at least let me help with that while we wait for lunch?"

"Thank you for asking instead of just doing." She set Zadie on the changing table and fumbled like a clumsy first-time mom with the dirty diaper. Thankfully, Jamison seemed unfazed by the entire situation. "First, we order. But I insist on paying, so do it from my phone. And I think that a fish fry sounds perfect. It's in my back pocket." Her hands were currently occupied with a wiggly baby. She glanced over her shoulder.

He stared at her with wide eyes, and his hands went up as if she were holding a gun to his head.

"I'm starving. And so is this kid."

Zadie let out a blood-curdling scream.

"Just do it," Bryn said.

"Don't slap me."

She felt a slight tug on her backside.

Thud.

"Crap. Sorry," Jamison said as he bent over to pick up her phone that had landed at her feet.

She couldn't help it, she giggled. She really shouldn't find a man getting so flustered by putting his hands on her butt funny, but she did. Maybe because it wasn't just any man, it was Jamison. However, she cleared her throat and opted to pretend that it hadn't happened and move on, going about the business at hand. "All of my tools and finished products are in the smaller suitcase and duffle bag. I was thinking that alcove in my bedroom would be a good place to set up a table, but I don't have one yet."

"Actually, you do."

She tossed the dirty mess her daughter had created into the diaper pail and sent a nasty look Jamison's direction.

He lifted his hands in the air as if she were holding a loaded shotgun to his chest. "Chip had an old desk in the attic, which we cleaned out while you were in the hospital. I thought maybe you might want that and a chair. It cost nothing but my time to wipe off the eight inches of dust, and the chair is my old one because I wanted a new one."

"I'm going to get tired of saying 'thank you.'" She

finished dressing Zadie, who was now screaming her precious little lungs out. "Is the chair in my room?"

"It is. And it's quite comfortable. I just wanted something a little bigger."

"All right. I'm going to sit in it and feed this little monster while I tell you where to put my tools."

"That sounds dirty."

Heat filled her cheeks. She didn't dare look over her shoulder as she made her way into her bedroom. It suddenly dawned on her that she'd be breastfeeding while he unpacked her things. She'd done that before, but he'd walked in on them in the middle of the feeding session. She hadn't started it in front of him.

She swallowed. "That doesn't look like an old chair."

"I've had it for about ten years. Swear to God." He rolled it to the edge of the bed before snagging the smaller suitcase and unzipping it. He glanced between the contents and the desk. He took a step back and planted his hands on his hips. "I think you need built-in cabinets over the desk for all this stuff. And maybe a bookshelf to house some of it." He waved his hands over her jewelry-making supplies. "The couple of drawers here aren't going to cut it."

"That sounds expensive and way out of my budget." She took one of the small blankets and tossed it over her shoulder. So far, Zadie had been latching on quickly, but every once in a while, it was a challenge to get her to take Bryn's nipple. That was something she hoped didn't happen right now. She didn't want to be rude and tell him to get the hell out. Because she wanted to buy him lunch, which had been ordered and paid for, and the idea of being alone in this house all of a sudden made her want to cry. "Maybe once I get my business going or find part-time work, I can swing it, but not right now."

He stood there with his back to her and scratched his head. "You're looking for a job?"

"I don't know about a job so much as I'm looking to find ways to make a little side money from home." She adjusted Zadie's head and cringed as her baby girl grabbed hold and started feeding.

"Would you be interested in working for me?" He turned. "I can't afford to pay you very much. As a matter of fact, it would have to be lead-based."

"What do you mean by that?" She leaned back in the leather office chair and patted Zadie's behind. Being a mother didn't feel natural, but it didn't feel foreign, either. All the doctors and nurses had told her to trust her instincts and never hesitate to call the office.

So far, she liked the pediatrician she'd met at the hospital, but what did she know?

"One of the reasons I want to build a website is to have a place for people to input their contact and project information, especially when I'm working at the station and can't return phone calls right away. But if I had someone who could do that for me and do quotes, I could manage my part-time work much better."

"I know nothing about being a handyperson," she said.

"You don't need to. You just need to know my schedule and cell number. I can answer short texts pretty easily at work. And some phone calls. But when I hang up on a potential new customer because I've got a four-alarm fire to deal with, they just go find someone else."

"I see what you mean. So, what exactly are you looking to have me do?"

"Answer emails and phone calls that come through the website. I can pay you per job I get."

"Are you serious? Because if you are, I'll take it, as long as we can set office hours."

"Absolutely. I wouldn't expect you to field calls after six or on Sundays, but if you could do Saturdays, that would be great."

"I don't even mind Sundays. Just not late at night." Trying not to expose herself, she lifted Zadie over her shoulder and patted her back in hopes of getting a good burp. Thankfully, Jamison kept his focus on her gaze and nowhere else.

So far, he'd proven himself to be a gentleman through and through, and she wanted to believe that he was one of the good guys. However, she would never get involved with him outside of working for him and being friends.

And not close ones.

That was all she could handle, and it might be all she'd ever be interested in since she didn't trust her ability to read men.

That and the fact that she couldn't afford for anyone to get too close for fear they might find out who she really was. That could be disastrous. If Timothy's parents ever found out that she and their unborn grandchild had survived the car crash, they would come for her, and they would do whatever they could—including lying—to take Zadie from her.

Bryn shivered.

"We can work out whatever kind of schedule works best for you that's within my budget." He held up a finger. "On one condition."

"I'm afraid to ask."

"You let me build whatever it is you need for your jewelry-making business and use it on my website as a demonstration of what I can do. Even though I've done a lot of work over the years, I haven't been very good at taking pictures of it."

"You drive a hard bargain," she said, just as the doorbell rang. "How about you get that while I finish feeding her?"

"Sounds like a plan."

She watched him practically sprint out of the bedroom. She shifted her daughter, who glanced up at her with wide eyes. "What have I gotten myself into, Zadie girl?"

5

*J*amison set all the food out on the kitchen table in the breakfast nook. He thought about eating outside, but he wasn't sure how Bryn would feel about that with the baby. It wasn't that hot out, but still, he remembered Nancy being weird about stuff like that, and he certainly didn't want to be too presumptuous, considering that he'd already overstepped his bounds.

More than once.

He twisted the cap off a beer that had been left over from the twelve pack he and Chip had brought over last night and leaned back in the chair, sipping his beverage and ignoring the smell of his sizzling burger calling to his tastebuds. He could wait a few more minutes for Bryn to finish feeding Zadie. Hopefully, the precious little angel would go right to sleep.

Though he'd been around enough infants to know

that didn't happen all that often, and even if she did go back to sleep, it likely wouldn't last very long.

He tapped his finger on the center of his chest in tune with his pulse. His heart broke for Bryn. It was one thing to get divorced. Even when it wasn't necessarily what you wanted but was what was needed. But it was another thing to lose the love of your life to death.

While pregnant.

And to be estranged from family during that time and have that tragedy not bring you and your family closer together had to suck even more.

He let out a long breath. It almost made him want to mend fences across the board.

Almost.

The sound of feet shuffling across the hardwood floor created butterflies in his gut. He mentally kicked himself in the ass. It was one thing to be attracted to her and quite another to want to pursue it.

He shouldn't be entertaining the latter at all.

And yet, she was all he could think about.

"All she does is eat, sleep, and make a nasty mess in her diaper." Bryn sat at the table, smoothing a napkin over her lap. "The nurses warned me not to get used to her sleeping. That her being this sweet little resting angel is an illusion."

He lifted a fry and dunked it in the hot sauce ranch mix he'd created. "They are correct. My brother's one kid had a horrible case of colic from age two weeks to three months."

"Don't you dare jinx me." She waved a fork in his direction before diving into her coleslaw. "Zadie is going to be perfect."

"She's your daughter. Therefore, she already is."

Bryn's jaw dropped. She blinked. Then she burst out laughing. Hard.

His first thought was that he had no idea what he'd said that was so funny. He'd paid her a compliment—and her baby.

That was until he replayed his words in his head.

"I guess that was kind of cheesy."

"In a sweet way," she said. "I didn't mean to make fun of what you said. I'm sorry."

"I'd pick on me." He dove into his cheeseburger topped with a fried egg and a few onion rings. He only allowed himself this kind of guilty pleasure once a week, at most, especially if he got all the fixings like he had this afternoon since he knew it would probably be his last meal.

However, he had eaten like this two days in a row now. Next week, he'd be working more and maybe skip the ritual since he'd already indulged.

He wouldn't feel guilty about it now. Besides, all he had in his fridge was a leftover quesadilla. Other than that, he needed to do a major grocery shopping trip, and that wasn't happening. At least, not today. He had a couple of other errands he needed to run, and he suspected that he would end up taking some measurements for above Bryn's desk and start on those built-in cabinets and shelves for her bedroom. He thought it might be a good idea for her to also have a way to display her work for pictures, and right by window would bring in enough natural light for some quality images.

"It was just the way you said it."

Regardless of how it'd tumbled from his lips, he'd meant it. However, he wouldn't repeat it. He wasn't sure if he could get rid of the cheese factor. For now, he'd keep the overwhelming flattery to himself.

"I'll work on my delivery." He continued chowing down on his food and sipped his beer. It had been a long time since he'd found the company of a woman so entertaining and comfortable. He didn't want to ruin it by being nosy, but he couldn't help himself. "Can I ask you a personal question?"

"I might not answer."

"Fair enough." He nodded. "Why Lighthouse Cove, Florida out of all the places in the country you could have started your life over?" What he really wanted to know was why she hadn't stayed close to where family was to try to work things out, and where home was previously. But he'd get to those questions eventually.

"That's a good question." She raised her soda bottle to her lips and took a good chug. "For starters,

I've never been to Florida, and I'm a huge Disney fan."

"Lucky for you the theme park is only a little over two hours away, but why not live in Orlando?"

She smiled. "I've never lived near the ocean, and that's been a dream of mine since I was a little girl. The idea that I can put Zadie in a little front snuggly pouch and walk to the beach is so appealing."

"I love living on the water."

"Do you have a place on the beach?"

He shook his head. "I'm on a canal just off the intracoastal in town." He pointed south. "It's actually only about three miles from here. You could walk if you wanted to, but it's in the opposite direction of the beach. Once you hit the traffic circle instead of going right, take a left, and I'm three streets down."

"Do you live in a house?"

"I do," he said. "I bought it when I got married, but my ex-wife wanted nothing to do with it. I love living on the water, so I kept it."

"As you should."

"This is none of my business, but you brought nothing with you from your past life. Don't you want your daughter to have things from her dad?"

Bryn glanced down at her plate and set her fork on the table.

Shit. Now he'd gone and put his fucking foot in his mouth. "I'm sorry. I shouldn't have asked that one."

She wiped the corners of her mouth daintily with her napkin.

He braced himself for either being kicked out or a lecture—both equally bad.

"I'm sure people will be wondering about Zadie's dad and why I'm alone, if they aren't already," she said.

"You don't owe anyone an explanation."

"You're right. I don't," she said. "And while I've never lived in a small town before, I suspect that what they say about everyone knowing each other's business or gossiping about it is true."

"The gossip part is true, but I doubt anyone will be assholeish enough to ask such an insensitive question to your face. Anyone but me, that is."

"Maybe not, but I can imagine how strange it must look from the outside for me to be a widow and not have a shred of evidence of my past." She swiped at her cheeks. "I know I'd be wondering what the backstory is and why I never have family or friends visiting."

Now he'd gone and made her cry. He really wasn't an asshole.

But he was an insensitive prick.

Pushing aside his food, he reached across the table and took her hand. "I didn't mean to upset you."

"It will be good for me to tell at least one person in this town. And if someone brings it up to you, well, maybe you can find a way to explain my situation in a kind way without getting into the nitty-gritty of it." She took in a long, slow breath and glanced around the room as if she were looking for the words. "When my husband died, his mom blamed me. And since she and I never got along, I felt it was best for me and my child to cut ties altogether."

"She doesn't know about the baby, does she?" A chill filled his veins and raced right to his heart.

"No."

Jamison bit down on his tongue. It wasn't his place to judge or express his opinion.

"I can tell you disapprove."

He relaxed his facial muscles, realizing that he'd scrunched his forehead—a dead giveaway for disliking something. "It doesn't matter what I think." One of these days, he'd have to learn to be a better liar. "It's whatever is right for you and Zadie."

"I appreciate that, but since you're my only friend and now my boss, I'm curious as to why my declaration made you look like you swallowed a lemon."

He chuckled. That's exactly how his mother described it. He quickly wiped the smile off his face and the memory from his mind. "If you go to the local market or get your hair done in town, you'll quickly learn this about me, which is why I might feel strange about keeping a baby from someone."

"Are you a father?"

"No," he said. "But my mother had an affair, and it resulted in me. However, my parents didn't think to tell me until two years ago. To add insult to injury, Steve, my biological father, is now dating my mom, and I'm just supposed to, all of a sudden, accept it all."

Bryn's eyes grew wide. Her lips parted, and she lowered her chin. "That's a lot to take in."

"It is. I'm also not very accepting. It's why I barely speak to my mom. I don't have a relationship with Steve, his kids, or my other brothers. And to be frank, all of this could have been avoided if some honesty had been shared from the beginning."

"Affairs aren't honest by nature."

"Nope. But by the time I was born, my father knew that I might not be his."

"So, are you not speaking to your dad either?"

He shook his head. "We've worked through our differences when it comes to the lie. I mean, he raised another man's child after his wife cheated on him."

She crossed her tanned, toned legs. Sometimes, it was hard to focus on anything but how pretty Bryn was, or maybe he was only using that to avoid the topic he'd brought up—which he slightly regretted doing.

"No offense, but that doesn't make him noble. I'm not saying that he's not a good man, but it doesn't mean he gets to be held to a different standard."

"No offense taken. However, in my mind, it does. Because he was trying to keep his family together."

"All right," she said. "But what do your brothers have to do with any of this?"

Jamison shifted uncomfortably in his seat. "I'm working on my relationships with them, but there was a time, when all this first came out, that they didn't see how it messed with who I thought I was. All they wanted was for Mom and Dad to be happy, and if that meant Steve was in our mother's life, then so be it."

"Well, I can see how that would be difficult for you." She held up her finger. "How old are you?"

He narrowed his stare. "Thirty-seven. Why?"

"Because when you were born, your parents had to make decisions, both selfish and selfless in order to protect you." She tapped her chest. "I know in my heart of hearts that I'm making the right decision for Zadie. If in thirty-some years, she meets up with her grandmother and ends up resenting me, I will still believe that I made the right decision in the moment, and I hope that Zadie will respect me enough to hear my explanation and try to understand what was going on at the time, at the very least."

The chill that had coated his system heated to a boil. He wanted to do what he did when he was with his family and bolt from his chair. Maybe knock it over and cuss like a drunken sailor. He clenched his fists against his thighs. "It's just that lying creates so many problems and hurt feelings."

"Let me ask you this question," she said. "Would

you have preferred to be raised by Steve? Or by the man you call Dad?"

Jamison fucking hated that question. "We both know the answer to that, and it's an unfair question. I had a lifetime of being Dalton Kirby's son. That's why it's not going to change. Biology doesn't make a person a parent. Which is why I get angry with my family. Steve knew of my existence. He knew I could be his. And instead of claiming me, he went off to Miami, got married, and had four other kids." Jamison squared his shoulders. "Obviously, this is a tough topic for me."

She scooted the chair closer and rested a hand over his. "I'm not saying that what your parents did was right, but there was more than one person involved. And while the way the truth came out really sucked, you're now in control. That's the key. You get to call the shots on how the relationships play out. But they had their reasons, and I suspect if you put yourself in each of their shoes, you might be able to understand."

He understood his father. What he did made sense. And maybe his mom because she only wanted to keep her family together.

But Steve's actions didn't make sense, and he didn't want to hear the man's excuses. So, Jamison always refused. He'd had no family when he left town. He'd walked away from the woman he supposedly loved and a child that might have been his, and

Jamison has always believed that actions spoke louder than words.

That action was pretty fucking loud.

"I appreciate what you're saying, and you have a valid point. I'm honestly working on all of this. However, you asked why I had an adverse reaction to you not telling your late husband's family about Zadie. Well, that's my reason. No matter what was going on, that's their grandchild."

"I respect that as long as *you* can respect that I had my reasons." She squeezed his hand. "I have to do what I believe is best for my daughter and me."

He couldn't argue with anything she'd said. He didn't have to agree with everything. The fact remained that her point of view made perfect sense. Even when she framed it around his life.

That was a hard pill to swallow. "That was a little deep for an impromptu lunch."

"Let's try to keep those kinds of conversations to a minimum."

He smiled. "I like the idea that we might have the chance to have a chat again. I enjoy your company." He glanced at his watch. "Crap. I've got to go. I promised my grandmother I'd fix her television before her show tonight. I'm sure her TV is fine. It always is, but she manages to mess up all her remotes so I bought her an Apple TV where she can have all her streaming stuff in one place and use just one." He lifted his plate. "Let me help you—"

"I can handle a few dishes." She curled her fingers around his waist. "Don't forget to get me all the information for your website. I'll start on it tonight."

"Thanks." Without thinking about what he was doing, he lifted her from the chair and held her by her forearms. He stared into her eyes, losing himself there for a long moment. He thought about what it might be like to kiss her but decided that might not be a good idea.

Yet.

Shit. There should be no future thought there, either. Not only had she just had a baby, she was still grieving.

They were friends. He needed to keep it that way.

"When you're feeling up to it, I'd like to show you around town. Better yet,"—he smiled—"why don't you come with me to my sister-in-law's birthday party? It's next weekend, so that gives you some time to recover. It's going to be huge, so you'll meet just about anyone who is worth knowing in Lighthouse Cove. And kids are welcome, so bringing Zadie won't be an issue."

"Oh, no." She shook her head. "I don't think going to a family party is a good idea."

"It's a great idea," he said. "Trust me. And, because I'll be giving Nancy a piece of your jewelry, it will be a great way to start talking up your business, especially if you're wearing some pieces. Hell. If you carry a men's line, I'd even consider displaying something as long as you don't make me look like I'm some freak or something."

She covered her mouth and laughed.

God, he loved that sound. If one could hear hot fudge being poured over cold ice cream, that's how he'd describe her laugh.

"I'm serious."

"And I'm seriously saying no. I'd feel like a fish out of water."

"You've got to meet people sometime, and this would be the perfect place to start. Besides, you'd be doing me a huge favor."

"How so?"

"Everyone in my family would be focused on you, your awesome jewelry, your adorable little girl, and not the fact that, for the first time since the world found out that Dalton Kirby isn't my real father, Steve and I will be in the same room."

"I see. You're just using me," she said with a wicked grin.

He'd thought he wanted to kiss her a few minutes ago, but now, he found her so insanely irresistible that he had to take a step back. "Not totally. I honestly believe it would be good for you. Not just for your business, but another of my brothers is married, and I think you'd get along with both Nancy and Farrah. Not to mention, there will be a lot of other ladies there around your age. It will be a good place for you to get to know the people of Lighthouse Cove."

"And for you to continue hiding and not dealing with your family."

"I won't deny that."

"At least, you're honest." She nodded. "Can I think about it? I have no idea how this new parenting thing is going to go over the next week. For all I know, she's going to become a holy terror."

He laughed. "I'll behave as if you're coming. But if you bail on me at the last minute, I'll understand."

"One of these days, I'm going to find out what your faults are."

"Oh. I've got plenty of those, trust me. Just ask my ex-wife. She'll be happy to tell you. While I wouldn't believe everything she says, some is true." He leaned in and kissed Bryn on the cheek without even thinking. "I'll be back tomorrow to start on your project. I'll text you in the morning to let you know what my day is looking like." He stood there for a long moment. Longer than what seemed normal to say a quick good-bye. It wasn't awkward, but if he didn't move, his mouth was going to crash land on hers, and the kiss would be wild and out of control

For fuck's sake. She'd just had a baby.

And he'd delivered that sweet little girl. What the hell was wrong with him?

"I can let myself out." He didn't wait for a response as he maneuvered around her and strode toward the front door. He didn't bother glancing over his shoulder as he hopped behind the steering wheel of his Jeep.

His gut hadn't been this tied up in knots over a woman in years. He didn't understand it. Even his ex-wife hadn't jumbled his ability to think straight, and he'd been madly in love with her in the beginning.

He hit the brake and pressed the start button.

Bryn was a good person and would make for a great friend. Besides, the last thing she needed in her life right now was a man. She'd made that clear without even trying.

6

---

*B*ryn bolted upright from a deep sleep. Her chest tightened as she gasped for air. Images still flashed before her eyes.

Timothy's rage-filled eyes staring at her with hatred.

His fist landing on her cheek.

She palmed the side of her face.

That wasn't her life anymore.

Timothy was dead. She'd attended his funeral. She'd watched as they lowered his casket into the ground. She'd even stayed to make sure the workers in the cemetery piled the earth on top of the wooden box. Two days after the service, she went back to check again.

She'd needed to make sure.

Zadie stirred in the bassinet next to Bryn's bed.

She checked the time. It was close to five in the morning. She'd yet to see the sun rise over the ocean.

Today would be that day.

"Come here, Zadie girl." Everyone told her not to wake a sleeping baby, but she would be in a full-fledged wail in a matter of minutes anyway. Besides, Bryn had learned over the course of the few days she'd been at home that leaving the house these days wasn't as simple as grabbing the car keys and walking out the door.

Not that she'd really left the house since she wasn't supposed to be driving yet.

But today, she'd venture the couple of miles to the public parking lot in town. She'd be driving for all of five minutes. And the walk from her vehicle to the beach would be another ten. The fresh air would do her and Zadie some good.

A little Zen under the morning sky.

Zadie greedily ate her breakfast, so waking her wasn't a problem. She didn't fuss too much while Bryn changed her, nor as she placed her in the car seat.

"We're going on an adventure," Bryn said as she pulled the belt strap, securing Zadie in the back of the vehicle.

Bryn glanced down the street in both directions. She was always on the lookout for anyone who didn't belong. Only she'd yet to get to know her neighbors, so she wouldn't know if someone out of place were strolling down the street or not. Her heart had finally calmed after her horrific nightmare. However, the feeling of unease had yet to leave.

Actually, she'd been carrying that sense around since she decided to fake her death. She wondered if it would ever go away. God, she hoped so. She didn't want Zadie turning ten with Bryn utterly petrified that the clown she'd hired to entertain the children at the party was a bad man hired by her in-laws to kidnap her precious daughter.

"Here we go." Bryn slipped behind the steering wheel and backed out of the driveway. The night sky gave way to the morning light. When she was married to Timothy, she used to slip out of bed and go sit on the balcony of whatever home they were in because they always had a balcony off the master. She'd grab a cup of coffee and sit there, staring at the sky and dreaming of a life of freedom.

She wished she felt free.

While she was no longer at Timothy's mercy or that of his family, she wasn't free by any sense of the word. She was still trapped in a world where she couldn't be who she wanted or see her family.

Tears stung her eyes.

She swiped at her face. This was no time to cry. This life was better than any other she could have had if she'd stayed. She'd made the right choice.

After finding a parking spot close to the walkway to the beach, she adjusted the front pouch and pulled

Zadie from the back of the car. She wrapped Zadie in the snuggle thing, which was a hell of a lot harder than she'd thought it would be. It definitely took more than the five minutes the store clerk had advertised when she'd bought it. But after fighting with it for about ten, she finally secured Zadie, and they were ready for a short walk—that's all Bryn would be able to handle on the beach.

She grabbed a towel and locked the car.

The sound of the waves crashing against the shore lulled Zadie to sleep in seconds, and it made Bryn forget all the demons lurking in the shadows.

This was why she'd moved to Florida.

This was her safe harbor.

She laid out the blanket and sat for a moment, patting Zadie's cute little bottom while she watched tiny white birds running back and forth as the water nearly took them out.

A man without a shirt jogged in her direction.

She was about to turn her head when she realized that it was Jamison. She blinked. His muscles flexed every time his bare feet hit the sand.

His gaze locked with hers, and he slowed. "Good morning," he said with a bright smile. "I didn't expect to see you out here, though it's a nice surprise."

"It's good to see you, too," she managed with a dry throat. She blamed it on the salt and the sand. Not the man looking like a Greek god, standing in front of her as the sun's rays began to show themselves where the ocean kissed the sky. There was no denying Jamison's sex appeal or the fact that she was attracted to him, but that didn't mean she had to act on it or allow him access to that knowledge.

"Did you come to catch the sunrise?"

"I've never seen one over the ocean before."

"Oh, my. It's beautiful," he said. "May I join you?"

"Sure." Who was she to deny him? It was a public beach, and the ocean and the sun belonged to everyone. She scooted over, giving up some of her towel so he didn't have to sit his ass all the way on the sand.

He glanced at his watch. "It will be about another ten minutes before the sun really shows."

"Do you jog on the beach every morning?" Perhaps this would become a morning ritual. She told herself that she was just looking, and as two more hard bodies ran past, she realized it wasn't a lie. She wouldn't only be gawking at him.

No one could blame a girl for checking out a nice-looking man.

"When I'm not working or being lazy. But I have to admit, sometimes the latter happens." He leaned back on his hands and stretched out his long legs.

Never in her life had she ever described a man as beautiful.

But he was.

They sat in silence, listening to the birds and the

ocean as the sky grew brighter. Zadie wiggled against Bryn's chest as if she wanted to be a part of it all.

A piece of the sun hit the blue sky. It was only a tiny sliver, but it slowly grew in size. All the beach walkers, joggers, and yoga people stopped, covered their eyes, and stared at the ball appearing in an array of blues, pinks, and oranges as if something magical were happening.

Her heart beat a little faster.

"That's amazing," she whispered.

"Takes my breath away every time, and I've lived here for my entire life."

"A girl could get used to this."

He took her hand and squeezed. "How about I take you for some breakfast? There's a great place right over there on the beach. Best coffee blend in town, and the French toast is to die for."

Her stomach growled. "Okay," she said before her brain thought better of it. She blinked. "But don't you need a shirt and some shoes?"

"Not if we're going to eat it outside on the picnic tables." He furrowed his forehead. "Or will that bother you? Because if it does, we can always have breakfast another day. It's not like we'll never see each other again."

Don't do it. You're not that hungry. "I don't care if you don't," she said. "But for the record, I'm just in it for the coffee."

He laughed. "Duly noted." He hopped to his feet faster than a jet racing down a runway.

She took the hand he offered, but only because standing with a five-pound baby strapped to her belly was about as hard as it was when she'd been pregnant.

If not harder.

"Thank you," she said, making sure she took her hand back as they strolled toward a big, blue building with a sign that read: *Safe Harbor Café*. It was a quaint place nestled between palm trees and overlooking the ocean. A park sat in front of it that had everything imaginable from tennis and pickleball courts, to shuffle ball, cornhole, and volleyball. They even had outdoor showers to rise off after a long day in the sand and sun. The park had dozens of tables as well as grills if you didn't want to eat at the restaurant.

Of course, she quickly found out that the *Safe Harbor Café* was only open for breakfast and lunch.

Jamison ordered two number five specials to go at the outdoor window where it didn't matter that he wasn't dressed.

She hung back and tried not to stare too long at his rock-solid body. Though if he noticed, she'd tell him that she was merely admiring his ink.

The small one he had on his biceps of a fire hydrant, and the design on his ankle that she couldn't quite make out.

"Why don't we sit over there?" He pointed to a table where they could see the ocean.

"Sounds good to me."

"Are you okay with Zadie? I don't mind holding her for a bit." He set the bag of food on the table along with the tray of coffees.

"She's passed out cold, but thanks."

"Bummer. I like babies." He winked. But his smile quickly turned into a frown. "You've got to be kidding me."

"What's wrong?"

"It's Suzie Walton. Excuse me a minute." Jamison stood and stomped off back toward the restaurant, leaving Bryn with her heart in her stomach.

She squinted, covering her eyes, the sun now out in full force. She swallowed the fear that nearly choked her.

Could Suzie know who she was?

"You'd better not be taking pictures of me," Jamison said with his hands on his hips, though he didn't see a camera or any of her people. Still, that didn't mean she wasn't up to no good. "Or my friend. Because if you are, you know what'll happen."

"It's nice to see you, too," Suzie said with a sarcastic smile. "And for the record, *your friend*, as you call her, isn't off-limits."

"The fuck she isn't. You know you're not allowed to have me as the subject of any of your YouTube video or podcast thingies without facing a lawsuit. Or, better yet, my mother arresting you."

"Your mom loves me."

He laughed. "No. My mom enjoys my ex-wife. She thinks you're a leech. Just because you were Cheryl's maid of honor or whatever doesn't mean that kindness transfers over, especially after what you did. I'm warning you. If you make Bryn or me the subject of any of your social media craziness, you will live to regret it."

"If Bryn wants to—"

"She's already said no."

"You don't speak for her."

"I'm not. I was there when she made herself clear. Besides, her story, the one where she gives birth in the middle of town, includes me. Therefore, you can't touch it without going to jail. So, I suggest you hop right back in your car and go back to whatever rock you crawled out from under."

"I have no idea what Cheryl sees in you." Suzie tossed her purse over her shoulder.

"I don't, either," he mumbled as he turned and headed back toward Bryn. He unzipped his shorts' pocket and pulled out his cell, pausing on the sidewalk.

Jamison: *Just ran into Suzie. I don't know if she was following Bryn or me, but we were both at the café on the beach,* *having breakfast. Can you give her a friendly reminder about what will happen to her if she runs a story about me?*

Dad: *Sure. Dare I ask? You're with Bryn?*

Jamison chuckled.

Jamison: *I ran into her while jogging and bought her a decent cup of coffee. That's it. Also, she doesn't want anything about what happened in town on some whack job's podcast. Make that clear, too.*

Dad: *Consider it done.*

Jamison rolled his neck. This next text would be a harder pill to swallow. He hated asking his mother for anything. He could ask one of his brothers, but it would be better if it came from the chief of police.

Jamison: *Are you on duty?*

Mom: *About to be. Why?*

Jamison: *Suzie is looking for a story again. She's using the girl who gave birth in the middle of town to get to me. She followed me to the park at the beach in town.*

He was careful not to use Bryn's name with his mother. He didn't want to give his mother any opportunity to make it weird for Bryn. And knowing his mom, she would.

Mom: *Why does she want you on her show anyway?*

Jamison's stomach roiled. As if his mother didn't know the answer to that question.

Mom: *I'm headed out the door. I'll handle it.*

Jamison: *Thanks. See you at the party.*

He tossed in the last comment for good measure but also to make sure his mother didn't keep texting.

But she would, and he didn't care to carry on the conversation. He'd come a long way in the last few weeks by taking a few phone calls and agreeing to be at the same party as Steve.

All steps in mending fences.

This was as far as he was willing to go right now, though.

He tucked his phone back into his pocket and strolled back toward Bryn. "I believe I made it clear to her that neither of us wants to discuss the day Zadie was born."

"Please tell me you didn't give her my child's name," Bryn said with wide eyes. "When any of the legitimate news channels reported on what happened, they were kind enough not to show pictures or share names."

"She knows your name, but not your child's. And if it makes you feel any better, both my mom and dad will make it very clear to her that if she comes near you, she could be facing charges."

"Jail time? Seriously?"

He took a seat across from her and pulled the top off his coffee. "She ran a story about who my real father was without knowing all the facts or having anyone's permission. That included mine, Steve's, and my mom's. That pissed us all off, and my dad took legal action. She comes after you, that's breaking a few laws. Actually, being within fifty feet of me is going against the restraining order I filed. That's kind of bogus, but still, it was fun." He pulled open his breakfast and dug in. "I'm going to get fat hanging around you."

"Hey. I'm the one needing to lose the baby pounds."

"You look fabulous. Trust me. The prettiest woman on the beach by far." He held the plastic fork in mid-air. "I'm sorry if that was inappropriate."

"It was sweet. Thank you." Bryn took a few bites of her French toast before setting her utensils on her tray as she stared at him with the kind of look his mother used to give him when he got caught sneaking out at night.

"What's wrong?" He decided to be proactive.

"Why does that Suzie person want to do a story on you so badly?"

"Because of my rich, biological father, my lawyer dad, and my chief-of-police mom. It's all juicy stuff that she can twist and turn into some ugly shit for her followers. I deal with enough judgments about what happened. I don't need to be the center of her gossip bullshit."

"It seems like that story is kind of old, though. No offense."

He laughed. "I wish this town would forget it. But they haven't, and since not much happens in this sleepy safe harbor, it seems my DNA is what everyone wants to talk about around the water cooler at work."

She glanced over her shoulder and then toward the parking lot.

"Are you worried about something else?" he asked.

"I don't want to be the center of any story or the excuse she uses to get to you. I don't want my sister finding out where I am, much less my mother-in-law."

"Ah. I see." He wasn't sure how to respond. He could relate to not wanting personal business plastered all over the internet for anyone to judge. It was no one's business, and she did have a child to protect. If she didn't want Zadie's name or image anywhere on social media, he could respect that.

What he struggled with was keeping her daughter from the rest of the family. Didn't they have a right to develop a relationship with Zadie?

Steve gave up that right when he walked away.

Now that Jamison was a grown man, it was up to him whether or not he wanted a relationship with the parents in his life. But those choices had been taken from him when he was a baby.

Was what Bryn was doing all that different?

Jamison really had no idea, because he didn't know why. And he wasn't going to ask. He saw the fear in Bryn's eyes. Whatever had happened had scared her to the point where she believed that running and starting over was better than staying and facing the music.

Jamison had chosen the latter because, deep down, he didn't want to lose his family.

Maybe Bryn did.

"I know you don't think I'm being fair or even doing the right thing, but it's not for you to decide."

"You're right. It's not," he agreed. "I want you to know that I will make sure Suzie stays as far away from you and your daughter as possible."

"Thank you. I appreciate that." She wiped her fingers on the napkin. "If you don't mind, I need to get going. I've got a website to finish." She smiled. "My boss is a pain in the ass."

He laughed. He enjoyed how she could so quickly lighten the mood. "I look forward to seeing it."

"Thanks for breakfast. I'll talk to you soon." Wrapping her arms around Zadie, who was bundled close to her chest, Bryn stood.

For a few moments, he contemplated racing up to her and offering to walk her to her car, but then he thought better of it. He understood how important it was for Bryn to be independent and do things for herself. It wasn't like the sun was setting, and he didn't need to worry about her being alone. This was a safe town, and the breakfast crowd had already started filling the park.

She was fine.

He, on the other hand, was not only out of his depth, but he'd also found himself wanting to ask a woman who'd just had a baby out on a date.

$\mathcal{B}$ryn spent the next week unpacking, building websites, making jewelry, and trying to get used to being at Zadie's beck and call. The hardest part was always figuring out what she wanted. The nurses had told her that, within a few weeks, she'd be able to tell based on her cries and the time of day.

But that hadn't happened yet. Of course, it hadn't been that long.

She put her feet up and leaned back on the chair on the back patio after checking the baby monitor. If all things went as they had last night, she had about forty minutes before Zadie started screaming.

Bryn tilted her head toward the setting sun.

No sooner did she let out a long, cleansing breath than her cell went off. It wasn't a text or a call. It was the front doorbell.

She raised her phone and stared at a policewoman standing on her front porch.

Bryn's feet hit the concrete patio. Her heart dropped to the pit of her gut. For a split second, she thought about not answering. Visions of grabbing her daughter and slipping out the back door filled her brain.

But she watched the national news every night. Hell, she'd even started listening to that obnoxious Suzie woman's podcast, just in case. If someone were looking for her, she figured she'd have heard about it, especially with how vocal her mother-in-law had been when Bryn's husband died. It had been hell. Worse than hell. It was like nothing Bryn had ever experienced. And when she found out two days after the funeral that she was pregnant, she'd known that she had to get out from under Barb Perish's thumb.

Bryn tapped the screen and cleared her throat. "Hello," she managed to croak out. "Can I help you?"

"Sorry to stop by unannounced. My name is Rebecca Kirby. I'm Jamison's mother." She held up a basket. "I brought over some welcome-to-the-neighborhood gifts in case you can't make it tomorrow for some reason."

"I'll be right there." It would be rude if she didn't let Jamison's mom in, even though Bryn really didn't want to entertain anyone. Especially a police officer. It wasn't that she didn't trust cops. Most of them were good people—the best. And they protected their communities.

But some could be bought. She'd learned this first-hand when she'd called one after her husband used her body as his personal punching bag.

However, she had no reason to believe that the chief of police and Jamison's mother was on the take or had ever heard of her late husband.

The nice thing about having Jamison around was that he did his thing with measuring or hammering with the built-in cabinets and bookshelves he was building, but he didn't require her to entertain him all the time. She liked that.

What she didn't like was how he made her belly hot with the kind of desire she hadn't felt for a man since she'd first met Timothy.

Thankfully, if Jamison felt the same attraction, he did his best to keep her at arm's length. He came over, he flirted with Zadie like there was no tomorrow, he went over his expectations for their employment agreement, and then he went to town on his work for her cabinets. Even though she enjoyed having Jamison around, she needed the project completed. She couldn't afford to become attached to him or used to having him in her home on a regular basis. She needed her independence.

"Hi," she said, pulling open the door with a bright smile. "You didn't have to come all the way over to drop that off." She stepped aside to let Rebecca in.

"Not a problem. I live right outside of town." Rebecca handed her the basket, which was filled with baby items. "Are you settling in?"

"I am, thank you." Bryn set the basket on the table in the family room. "Can I offer you something to drink?"

"I'd love a water. Thank you."

"My pleasure. Would you like to sit out back?" Again, not that Bryn wanted to entertain, but she wouldn't send the woman packing, either.

"I can't stay very long," Rebecca said as she took the water bottle and followed Bryn to the backyard. "But I did want to stop by and assure you that Suzie Walton will not be bothering you again."

"Oh. Um. Thank you."

"Jamison told me she was trying to get you to talk about the delivery. And, to be honest, she'd turn around and make it all about Jamison and start asking him personal questions that he doesn't want to discuss."

Bryn wasn't about to let on that she knew anything about that. It wasn't her business. "Thank you. I'm a private person and don't want my daughter's image all over the news. Besides, it was kind of embarrassing."

"I can imagine." Rebecca smiled, and Bryn saw a bit of Jamison in the grin.

"My son hasn't told me very much other than he

helped you deliver your baby in the middle of the road."

Bryn found that statement interesting since that had made the evening news, which she still worried might make it back to Barb and Mark Perish. If anyone recognized her or thought she looked familiar and sent the story to her late husband's family, Bryn didn't know if she had it in her to disappear again.

She knew she didn't have the funds. Every penny she'd hidden from Timothy over the years had gone into making sure she could start fresh.

"There isn't much to tell," Bryn said, wondering if this would become a fishing expedition, and Bryn was the catch of the day. She remembered all the questions the police had had for her when Timothy died and how they treated her as if she'd been the reason his car had wrapped around a tree.

At one point, she'd thought the cops—and his family—totally disregarded the fact that he'd been high on cocaine and drunk.

The worst part had been that his parents actually believed the only reason he was under the influence was because he and Bryn had gotten into a fight.

Only, they fought every day.

Because he was high every day.

Rebecca leaned against the fence and pushed her sunglasses back over her eyes. "What do you do for a living?"

"I make jewelry."

"Really," Rebecca said. "How long have you been doing that?"

That was a loaded question. "I've dabbled in it since I was in high school but didn't decide to make a business out of it until recently."

"That's fascinating. Do you specialize in any particular kind?"

"No, but I try to create unique pieces that you can't find anywhere else. I also do custom work." Bryn pulled her cell from her pocket and tapped the picture icon. "I made this matching set from someone's wedding dress."

Rebecca took the phone into her hand. "Wow. That's beautiful. You're incredibly talented."

"Thank you." Bryn couldn't help but puff out her chest a little in pride. Timothy and his family had never taken her so-called hobby seriously. As a matter of fact, the last two years of her marriage, Timothy had forbidden her from even making anything for herself. He called it cheap and pathetic. He often told her that no wife of his would wear some homemade piece of crap when he could afford the real thing.

"I might have you make some pieces for me. If you're interested."

"I'd love to," Bryn said. "Maybe we can set up an appointment next week when you're not working to go over exactly what you're looking for."

"I'm having a big party for my daughter-in-law and I don't have time before that, but I would like to have some things remade from my collection for my daughters-in-law and my granddaughters."

"Oh. I love that," Bryn said. "Just let me know when you're available. Let me get you my number."

"Perfect. I'll send you a couple of dates that will work for me and we can go from there." Rebecca took out her cell and typed in the numbers that Bryn rattled off. "Jamison's wife would love this stuff. She's really into jewelry."

"Isn't he divorced?" Bryn asked.

"He was going through some stuff when that happened. I think he rushed into it and it's only a matter of time before he realizes that he made a mistake."

That's not what Jamison had told Bryn, but who was she to question his mother?

"So, where did you move from?" Rebecca asked.

Hatti had told her to keep the lies as close to the truth as possible. That way, she wouldn't confuse them and get caught. It made sense. Over the course of the last few months, Bryn had worked out a past history that she thought was foolproof. But now that she was living in the real world and not running from one horrible hotel room to the next, she wasn't so sure— especially since she was conversing with a police officer.

And not just any cop. The chief.

"Colorado Springs," she said.

"Is that where your family is?"

Bryn wanted to ask Rebecca if Jamison had said anything at all about Bryn, because it felt like the woman had no information at all, but that would be rude, and it would also imply that Bryn knew something about their relationship. That wasn't a good way to start any kind of relationship, even if she planned on it only being casual. Bryn had to live in this town, which meant she had to know the players, understand how they operated, and find a way to fit in while remaining on the outside.

If that made any sense at all.

"No. That's where my husband's family lives."

"That's got to be hard on them now that you and your daughter are here." Rebecca raised her arms and rested them over the posts.

This was not the conversation Bryn wanted to have with anyone, especially a police officer. "It's complicated," she said.

"All families are." Rebecca nodded. "Was there a specific reason you chose south Florida?"

"Just the sunshine and its proximity to Disney."

"Two very good reasons." Rebecca smiled. "When my boys were little, I took them to the theme parks at least three or four times a year. As a Florida resident, you can get discounted passes. Actually, when your little one gets older, I suggest buying annual passes. You only need to go twice to cover the costs."

"I'll keep that in mind, thanks for the tip."

"Sure thing." Rebecca polished off the rest of her

water. "Well, I'd best get back to work. I appreciate the hospitality and the—"

"Mom? What are you doing here?" Jamison asked as he came around the corner.

"I stopped by with a gift basket, but I was just leaving. Duty calls." Rebecca tapped her weapon strapped to her hip. "Why don't you walk me to my vehicle?"

"I have some things to discuss with Bryn," Jamison said as he stepped into the backyard.

"Oh. Are you doing work for her or something?" Rebecca asked.

Bryn always hated it when someone talked about her as if she weren't in the same space. Her in-laws used to do that.

"I am, but that's not why I'm here," Jamison said.

"I see." Rebecca looped her fingers in her belt. "This will only take a few minutes."

"Mom. Say what's on your mind." Jamison had a sharp edge to his tone.

Rebecca shrugged. "I ran into Cheryl this morning. I can tell she's miserable and misses you."

"We're not having this conversation," Jamison said. "Not now. Not ever. Besides, didn't you say you needed to get back to work?"

His mother let out an exasperated sigh. "It was really nice meeting you, Bryn," she said. "Don't get up. I can see myself out."

"Thanks for stopping by." Bryn waved.

"I'll be in touch about those jewelry pieces." Rebecca nodded in her son's direction before stepping through the gate and disappearing around the side of the house.

"I'm sorry about my mom, especially that last exchange."

"No worries," Bryn said. "I wasn't expecting you tonight." She sat up a little taller.

"I was worried when I drove by on my way home and saw my mom's patrol car. When I got out of my Jeep, I heard voices, so I walked around back here. Is everything okay?"

"She was just being friendly and gave me a basket filled with baby stuff. She also informed me that she took care of Suzie." Being in the middle of a family feud was the last place Bryn wanted to be; however, she needed to find some middle ground. She needed to build her business. If Rebecca was going to have her build custom pieces, staying in her good graces so she'd rave about Bryn's work was imperative.

Of course, she needed Jamison, as well.

Talk about having to walk a tightrope.

"I'm glad about Suzie. However, the one thing you'll learn about my mom is that as sweet as she can be, she's always got an agenda." Jamison took off his baseball cap and ran a hand over his freshly buzzed head. "Based on what she said just now, one of them is she thinks that I should be with my ex-wife, and she wanted you to know that. But that's never going to happen."

"I think you've made that abundantly clear."

"I wish my mom understood that." Jamison laughed. "Since I'm here, is there anything you need done around the house?"

"Not that I can think of, but you're not my personal handyman."

"Point taken," he said with a big smile.

It was hard not to be at ease around him, and there were moments she didn't care how much she enjoyed his company.

"Have you eaten dinner yet?" he asked.

She shook her head as her stomach growled so loud he had to have heard it. She had some leftover pizza in the fridge, but that wasn't overly appealing. There might be salad fixings she could put together, but that didn't do anything to excite her taste buds.

What she really craved was a big, fat, juicy steak, mashed potatoes with sour cream and chives, and some grilled asparagus.

Damn, that made her stomach do a little dance.

"I was going to head over to this great little place on the water to grab a bite. I don't mind eating alone but would prefer your and Zadie's company."

Bryn contemplated Jamison's proposition for a long moment. Ever since Timothy had died, she'd decided to live her life by the cliché that if it was too good to be true, then it often was too good.

She wanted to believe that she was a stronger woman than she'd been when she met and married Timothy. Of course, he'd gaslighted her into thinking that she wasn't worth shit. That she was useless and, without him, she'd never make it on her own.

Thankfully, today, she knew that to be total bullshit.

"I need to pay for my own meal."

Jamison chuckled. "Dutch, it is."

Like perfect clockwork, Zadie started to fuss over the baby monitor.

"Give me a few minutes to change her, and then we can go." She stood and brushed her hands down the front of her jeans. "Am I dressed okay?"

"You look amazing," he said. "I can't believe you had a baby about a week ago."

It was hard not to smile. "You're sweet."

"I have my moments." He winked. "I'll wait for you by your car."

She blew out a puff of air and tried not to stare at his ass as he walked away, but that proved impossible. She should have just said "*no thank you*" to dinner and suffered with the leftovers in her fridge, but she hadn't, so it was time to suck it up and enjoy whatever Lighthouse Cove had to offer.

Besides, Hatti had told Bryn the last time she'd seen her that this was her chance to have the life she deserved.

Jamison polished off the last of his steak and pushed his plate aside. He was quite impressed with how much food Bryn had managed to eat. Even more impressed by how she handled breastfeeding Zadie in public, and how Zadie barely made a peep.

Of course, he'd probably jinxed that by thinking how great the little girl had been.

He took a sip of his beer, trying to make it last a little while longer, knowing that when he was done, dinner was done, and therefore, it would be time to take Bryn and Zadie home.

"This has to be the best dinner I've had in a long time," Bryn said as she stared out over the intracoastal. "And the view is amazing."

"This is my favorite restaurant. I eat here at least once a couple of times a month if not more. If not physically right here, then I order out and bring it home."

"Is this where we got that burger or the fish fry?"

"No. That's a little place by my dad's office. Just as good, but it's not on the water. This is a little more decadent."

"Yeah. You can say that again." She waved her fork that had been loaded with some cheesy potatoes. "I'm full, but I don't want to stop. I mean, I haven't had food this good in months."

"I think you've got baby brain," he said. "I'm sure

they have fabulous restaurants where you lived before."

"I don't remember ever having a meal this good." She tossed her utensils onto her plate before pushing it aside. "It's like having a little party in my mouth."

He let out a hearty laugh. "That's a perfect phrase to describe the food here." The second his gaze landed on his ex-wife, Cheryl, his giddiness was cut short. He tried to look away but Cheryl lifted her hand and wiggled her fingers as she made a beeline across the room.

Fucking wonderful.

At least Suzie was nowhere to be found.

He shifted in the booth. The last thing he needed was to get into it with his ex-wife. He never knew who he would be getting: the woman who'd cheated on him and blamed him for it because he'd been going through an identity crisis, or the one who wanted him back, even though she was still in an on-again/off-again relationship with the man she'd had the affair with.

"I should have known I'd run into you here," Cheryl said as she stood at the end of the booth. She folded her arms under her large, fake breasts. They barely moved. He'd been so angry when she'd gone and gotten them.

It wasn't about the surgery. It was that she hadn't told him, especially after they'd had numerous conversations about whether or not she should do it. Of course, he understood that it was her body to do with as she wanted, and he'd told her that he'd support her decision. She'd always been sensitive about the size of her breasts, and she'd been picked on as a little girl. Another thing he understood. He wanted his wife to feel good about herself, but he loved her the way she was, and he wanted her to feel how much he adored her. Still, she sought that approval from others, and instead of going through the process together, he'd had to find out about his wife's boob job from the neighbor.

"I'm shocked that no one told me that my ex-husband is now dating someone who has a kid. Of course, your family is pretty good at keeping secrets. Though I just saw your mom this morning and she was talking about Nancy's party and how you and I should go together. She said you were going to call me. What am I missing?"

"The fact that I don't speak to my mom and that it was wishful thinking on her part *and* yours," he said under his breath, wishing he could control his temper. Getting into a fight with his ex wasn't a good way to impress—shit—he didn't need to dazzle a friend.

"Are you going to introduce us?" Cheryl asked. "Or are you going to be rude as usual?"

"Bryn. This is my ex-wife, Cheryl." Jamison stretched his arm over the back of the booth and wiggled his fingers, hoping that would get rid of the pent-up frustration. "What are you doing here? This was never your favorite place."

"No. It was yours, and you've always been a creature of habit." She tossed her long ponytail over her shoulder and laughed. "Getting you to go anywhere else was always a chore."

"If you say so," he said, shaking his head. "Did you need something?"

"Your mom said I should get the details for Nancy's party from you and possibly hitch a ride since my car's in the shop."

"You'll have to find another ride," he said.

"Why?" Cheryl asked. "We're both going."

"Because I'm busy." Jamison didn't owe his exwife an explanation, and he wouldn't give her one.

"Are you serious? It's not like I live that far out of your way."

"I'm going to be running late because I'm working a couple of extra jobs. I'm sorry. I just can't."

"Fine." Cheryl leaned over, tucking a few stray strands of hair behind her ear, and cooed at Zadie, who was half-awake in her car seat next to Bryn. "She's so stinking adorable."

"Thank you," Bryn said.

"You must the lady that delivered her child in the middle of the road last week," Cheryl said.

"That's me," Bryn said.

"So, is this a thank you dinner, or a date? Because if you think it's a date, I should warn you about him."

"I'm not sure that's any of your business." Bryn smiled the wicked grin that made Jamison want to scoop her off her feet and kiss her like tomorrow might never come.

Cheryl jerked out her hip. "You don't understand the situation you're getting involved in."

"I know more than you think I do," Bryn said. "Regardless, it's still none of your business."

Jamison rested his hands on the table. He enjoyed this exchange a little too much.

"Now, if you don't mind, we're going to try to enjoy dessert before my daughter decides she's had enough and starts screaming," Bryn said.

"Wow. You've got yourself a spunky girlfriend." Cheryl stood tall. "I can take a hint."

"I doubt that," Bryn said under her breath.

Cheryl cocked her head. "You're a novelty. You'll wear off. They always do." She turned on her heels and stormed off toward a group of women standing around the bar. They all glanced in Jamison's direction. He recognized two of them as they pointed and looked as if they'd eaten something that'd soured their stomachs.

"Sorry about that." Jamison rolled his neck. The tension that'd built after being around Cheryl for only a few minutes had knotted into tight balls, creating the kind of pain that he used to carry around every day. No massage therapist would be able to work out the kinks. "She knows how to rile me up, and for some reason, she enjoys doing it whenever she gets the chance."

"She's still in love with you," Bryn said matter-of-factly.

"She should have thought about her feelings for me before she cheated on me." Jamison's brother, Miles, constantly told him how much his ex-wife still carried a torch for him. Part of him knew that was true. However, the last six months of their marriage had been a living hell. It was as if he'd landed a role in a horror movie and it wasn't one where he would survive to the end.

"I'm sorry she did that to you."

He shrugged his shoulders. When he looked back on it now, Cheryl had done him a favor. She'd given him a reason to get mad enough to bring up divorce. She might have been the one who did the leaving, but he was the one who'd suggested they call it quits. And if he were being honest now, they had been doomed *before* she cheated. They were like oil and water, and he knew he would never be able to make her truly happy unless he changed everything about who he was—and he wasn't willing to do that. If he did, then he'd have been the miserable one, and their marriage still would have been horrible.

"There was a lot going on with me at the time. A year before Cheryl and I called it quits, I found out that my dad wasn't my father, and I wasn't easy to live with."

"That doesn't give someone permission to cheat," Bryn said. "She was your partner. She was supposed to support you and be a sounding board."

He laughed. "Steve is rich. She wanted his money because I don't make much. Better yet, she wanted me to ask Steve for a job. Cheryl's very much into appearances. She grew up dirt-poor. I get it. She wanted more. She also wanted respect. When her mom and mine became friends, Cheryl saw how everyone in this town looked at my mother and she wanted that."

"Not much is more honorable than being a fire-fighter."

"Thank you for saying that. However, the salary isn't great. Even at the level I'm at. And Cheryl has expensive tastes. She wants fancy cars and fine jewelry." He chuckled at the memories popping into his mind. It wasn't that he hadn't wanted to give his wife those things, he just couldn't afford everything she coveted. They'd had to live within their means. He'd worked hard—still did—and he was willing to work more, but they would never have been millionaires.

"I thought I was being such a good husband when I bought the house I'm living in now for our first anniversary. Well, let me tell you, Cheryl was not happy. She actually told me that she'd be embarrassed to entertain her friends in something that needed to be completely gutted. When she said that, I burst out laughing because the people I bought it from had done a fair amount of work. There wasn't much left to do. Granted, it still needed some updating, but it's a nice house, and the view is spectacular. I get shit living in it because people always wonder how I can afford it. I usually laugh and say it's mortgaged to the max."

"I have to ask, considering the size of my place, what's your definition of *small?*" she asked as she brought her straw to her plump lips and sucked.

He inwardly groaned. "It's not tiny at twenty-four-hundred square feet," he admitted. "But we were talking about starting a family when I bought it, and I'm one of six. She's one of four, so the three-bedroom thing I knew might be an issue. But given where I bought, we could have built up. So, we could have added bedrooms if we wanted."

"You bought it without her knowledge?"

He nodded.

"I'm sorry. I don't want to take her side because of how she just behaved, but I'd be mad at you too if you did that. It's insanely controlling, and she seems like the type of woman who would resent that."

Zadie fussed, and Bryn reached over and rocked the car seat.

"Cheryl loved grandiose gifts. One of her friend's husbands bought his wife a car. And not just any car, a Porsche. He did so sight unseen, and Cheryl thought that was the most romantic thing ever and hinted that something like that would be okay for me to do. Silly me to think a house would be on the same level."

"A vehicle that you drive is very different from a place you live," Bryn said with her forehead scrunched just enough to make a few creases.

Jamison didn't have his mother's and some of his brother's cop skills, but he didn't need them to read her face.

Something about the idea of Jamison making a decision for both him *and* his ex-wife bothered her to the core.

"I understand that," he said. "However, we discussed exactly what she wanted, and we even looked at a few places together. Of course, they were all out of our price range, which I explained to her. I also told her that we could do it if we scaled it down."

"And what did she say to that?"

"She told me to show her some places. My house was about to come on the market, so I put an offer on it because I knew it would go fast—"

"That was a mistake. You should have showed it to her first."

"In Florida, you can back out of a deal after thirty days, no questions asked. So, we could have walked away. It was her call," Jamison said with a little more kick than intended. He was tired of defending his actions when it came to Cheryl. He wasn't the one who'd checked out on their marriage. He wasn't the one who'd decided that his career wasn't good enough. His money wasn't enough. That nothing about him would ever be good enough.

"I don't mean to be judgmental, but that's a lot of pressure to put on someone, especially when I suspect you were super-excited. If she said, 'No freaking way. I don't want it,' she would be crushing your dreams and putting a hole in your heart."

"That's kind of what she did," Jamison said.

"But you said that was on your first wedding anniversary. Had your marriage already gone bad that early?"

He curled his fingers around his beer glass and took a long, slow sip. He thought long and hard about his marriage and their courtship. He'd honestly loved Cheryl, faults and all—and she had a few. His father had once asked him if he'd thought he could change her. Jamison had known that he couldn't, but he'd always believed that she'd grow and learn, like everyone did.

Being eight years younger than Jamison wasn't that big of a deal. The problem was that Cheryl wanted more than she had. Always. Her family had struggled financially for most of her life, and Cheryl had spent her childhood being jealous of those who had more. The problem was that she didn't do anything about it and simply expected others to take care of her—starting with Jamison.

He had promised her that when he hit twenty years as a firefighter, he'd retire and find a second career. But he still hadn't hit that mark, and now he was glad that he was divorced because he thought he still had another ten or so years in him.

"No. Not really. I mean, we had our problems like every couple," he said. "When I showed her the house, I explained that we didn't have to take it, but I also had an interior decorator walk the property with us, talking about what we could do in the future. How the house could grow with us. Cheryl seemed to be on board and decided it was okay to keep it. Only, when we couldn't do everything right away, things started to go bad. We fought over what needed to be done first. Still, we formulated a plan, one that we were both happy with. Or so I thought. Until Steve and my mom showed up on my doorstep wanting a DNA swab."

Bryn lowered her chin. "They literally dropped by like that?"

"My mom is quite forward. I both love that about her and resent the fuck out of it."

"If you don't mind me asking, what does that honestly have to do with you buying and keeping your home?"

"I don't mind," he said. "Because Steve is rich and my biological father, she believed he owed me and thought I should ask him for the money we needed to make the house exactly like she wanted. I don't want to owe anyone. Not him. Not the man who raised me. Not my mother."

"I can relate to that, but I still have to side with

her on buying the house in the first place. I would have appreciated seeing it before the offer went in."

"Trust me. I've learned my lesson, though I doubt I'll ever get a chance to make the mistake a second time."

"Why do you say that? You don't want to get re-married?"

"I don't want to move," he said with a smile.

"Fair enough." She pushed Zadie back and forth in the car seat. "Can I ask you a really personal question?"

"Sure," he said.

"When did the affair happen?"

"I think it started right when I found out about Steve."

"Shit. That really sucks. I'm sorry." Bryn reached across the table and squeezed his hand. "Is she seeing anyone now?"

"She's in an on-again/off-again relationship with the man she cheated on me with. A guy by the name of Troy. Unfortunately, it's someone I work with."

"Wow. And she still wants you back?"

"It's a bit fucked up," Jamison said.

"You can say that again."

"I do wish the best for her, but she doesn't make it easy." Thing was, he actually meant that. He didn't want to have any ill will toward Cheryl, but she made it so damn easy.

"How long have you been divorced?"

"Just a year," he said.

"That's still pretty fresh." Bryn picked up a fussy Zadie. "And I stand by my observation that she's still in love with you."

"Perhaps, but I'm not in love with her anymore." And that was the truth. His love had died the day he'd caught her in bed with Troy. It was bad enough that his wife had cheated.

It was worse that it was with someone he'd once called a friend. And someone he missed and wanted back in his life.

"We'd better get that girl of yours home. It's getting late, and I'm sure you want to get a routine going." He waved to the waitress to get the check.

"Thank you for tonight. It was nice to get out."

"You're welcome." He glanced at the bill and tossed a wad of cash on the table.

"Hey," she said, "we were supposed to split that."

"You can pay me back for your half however you see fit. I kind of just want to get out of here, if you don't mind."

"I can appreciate that." She gently placed her daughter in the car seat and slipped from the bench. "But the next dinner is on me."

"I'm just tickled that you're agreeable to a second date."

"Don't call it that," she corrected. "I suggest that it's a business dinner."

"I can live with that." Jamison waited for her to

secure Zadie in the car seat before taking it from her hands and leading the way through the busy maze of people. He wasn't sure what to think of how comfortable he felt being in Bryn's company or the fact that, for the first time in the last year, he didn't actually care what his ex-wife thought.

8

*B*ryn stood in front of her Keurig and tapped her foot, waiting for her decaf coffee to finish percolating. She glanced over at her little girl, who was taking her morning nap in the portable bassinet that Jamison had bought. The man had managed to get her everything she needed, and relatively inexpensively. She knew this because she'd looked everything up online and checked the receipts he'd left. She wanted to return any overpriced items for less-expensive things, but he'd really done some bargain shopping.

She smiled as Zadie stretched but didn't wake. She was sure that she had the best baby on the planet.

Zadie went to bed at night around one in the morning and didn't wake up again until eight. That was pretty darn good. Of course, she didn't sleep much from seven at night on and demanded to be held, swaddled, cooed at, and fed pretty much all the time before she went down for the night. However, Bryn figured this routine would change in a few weeks. During the day, Zadie was pure sweetness, giving Bryn enough time to build her website and populate it with some products, as well as Jamison's. Now, both were live, and she was fielding emails and phone calls from both.

All she had to do was decide about going to Jamison's sister-in-law's party or not.

The more time she spent with Jamison, the more conflicted she became. On the one hand, he wore his emotions on his sleeve. When he walked into a room, she could tell what he was feeling. Or, at the very least, she could sense how others affected his mood.

She admired how he controlled his actions, though he dealt with things with a heavy dose of sarcasm. His bottled-up anger, which covered up his pain, gave her pause. He appeared to be a giant teddy bear, but she'd thought that Timothy had been romantic and sweet when an evil monster hid under all that generosity.

The doorbell startled her, and she jumped. She picked up her cell and opened the app that allowed her to see and talk with whoever was disturbing her morning ritual.

Mrs. Willamina Campbell from next door. Sweet old lady with some of the funniest stories.

And she missed her best friend.

From what Bryn had gathered, Chip's mom, Elenore, had been the life of every party, and the entire town missed her dearly.

Bryn made sure the bassinet was settled in the middle of the table before scurrying from the kitchen to the front door. "Hi, Mrs.—"

"I've told you a million times to call me Willa."

"Hi, Willa," Bryn said with a smile. "I was just making some coffee. It's decaf. Would you like some?"

"I'd prefer tea. Do you have that?"

"Of course. It's just basic tea. Nothing fancy. Is that okay?"

"That would be perfect. Thank you. I actually haven't had my morning cup." Willa strolled—no, more like waddled like a duck—into the kitchen and took a seat at the table. She rested her hand on Zadie's belly and gave it a little pat. Willa loved coming over and sitting with Zadie. She'd spent two hours with her yesterday while Bryn did some website work and made some jewelry. It was nice because Zadie would get a little fussy, and Willa would scoop her up and rock her, but she wouldn't take any money. "I was hoping to borrow a bag of tea, but since you offered, I certainly won't pass up a little company. And I have a favor to ask."

Bryn went about fixing a mug of hot water and tea, making sure she grabbed a few extra bags so Willa could take some home. Not that she minded the woman coming over, but she knew Willa would likely go through two or three a day.

"Before we get to your favor, I made you a little present," Bryn said.

"Oh, no, dear. I told you not to do that."

"Well, it's not exactly for you." Bryn set a cup in front of Willa. "You mentioned that your grand-daughter is turning eighteen next month and that she's always loved dolphins."

Willa nodded.

"I made her a dolphin necklace. Let me go get it." Bryn raced to her bedroom and opened the top drawer of her desk. A shadow outside caught her attention. She gasped.

A man, at least she thought it was a man, wearing a hoodie, hunched down in her bushes. When he realized that she saw him, he took off running.

Bryn stood there, frozen, staring out the window, her muscles so tight she couldn't move. She opened her mouth and gasped but covered it quickly, not wanting to scare her elderly neighbor. Whoever was out there could be here just for her and no one else.

Or maybe it was that bitch, Suzie.

She should call the police, but if Barb and Mark Perish found her, the police wouldn't be able to help her because her in-laws would bribe the entire department. No one touched the Perish family. They could, and *did*, get away with murder.

She wiggled her fingers. She'd know if the Perish

family or anyone in their organization thought Bryn was alive. It would be an all-out witch hunt.

It was best if she called the authorities.

No. Then she'd be in the system. She couldn't afford that.

Another reason not to go to Nancy's birthday party with Jamison. He could show off the piece that he'd picked out and they could go to her website if they wanted more information. She could tell him that she and Zadie had had a tough night and that she needed rest. He'd believe that and leave it alone.

She hoped.

"I think your granddaughter will love this." Bryn strolled into the kitchen and set the open necklace box on the table.

"Oh, my. That's just beautiful." Willa fingered the silver dolphins. "I can't take this without paying you."

"You can. And you will." Bryn squeezed the kind woman's shoulder. "You can tell everyone where you got it, and they can come buy more pieces from me."

Willa waggled her finger. "You're a clever one."

"Why, thank you." Bryn did a little bow as if she were on stage. She'd fallen in love with Willa. It was like spending time with her grandmother. Or her favorite aunt, who had passed when Bryn was fifteen. She felt safe with Willa. "Now, what was the favor you wanted to ask me?"

"Well, as you know, I can no longer drive, so I was hoping to catch a ride with you to Nancy's party."

How could she say no to Willa? That would be like saying no to a well-behaved child on Christmas.

Impossible.

"You are going, right? Jamison said you would be."

He shouldn't have said she was definitely going. That was a bit manipulative on his part, and she'd make sure that she let him know how much that annoyed her later.

But there was no point dragging a sweet old lady into it.

"Yes. I'm going. And I'd be happy to drive you. Can you be ready at twelve-thirty?"

"With bells on." Willa lifted her teacup to her lips and took a slow sip. "Oh. That's some good stuff."

Bryn sat across from Willa and sipped her coffee. She'd learned in the short week she'd lived in Lighthouse Cove that you didn't push Willa out the door too fast. And, right now, Bryn was fine with that. She hadn't realized how lonely she'd been all these months living in solitude, only leaving one dingy hotel room to go to the next one.

There was a three-week period where Bryn swore she hadn't seen the sun. During that time, all she could think about was never seeing her father or sister again. She knew what it was like to bury a parent. And she missed her mother every day. However, when someone died, it was final, and you knew it. At some point, you had to accept it.

When Bryn left California, she'd known that her father and sister were alive. However, if something were to happen to them, she'd never know. It tore her at her insides that they were grieving her death when all she wanted to do was go running up her father's driveway screaming, "*I'm alive.*"

But she needed to remain dead.

"Where did you go, honey? Because it's not here in Lighthouse Cove." Willa rested her wrinkled hand over Bryn's wrist. "Sometimes, when we sit and chat, you disappear for a minute or two. I don't usually say anything, but right now, you have this sad look about you, and it breaks my heart."

Bryn had told Jamison that she was estranged from her sister. It was a story she would stick to. It was believable, and while everyone had an opinion, it wasn't like anyone would meddle because her fabricated sister would be unreachable, and she'd never show her face in Florida.

"I was just thinking about the party for Nancy, whom I haven't met yet, and how I wish things were different with my sister and me."

"You've only mentioned that you have one and that you aren't close."

Tears threatened to fill Bryn's eyes. That was so far from the truth, and it hurt. She and Anna, who she was going to call Arleen from now on, had been best friends. Her sister had been Bryn's confidante. The one person, besides Hatti, that she could count on until Timothy turned into an asshole. That's when Anna, aka Arleen, had had enough. She told Bryn that if she didn't leave Timothy, she would stop giving her a safe place to land every time he raised his fist to Bryn's cheek.

And that's exactly what she did.

So, it wasn't an untrue statement to say that they were estranged. However, Arleen had told her that if she ever left, she'd be the first one to open her doors, her arms, and her heart.

"We're not, and I was just thinking about how close Jamison's family is and how sad it is that he's struggling with it all. I mean, they're all still here and have a chance to mend things. I won't ever have that with my sister."

"That's too bad," Willa said. "Why do you say that?"

Because she thinks I'm dead, was the first thing that popped into Bryn's head. "It's complicated."

Willa laughed. Not loudly. She never did that. It was always this quiet chuckle where her shoulders bobbed up and down, and she shook her head. "All families are complicated. Take Jamison and his family. He tries so hard to be mad and to hate them and not speak to them. Jamison has done a pretty good job of shunning Steve, his kids, and both his parents, but then his marriage fell apart, and it was his dad who helped him pick up the pieces there. His mom tried, but Jamison wouldn't let her in. I think he should, but what I do I know?"

"I'm sure the sting of being cheated on by his wife didn't help the relationship with his mom."

"Like I said, you're a smart cookie." Willa pointed to a squirmy Zadie. "May I pick her up?"

"She's going to be fussy for food soon, so be my guest." That's another thing that Bryn enjoyed about Willa. She always asked before randomly picking up her kid.

Willa lifted Zadie over her shoulder and patted the baby's behind. "Jamison's the youngest of six boys. Imagine that growing up. And his older brothers were hard on him. Relentless at times. But that young man let it all roll off his back like he hadn't a care in the world. When he found out about his paternity, it was like his entire existence had been washed out to sea. He didn't know who he was or how he fit in anymore. At first, his brothers were just as angry and upset as he was, especially when their parents finally called it quits." Willa shifted the baby to her other shoulder as Zadie squirmed more.

"It sounds like Jamison's parents had marital problems for a long time."

"They did, and they probably should have divorced after they had kid number three, but they didn't. Truth be told, Steve coming back was the catalyst, but not the reason, and when the older boys realized that, they accepted the relationship. But Jamison, because he's the product of the first affair, he can't seem to come around."

Part of Bryn could totally understand where Jamison was coming from. His identity had completely changed. The biology of who he thought he was, and the reality of the DNA, were two very different things.

However, that didn't change who he was or who he'd become. He was still the same man, and that was the disconnect for Bryn. Jamison held onto his hurt and pain like a medal and displayed it as if it were a scarlet letter. Factor in a cheating wife, and it was the perfect storm.

One thing Bryn had learned from being married to a control freak: The more Timothy pushed her to do what he wanted, the more she wanted to rebel. However, when he became violent and stripped her of all her self-worth, she'd lost herself and became someone she didn't recognize anymore.

She couldn't figure out if Jamison was the kind of man who had controlled his wife to the point where she lashed out by having an affair, or if he was the type of man who had a kind heart that people tended to put a knife in, which meant he was bleeding out all over the floor now.

It was a hard thing to figure out because Jamison sat on two fences. He was a victim in his parents' mistake.

A victim in his wife's affair.

But he tended to control and take action where a little communication would be more efficient.

It was the latter that made Bryn want to keep Jamison at arm's length. But he paid her a decent wage that would help her pay her first month's rent and get more supplies for her business. Right now, she needed the pesky firefighter with his side handyman job. But she'd keep her wits about her, and she'd make damn sure he stayed in his lane.

"Maybe if they backed off and gave him space instead of constantly telling him what to do, he might decide to have the necessary conversations to mend fences all on his own." It felt like Jamison wanted to do that, but he wanted to do it on *his* terms. Not his mothers, or Steve's, or even his brothers'. But the longer he waited, the harder it became. Bryn understood. This was completely different than her marriage to Timothy, or what his family had done as they stripped her of her power.

Yet Jamison was holding on to what little control he had over his life.

She'd done that with eating. She chose what went into her mouth, how much or how little, and how often. Her weight went up and down like a rollercoaster. It became another thing for Timothy to hit her over, but still, it was the one thing she had a say in. Jamison had decided who he wanted to have a relationship with and who he didn't.

"That's what his father keeps telling everyone, but

his mom pushes." Willa kissed Zadie on the forehead. "Jamison and his mom are a lot alike. Stubborn. Know-it-alls. And they like to do things their way. Once, when Chip and Jamison were over here building that carport, I heard those two boys yelling and screaming at each other. I swear, I thought they might get into a fistfight. Not kidding."

"What were they fighting over?"

"I'm not exactly sure. But it had to do with the best way to build it. Chip eventually threw his hands up and caved, deciding it was better to do it however Jamison wanted than to stand there and fight with his best friend."

Another reason to keep Jamison at a safe distance. She was sure that Jamison wasn't like Timothy in the sense that he was a wife-beater. But being a control freak had its pitfalls, too. However, Bryn would never be ready to let a man into her life.

Never.

Not even when Zadie was grown.

"Jamison is a perfectionist. Chip, not so much. So, I think it was a good idea to do it Jamison's way. But sometimes he's so stubborn he can't see past his own nose, and that can be a problem."

"It sure can."

Zadie squirmed some more and started to cry.

"I think this little one is getting hungry." Willa handed Zadie over. "And I best go get ready for the barbecue. Thank you so much for taking me, dear."

"It's my pleasure." Bryn stood, taking Zadie. Her confidence as a mom had expanded, and she felt as though she were getting to know her child's wants and needs. She wanted to believe it was intuitive; however, it was more a combination of trial and error and paying attention to behaviors.

That and sheer luck.

"Oh, no, honey. Don't get up. I can see myself out."

Bryn nodded. She leaned back in the chair and adjusted her clothing. So far, she'd mastered the breastfeeding thing, but in another week, she'd start giving Zadie a bottle. She wanted that freedom. Not that she ever planned to leave her precious little girl, but she wasn't sure how long she'd be feeding this way, and she knew Willa wanted to be able to feed Zadie. It would be nice to have three or four hours so she could exercise, take a long bath, or even go to the grocery store alone.

But she'd insist on paying Willa.

Bryn would never be indebted to another person again.

9

*F*amily gatherings these days made Jamison itchy. He scratched his neck and shoulder as he stood in front of the grill. He couldn't believe that he'd agreed to step foot in Steve's ocean-front mansion. Of course, he didn't buy the lame excuse that the venue had changed last minute. Nope. Best kept fucking secret in Lighthouse Cove.

Shit. Wait until his ex-wife showed up. She'd be all up his ass about how he could be working for his biological father and living on Lighthouse Island in a twenty-million-dollar home, too. Well, no fucking way. Besides not being able to wrap his brain around that kind of wealth, he couldn't see himself living like this. It was over-the-top and way too indulgent.

As he'd told Bryn, he could imagine building a second story onto the house he owned now. But that would cost a few pretty pennies.

And he didn't have enough of those saved up yet. But he would. Someday. Especially now that he had a website and was working off more than word of mouth.

He lifted the grill, and steam and smoke hit his face. He took the spatula and flipped the burgers, pushing around a couple of the hot dogs and potatoes. His mother had been happy that he'd agreed to do the grilling. However, she'd also wanted him to mingle with the hundred-plus guests that'd shown up.

"Hey, baby brother," Seth said as he slapped his shoulder. "Looks like you're still trying to avoid all of us by cooking." Seth was ten years older. But growing up, they had been tight. Not to mention, Seth had married a woman that Jamison had dated. Sort of. And Farrah and Jamison had been friends all through school. She was still someone Jamison admired and enjoyed being around, though the current climate of the family made that difficult.

He wished things were different. Especially with Seth, though that relationship was getting better. If Jamison had needed advice about anything, he'd call Seth before going to any of his other siblings. It wasn't because he was older and wiser, though that was part of it. It had more to do with the connection he felt with Seth. As if he always understood where Jamison was coming from and knew how to help solve whatever problems his little brother was faced with in life.

Until Steve had come into the picture.

Seth had been one of the first to accept Steve and his family, and that hurt in ways Jamison couldn't describe. It was a betrayal that'd burned through his core faster than when his wife had cheated on him.`

"Actually, Dad set me on this task."

"That shouldn't surprise me." Seth handed him an ice-cold beer. "Mom said you're bringing a date."

"We're not dating," Jamison corrected. "Bryn doesn't know anyone in town, and I thought this would be a good place for her to meet some people. Plus, she's got a jewelry-making business that she needs to get off the ground."

"Yes. I've heard. Mom is showing off her website to everyone who steps through the doors and talking about how she's going to use her to make some custom pieces. But Mom thinks you're bringing Cheryl as your date, not Bryn, and she's telling people that you're going to have special jewelry made for her as if you're getting back together."

"That, right there, is why I'm not staying long." He arched a brow. "I don't know what's worse. Mom pushing Cheryl on me or Steve."

"Jamison, don't start." Seth took a quick swig of his beer and gave him that big-brother look of disappointment. "Mom just wants you to be happy, and Cheryl is in her ear telling her things and influencing her. You're not."

"I can only imagine what Cheryl has been saying. But what's worse is that Mom is even listening, much less believing her. I'm divorced, and there's a reason for that. I don't want Cheryl in my life, and Mom needs to respect that."

"Well, you need to respect that Steve is in Mom's life, so don't go and pick a fight with them today. Or Orlando. He's struggling with all this, too."

"He's only worried I'm going to take his trust fund." The second the words left Jamison's mouth, he regretted them. He had no idea what his new siblings really thought because he refused to give them the time of day. And, honestly, they hadn't tried too hard to reach out to him, either.

"That's not true."

Jamison chuckled. "It's partly true, and you know it."

"Only because of Cheryl," Seth said. "For the record, we've all told Mom that Cheryl isn't the one for you."

"Thanks."

"But I'm asking you to be on your best behavior today."

"Keep Steve away from me, and we've got nothing to worry about."

"Come on, man. It's been two years since all this came out. Why can't you let it go?" Seth leaned against the outdoor kitchen counter. He looked identical to their father.

To Dalton.

It was a painful reminder that the biology wasn't there for Jamison.

"I could if everyone would stop trying to force a man who isn't my father on me."

"All right. But he's Mom's boyfriend. He loves her, and she loves him, and I wouldn't be surprised if a wedding's in the near future."

Jamison closed his eyes for a brief moment and inhaled sharply. The thick, rich scent of sizzling meat filled his lungs. He allowed the aroma to linger for as long as he could. He needed the pleasantness of it to crowd out the bitter emotions filling his heart.

He blinked. He had no desire to fight with his brothers, but they didn't make it easy. "Have you ever once put yourself in my shoes?"

"I've thought about what it must be like for you. And I know, initially, I'd have been upset, too. But dragging it out this long, I don't understand that."

Of course, Seth didn't have a clue because, at the end of the day, it didn't affect him or how he looked at himself in the mirror. Jamison woke up every day and, before he let his feet hit the floor, told himself that he wouldn't allow this to control his world.

But the second he brought that razor to his cheeks; he saw how different he was from the five brothers he had been raised with and how much he looked like the four siblings he'd hadn't known he had. It wasn't major things that stood out, but tiny details. Like the fact that he was the only one in his family who was left-handed.

Like Steve.

Like Steve's sons, Orlando and Melbourne. Or the girls, Tallahassee and Miami.

Or that Jamison wasn't as tall as his brothers, who were all at least six-one.

Steve was five-ten. Orlando and Melbourne were five-eleven.

Jamison could rattle off a dozen other tiny differences that many wouldn't notice, but they smacked him right between the eyes, and they mattered to him because they made him feel as though he wasn't part of *his* family. It sounded crazy, even to him.

However, inside, his heart and his soul had shattered into a million pieces, and he couldn't find them all to put them back together again, no matter how hard he tried. It became this impossible game of trying to fit into something that he'd thought had been his home but had turned out to be a lease all along.

Yep. Crazy.

"We're still brothers. Nothing and no one can take that away from us," Seth said.

That was a true statement, but things *were* different. They no longer shared the same biology. Not completely. There were differences, and as subtle as they might be, they existed, and Jamison couldn't shake how distant it made him feel from his family.

"I'm trying to make things right with you and all our brothers."

"But not Mom and Steve," Seth said as a statement and not a question.

"Why do you care so much about me having a relationship with him? Why does it matter to you?" Jamison tossed a bunch of the hot dogs and hamburgers onto a tray and handed them to one of the servers before placing more raw meat on the grill. He could stand here all day as long as he had a beer in his hand.

"Because it matters to Mom. I love her, and I love you. And believe it or not, it matters to Dad."

Jamison took a nice big swig of his cold beverage. His father wanted him to bury the hatchet. He wanted his boys—which included Jamison since he'd raised him as his own—to stay as one big, happy family.

And Jamison wanted to give that to his dad. He just couldn't stomach being around Steve. His therapist had once asked him if he felt abandoned by Steve.

His quick answered had been no.

But that wasn't true.

Only Jamison wasn't willing to admit that out loud.

"I'm here. And I'll be at family parties. But I'm not going to welcome Steve and his kids with open arms. He didn't want me in his life when I was born.

If he did, he would have stuck around instead of letting Dad raise me."

"It's not that simple. And if you'd let anyone tell you what—"

"Don't go there, big brother." Jamison slammed the lid on the grill. "It doesn't matter to me what the reason was. He wasn't a teenager. He was a grown-ass adult who had an affair with a married woman. They both knew what they were doing, and Mom got pregnant. He didn't want me. Dad did."

"I've never met anyone as stubborn as you," Seth said. "Except for maybe our mother." He pushed from the counter and strolled toward a group of people who had gathered by the hot tub.

No sooner did Jamison catch his breath than his mother appeared.

Wonderful.

Well, rumor had it that she'd moved into Steve's place. And it *was* her party that she was throwing for her daughter-in-law, so he knew he couldn't avoid her forever. He just hoped that he wouldn't have to speak too much to Steve. That was always awkward and painful.

"Where's Cheryl?" his mother asked.

"She's my ex. I wouldn't know, and I honestly don't care."

"Why do you have to be like that?"

"Because you keep trying to push me back together with a woman who cheated on me with a friend of mine. Who is *still* sleeping with him. And you don't seem to understand why I don't want to be with her anymore." He glared.

"I've never thought you gave your marriage enough—"

"I don't care what you think about that subject. Now, drop it."

"Fine. What about your friend who makes the jewelry? What's her name? Isn't she coming?" his mother asked.

"Her name is Bryn. She'll be along soon enough. She's bringing Willa with her."

"That's nice of her to do. Willa is so sweet. I'm glad she can make it."

"Bryn's a kind person." He rounded his shoulders and did his best to calm his fucking nerves. He'd promised his dad that he wouldn't start a fight today and that he'd do his best not to be sarcastic and grumpy as his father described him.

He hadn't gotten off to a great start.

His mother waved Nathan over. "I need to speak to you for a moment. Privately."

Fuck. Whatever this was about, he wanted nothing to do with it. "Now? We're in the middle of a party. Can't it wait?"

"No. It can't." She took the spatula from his hand and gave it to Nathan, who immediately stepped in front of the grill and started flipping the burgers.

His mother looped her hand through his arm and

tugged him toward the kitchen. Jamison had never been inside Steve's house, and he really didn't want to see it now. But it looked like he wouldn't get a choice.

This was why he needed to stop making promises to the people that mattered in his life.

He stepped through the largest sliding glass door —no, scratch that, it was more of an accordion-style thing. The kitchen was not only massive, but it also had all state-of-the-art appliances. He was afraid to touch anything for fear he'd break or stain it.

His mom led him through a family room the size of Bryn's entire house. The television had to be one hundred inches, at least. It was incredible. He'd never seen anything like it before in his entire life. Watching porn on it would probably be more like viewing a horror flick. He pushed that thought right out of his brain as he followed his mom down a hallway, around a bend, and into an office.

"Oh, no," he said, backing up.

She grabbed him by the wrist and tugged. "Ten minutes. Just give him that."

He met her stare, ignoring the man sitting behind the large, cherry wood desk. "Why should I?"

"I know if I were to say because I'm asking you to, you'd laugh."

"I wouldn't go that far," he said. "However, I don't owe either of you anything."

"No. You don't," Steve. "But I'd like the chance to talk to you. Man to man. And since you won't take my calls, this was the only way I thought that might happen." Steve stood and waved his hand toward one of the big leather chairs in front of his desk. "Why don't you take a seat?"

"I'd rather stand, thank you." Jamison folded his arms across his chest, keeping himself closed off emotionally.

His mom curled her fingers around his biceps. "All I'm asking is that you listen to him." She squeezed. "I'll be out back."

Jamison said nothing. He just stood there. He'd hear the words, but he wasn't sure he'd take them in. What difference did it make? Steve had made his choice. There were no do-overs when it came to becoming a parent. Especially this late in the game.

Steve pressed his hands to the top of his wood desk. He glanced between the glass doors that looked out over the patio and Jamison. "I've lived here for three years, and I believe you and I might have shared ten sentences with each other."

"I'm standing here not because my mother wants me to, but because I'm tired of being mad at my brothers and I miss them. I am doing this for them. And for my dad. No other reason. So, speak your mind."

"You remind me of your mother."

"I get that a lot," Jamison admitted. In the past, he'd have taken that as a compliment. Actually, he still did. He was proud of his mother. Being the chief of police was no small feat. And she was good at her job. She was a kind woman, too. A good mother.

But she'd made some shitty choices, and he'd paid the price.

"I think this calls for some liquid courage." Steve stood, turned, and opened a cabinet behind his desk. "Do you like a good tequila?"

"As a matter of fact, I do." While he generally considered himself a standard beer drinker, when he went for the stronger stuff, he preferred tequila over anything else.

"Orlando and Tallahassee love tequila, but my other two kids, not so much." Steve handed him a glass of clear liquid with a couple of ice cubes but thankfully didn't ask him to clank glasses because that's where Jamison would draw the line.

Jamison took a sip, expecting it to burn, but it went down smoothly. It was like nothing he'd ever tasted. He was tempted to ask for the brand name, but he figured it was probably something like a thousand dollars a bottle. He also wanted to know why Steve had named his kids after cities in Florida, but that might be seen as an exercise in getting to know someone, and that wasn't something he wanted.

Yet.

"I had this entire speech planned out. I've been playing it over in my head for years, but now that you're standing here, and we're alone, I don't know where to begin." Steve sat on the corner of his desk.

He set his drink on a coaster and let out a long sigh. "You've never once asked why I left."

"It's kind of obvious."

Steve chuckled before lifting his glass, giving it a little twirl, letting the ice rattle, and raising it to his lips. He stared past Jamison and swallowed. "How so?"

"I'm not going to play this game. You brought me here to tell me something, so say it."

"I'd like to know what's going on in your head, though. What it is that you think. Because if you believe I left because I didn't want you, then you're wrong. I left you behind because I believed it was the right thing to do and—"

"It was right for you."

"Not just me, but for everyone involved. And it was what your mother wanted," Steve said.

"Can I ask you something?" If Jamison was going to do this, he would do it his way and get the answers he wanted.

"Of course."

"Were you involved with your wife at the time you had the affair with my mom?"

"No. I didn't meet my ex until I moved to Miami," Steve said. "You have to understand, there was always a chance I wasn't your biological father. And because your mom and dad wanted to try to work things out, I stepped aside."

"That's not entirely true." One of the things

Jamison had learned when Steve came back into town was that Steve and Jamison's mom had always been in contact. There hadn't been a time in history where they hadn't communicated with each other. And that not only broke Dalton Kirby's heart, it had killed any chance Steve had for having a relationship with Jamison.

It'd also destroyed the bond that Jamison had with his mom. He could no longer trust anything she said or did. It was all suspect.

Cheryl cheating had made it all worse. It was like pouring salt on an open wound, and Jamison had already lost his family.

"What are you talking about?" Steve narrowed his gaze.

"You never took a back seat in my mother's life. And don't try to deny it."

"I'm not sure what you're implying."

"You kept in contact with my mother after you left Lighthouse Cove."

"No. We didn't speak to each other until you were two years old, and she heard that I'd gotten married. She knew in her heart that you were my son. She reached out to me, but my wife was about to give birth to our first daughter at the time. It was then that I understood why it had been so important for your mom to keep her family together, and I was going to do the same with mine. Your mom and I didn't begin our friendship again for another ten years."

Jamison downed the rest of his drink and set the glass on the desk.

Immediately, Steve moved it to a coaster.

"I'm not sure I'd classify what you were as *friends*," Jamison said. "You might not have been sleeping with my mother during those years, but it was still an emotional affair."

"I won't deny being in love with your mom for as long as I've known her, but she wanted to try to keep her family intact, and I wanted to do the same with mine. It was a complicated situation, and we made a lot of mistakes. As a matter of fact, when she first found out that she was pregnant with you, she didn't tell me. She actually called off our affair. Told me she could never see me again. That it was over. However, Dalton found out about us when she was seven months pregnant and, for a short time, your mom contemplated leaving him."

Jamison's breath caught. It wasn't that he didn't know this, but hearing it from Steve seemed highly inappropriate and hurtful.

"She wanted me to move back, but I couldn't. And if she were to leave, your dad wouldn't have let her take your brothers."

There was a reason Jamison didn't want to hear this. "I take it if it had been proven that I was your kid, she would have been able to take me."

Steve nodded.

"And you met your wife, so you told her no."

"Actually, that relationship was new, and I was madly in love with your mom. I would have blown up my life in a heartbeat."

"Why didn't you?"

"Your mom couldn't move to Miami," Steve said. "And I couldn't leave."

"Why the fuck not?" Jamison asked with a fair amount of anger. He had no idea where it had come from.

Actually, that wasn't true.

He felt abandoned.

By his biological father.

"There were things I needed to take care of in down south. And considering the situation and with Dalton knowing about the affair, I felt as if I needed to make a sacrifice so that you could have the best life. I called Dalton. We agreed not to find out who the father was and to put him down on the birth certificate. I'm sure it wasn't easy for your dad. I know how hard it was for me. But I wasn't looking at your face day in and day out, and I asked Rebecca not to send me pictures. The one time she did, I knew immediately that you were my kid." Steve leaned across his desk and pulled open the center drawer. He pulled out a photograph. "I guess this was the day you got your driver's license."

"Wow. I remember that day." Jamison took the image. His hand shook as he stared at his younger self.

He couldn't help it. He glanced between the photo and Steve.

He looked just like him. There was no denying that.

He glanced at all the pictures of Steve's two boys and two daughters lining the bookshelves behind his desk.

Jamison and Melbourne looked as if they could be twins. Orlando had a bit of a different look, but there was still a huge resemblance. And, of course, he saw the similarities to his half-sisters.

It was hard to comprehend that he had four more siblings to add to the five he already had.

"Dalton told me that if we were going to do this, I had to go away and never come back," Steve said.

"I guess you're not a man of your word."

"That's not fair. Because I did exactly that until you well into your thirties." Steve puffed out his chest. "I left you alone. I raised my family. I did the best I could to stay in my corner. But you are right when it comes to Rebecca. She and I broke our word to your dad by remaining friends. When I returned three years ago, your father asked me if I was going to come after you, and I said no."

"But you did anyway."

"Put yourself in my shoes. Wouldn't you want to know?"

That was a question no one had ever asked Jamison, including himself and his therapist. And he didn't have an answer. He wasn't prepared to dig deep and examine the question.

Only, the tickle in his heart told him that maybe, just maybe, he might want to know if he were Steve.

"And, for the record, I didn't break up your parents' marriage. And you know that. They separated a dozen times. I know because your mom called me each and every time."

"You can stop right there." Jamison had heard enough. "I know what it's like to have a wife cheat on me. While I understand that Cheryl and I had other issues, it was the affair that put the final nail in that coffin. You put a few of those in my parents. All those letters, emails, and late-night phone calls, they did a number on their relationship."

"Perhaps. But at the end of the day, we all tried to protect you. That includes both your dad and me."

"If that's the case, why did you feel the need to tell me the truth after all these years?" Jamison had never asked anyone that question, and whenever his dad tried to explain, he shut him down.

Same with his mom.

That had been before his divorce. Once he and Cheryl split, everyone cut him some slack, but now it was all building again since Steve and his mom were all lovey-dovey.

"Your parents had separated. I moved back. People were gossiping about it. Your mom and I wanted to know. So did your dad."

"And you didn't think about how it would affect me? My brothers? Your other children?"

"Of course, we did," Steve said. "However, you're not a child. You're a grown-ass man. We didn't think you'd all but cut your mom out of your life."

"That's just it, Steve. You didn't think about anyone but yourself. Neither did my mom. And for the last two years, I've had to listen to why I should accept you, simply because we share the same biology. I'm told I need to forgive and forget. That the past lies don't really matter. But you have no idea what you've done to me or how this has affected all aspects of my life, and I'm damn fucking tired of explaining it. You've had thirty-seven years to come to terms with being my father. My dad made a conscious decision to raise me, knowing I might not be his kid. That takes a man with honor and a whole lot of love, which Dalton Kirby has in spades. He's never wavered, either. Not even when you waltzed back into our lives as if you belonged in them. I mean no disrespect, but you are not my dad. You never will be, and just because you and my mother are in a relationship doesn't mean I'm going to welcome you in any capacity. You've fucked with my identity, and now I need time to figure out some things about myself. Maybe that sounds childish or immature, but that's my truth. And even when I *do* get all that straightened out in my mind, you'll never be my father. That title is reserved for the man who cared enough to be there when things got tough." Jamison tried to swallow but he couldn't. The harshness of his words was too much. He'd gone too far, and he knew it.

"You know what, fuck it," Steve said under his breath. "You talk about what all this did to you and how damn tired you are and that I'm some selfish monster, but you missed out on some key information. Do you even know why I left town?"

"Yeah. To build your empire and because you and my mom—"

"No. I left because my mother was dying, and I needed to go back to Miami to take care of her. I have money and means, and I wasn't about to have other people taking care of her in her final days. I wanted to do that, especially if there was a chance she could live longer. I wanted to make sure she had the best treatment money could buy." He stood and found the bottle of tequila, refilling his glass and downing half of it. "I promised Rebecca that I wouldn't tell you this shit because she didn't want you to feel like I was justifying or putting my family's needs over you or some bullshit. She thought that would fuck with your fragile psyche more. Well, fuck that. You're not fragile whatsoever, and you're a grown-ass man."

"That's correct," Jamison said.

"My mother hung on for five years. She lived to see me get married and was there when Tallahassee was born. My biggest regret with my mom was that she didn't know about you," Steve said. "The cold, hard facts are that as parents, we make some pretty questionable decisions. Plain and simple, we fucked up." He swiped the tears that rolled down his cheeks.

"I can agree with you on that point."

Steve laughed. "When I told Rebecca I was leaving for Miami, I asked her to come with me, but we know that wasn't possible. I wouldn't stay because of my mom, but I told Rebecca that I'd try and talk my mom into moving and that I'd help her raise you. But once she decided to stay with Dalton, I felt I had no choice, and my mom became my priority. I loved you. I wanted you, but I no longer had a say in the matter."

Jamison leaned against the doorjamb. "You always have a choice. However, I can respect wanting to take care of your mom. What I don't understand is why you didn't do the DNA test sooner?"

"That was my fault," Steve said. "Once your parents decided to stay together, I told your mom that was it. That things needed to stay that way for your sake and for my mom and me. I didn't want her to be on her death bed thinking I had a child she couldn't get to know. That would have been heart breaking for her, and I was afraid I'd do something crazy like try to get visitation or something, and that would have been a shitshow not just for you, but for your brothers, as well."

Jamison had to admit that all made sense. "What

about when you returned? You had an entire year before you told me."

"Your parents and I fought about that. But even I thought I'd be okay. What difference did it make if you knew or not? I was in town for six months before I broke down and told Rebecca that I had to know for sure."

"Were you and my mom a thing yet?"

"It was on and off. Mostly off because there was a hole in my heart because of you."

"All very selfish, if you ask me."

"I won't deny that," Steve said. "Look. If I weren't your biological father, would you be having such a hard time with your mom and me being in a relationship?"

"Honestly, I don't know," Jamison said quickly. "You had an affair. You and my mom both betrayed my dad and me and my brothers. And, as a husband, I know what that feels like. It sucks. I have some serious issues when it comes to honesty and loyalty. I don't know if you have any idea what that's like, but you end up questioning everything that people say and do. It's an exhausting way to live, and I don't want people in my life that I have to worry about, wondering if they are being truthful."

"I've only lied to you about one thing."

Jamison ran a hand across the top of his head. "And that's supposed to make everything okay?"

"No," Steve said. "I'm going to ask your mom to

marry me. I'm not going anywhere. All I'm asking for is the opportunity to get to know you as a person. Not as a father. You have one, and to be totally honest, I knew I was leaving you in the best of hands."

"I guess that's something," Jamison said.

Steve glanced over his shoulder. "Oh shit," he mumbled. "Your ex-wife just arrived."

Jamison leaned forward and glanced toward the pool area. "Why can't my mother get that I want nothing to do with Cheryl?"

"That is something I don't have an answer for. I've told her I don't think you're compatible."

Jamison burst out laughing. "I'm not sure if I find this funny because you're right or that my mom isn't listening to you."

"She won't listen to your dad, either. He told her flat out this morning when we were setting up that she shouldn't be inviting Cheryl to things. I think Dalton called her a manipulative bitch."

Jamison had to appreciate the way Steve used the word *Dad* to describe his father. It meant something. "Sounds like my dad."

"He's a good man."

Jamison nodded.

"Thank you for hearing me out. I hope you understand me better now."

"I do, but please don't take this the wrong way… One conversation isn't going to solve our problems."

"I know. But it's a start."

"Agreed," Jamison said. "Now, if you don't mind, I'd like to go find Bryn and find ways to avoid my ex-wife."

Steve chuckled. "You're really good at avoiding people."

Jamison nodded. He made a beeline for the pool area, but at the last minute, decided to go straight for the beach. He needed a few moments to collect his thoughts before mingling with half of Lighthouse Cove. He figured everyone at the party was wondering how he and his new *daddy* were getting along.

Before he started fielding questions, he wanted to get his answers straight in his head.

10

*B*ryn had spent the last ten years of her life resenting the fact that her husband was wealthy. Timothy and his family hadn't earned their fortune the legal way, for one. And Timothy had kept her on a tight leash. Sure, she could spend to her heart's content when it suited Timothy. As long as she looked the part, he was happy. But the second she bought something he disapproved of, she ended up having to spend a small fortune on better makeup to cover all the bruises.

"Why don't you let me take her for a little bit?" Willa said. "She's fed. She's happy, and I saw Jamison head out toward the beach. Why don't you go join him?"

The entire ride over, Willa couldn't stop talking about how wonderful Jamison was and what a great husband and father he'd make. The last thing Bryn needed was a man. She could raise her child and support them both all by herself. However, the crowd and everyone coming at her, asking her a million questions, had been overwhelming. She could use a little walk along the shore.

"Sounds like a plan. Just text me if you need me, okay?" She kissed her little girl and placed her back in the stroller.

"Don't you worry about us. You go find that handsome young man and have a romantic—"

"Willa, for the last time, it's not like that. We're just friends."

Willa smiled. "For now."

Bryn rolled her eyes and chuckled as she dodged the people mingling on the patio. The older woman meant well, but Jamison had a moodiness to him that Bryn didn't want to deal with. As a friend, he was solid.

As a boyfriend, he couldn't be trusted. Not that he was a cheater. Or an abuser. She didn't believe that. But he had his faults, and they kept popping up like an old-fashioned tin of Jiffy Pop Popcorn.

"Excuse me, ma'am?" a male voice called.

It couldn't be for her, so she kept heading toward the pathway to the beach.

"Oh. Miss. Can I speak to you for a second?" the same voice asked a little louder. "Bryn Tinsley, is it?"

She paused by the edge of the sandy path and turned.

A gentleman, maybe age forty or so, stood five feet away. He wore white shorts and a blue and white golf shirt. His sunglasses were designer and dark, so she couldn't see his eyes.

"Can I help you?"

"Are you Bryn Tinsley?" the man asked.

"I am." She clasped her hands together and fiddled with her thumbnail. "And you are?"

"My name's Jon Kaplan." He held out his hand. "I was hoping to interview you."

"Oh. You're a reporter?" Her insides shook like an earthquake. She searched her brain for the name that Jamison had given her if she ever wanted to do an interview for her jewelry. Maybe it was Jon Kaplan.

It sounded familiar.

"I am. I work for a local magazine. You might have heard of it. *The Lighthouse Cove Living*. I heard about how you gave birth in the middle of the road. That must have been scary."

"It was, but Jamison Kirby kept me calm."

"He's a good man. And one of the best firefighters this town has," Jon said. "He might have told you about me?"

"Yes. He did."

"I was hoping I could do a feature about you and your new business."

"Oh. Well. I guess that would be okay." She fiddled with her thumbnail some more. She hadn't thought too much about this kind of advertising, but it would be good for business. "How much reach does the magazine have?"

"It's mostly local, but it's great when tourists come to town, and we get a lot of those. And since yours is an internet business, you could receive a lot of online orders. Are you interested?"

"I am. Thank you."

"Here's my card. Give me a call on Monday to set something up. I'd like to take some pictures of you wearing your jewelry if that's okay."

"Sounds great." She tucked his card into her pocket. "I really appreciate it."

Jon tilted his head and looked her up and down. "You look familiar."

"I was just on the news," she said nervously. When she'd watched the program, she had been thankful that they'd barely shown her face. It was more Jamison than her and Zadie.

"No." He shook his head. "I thought I'd seen you before when I saw the story about you and your baby."

"I've been told I have that kind of face."

He waved his hand wildly around his head. "The hair is different, but I swear, you look like…" He let his words trail off. "Now that I'm standing next to you, I must be mistaken."

Her heart lurched to her throat and then did a nosedive to her gut. She smiled as best she could. "I've always had one of those faces that reminds people of someone else, so I'm sure it's that."

"I'm sure you're right," Jon said. "Congratulations on your little girl, and I look forward to talking with you soon."

"Thank you. I do, as well." She smoothed down the front of her sundress and headed toward the beach. She wondered if she'd ever stop worrying that someone would recognize her or put her with her late husband's family.

One of the reasons she'd started an online business was that she could pack up and move if she needed to, and she had every intention of doing so in maybe a year or two.

Or less.

It all depended on money and how safe she felt.

Right now, between Jon the nosy reporter, and the random guy jumping out from her bushes, she wasn't feeling very confident that she would be staying too long in Lighthouse Cove, and that made her sad.

She really liked it here so far.

Jamison sat in the sand about twenty feet away. He had his knees to his chest and his arms draped over his legs as he stared at the water crashing against the shoreline not too far from his feet. Hopefully, the tide was going out and not coming in; otherwise, he would be soaked shortly.

"Hey, you," she said softly.

He turned his head and smiled. "You're a sight for sore eyes."

Why did he have this uncanny ability to make her feel like a woman? She didn't want to feel attractive. Hell, she'd just had a baby two weeks ago. She should feel like a puffy marshmallow.

He held out his hand and helped her to the sand. "Where's Zadie?"

"I left her with Willa."

"She's in good hands, then." He leaned back and stretched out his legs. "What brings you out here?"

"That's one hell of a house, and the number of people was slightly overwhelming. I thought it would be nice to check out the water, and Willa saw you come out here."

"I'm glad you joined me."

She crossed her legs and studied his expression.

He always had a contemplative look unless she had him engaged in conversation. She couldn't help but wonder if that was his natural state or a byproduct of the events of the last three years. "How are you holding up?" she asked.

"Honestly? I'm numb."

"Why? Did something happen?"

He nodded. "I had a chat with Steve. It went well, and I have a better understanding of what happened." He reached out and tucked some of her hair that was blowing in the breeze behind her ear. "But in some ways, it conflicts me more."

"Why?"

"I'm not sure I even want to voice it. He made choices because of his family, and I can respect them. But all of a sudden, I feel abandoned by him, and I hate that feeling. I left his office thinking maybe we'd turned a corner, but then I thought about the affair and all the secrets and how it turned everyone's life upside down, and I ended up angry all over again."

Bryn reached out and ran her hand across his shoulder, massaging gently. "Holding grudges is exhausting."

"I've been holding one for two years," he said with a sarcastic tone. "The problem I keep having is that every time I think about having any kind of relationship with Steve and my mom, I feel guilty about my dad."

"But isn't he pushing you to have one?"

"He is. But then he does things like showing up today for an hour or so and then leaving."

"What? Your dad's gone already?"

"He left about ten minutes ago," Jamison said. "He brought his girlfriend, Lanie, but they left. I don't know why. I have to assume it had to do with Steve and my mom."

"That's a big assumption. Did you ask him why he was leaving?"

"Well, no."

"Did you tell him what happened and how you're feeling?" She felt compelled to help him sort through his emotions for some reason. She didn't understand why. Perhaps it was because she'd never have this kind of attachment to family again. And he was the only friend she had in Lighthouse Cove.

Sure, she had Zadie, but it would be a few years before she was old enough for them to develop that kind of mother-daughter bond.

"We talked out here for a good half an hour. He doesn't believe I have any reason to feel guilty and said the only reason he felt the need to leave today was because Grandma wasn't feeling well. Which is true. She wanted to go home and rest."

"Do you think maybe you're using your dad as an excuse not to get to know Steve and to hold onto your hurt feelings?"

Jamison laughed. "That's exactly what my dad, Lanie, and grandma think. But I also believe there's more to it than that. It's like I have this emotional block and can't get past the idea that I'm not a Kirby."

"How do you think someone who's adopted feels?"

"Wow. You sound just like my grandma."

"Dalton is your dad. You have a father-son bond that can't be taken away. Not even by Steve, who you share biology with."

"Have you checked out how much I look like Steve?" Jamison shifted his body, pulling her between his legs.

For a split second, she considered moving out of his embrace. Instead, she leaned back against his firm chest and closed her eyes. She focused on the sound of the waves lapping at the shoreline. She inhaled deeply, letting the salty air tickle her lungs before expelling it back out into the elements. She felt safe, secure, and cared for, and that was an uneasy sensation. But not so much that she was willing to pull away.

Not just yet anyway.

He rested his chin on her head. "I look at him, and it's like looking into a mirror to the future. My mom showed me pictures of him when he was my age, and it was like looking at me in bad clothing choices."

She chuckled.

"I know I'm beating a dead horse with all of this, but I can't shake it. As soon as I let a little of the anger go, something happens, and I'm reminded that my entire life was one big lie."

"Did your parents love you?"

"Yes," he said.

"Did you have a good childhood?"

"That's a bit of a loaded question," he admitted. "My mom and dad fought a lot, and my dad left a few times. So, the answer is…yes and no. It was dysfunctional, but it wasn't horrible."

Bryn decided to make up a truthful lie. If she could help Jamison get past this hurdle where he could be a part of his family again, then it was worth a little dishonestly birthed from part of the truth. "I grew up in an abusive home."

He wrapped his arms tighter around her body. "I'm sorry to hear that."

She gripped his forearms. The memories of Timothy's fists connecting with her cheekbone were all too real. She needed to tell this as if Timothy were her father, not her husband. It was the only way she could help Jamison. And he'd never find out about her lies. If he did, he'd hate her, because the one thing she knew about him was that he couldn't tolerate that kind of betrayal.

"My dad hit me." It wasn't her dad; it was her husband. That was a distinction she needed to remind herself of.

"Shit," Jamison said. "That's fucked up."

"You're right. It is. It's the worst kind of betrayal." Timothy used to tell her that he hit her because he loved her. That if he didn't care that much, he wouldn't bother. At first, she'd found that statement laughable. But near the end, she had begun to believe it.

Jamison hissed.

"The hardest part of all was that the other people in my life who were supposed to protect me, turned a blind eye to it all." Not that her father and sister hadn't paid attention—because they knew what was going on—but they had become so fed up with Bryn, her calls for help, and her unwillingness to do anything about it, that they had told her they would be there for her when she was ready to leave.

For good.

But if she kept going back to Timothy, then they couldn't help her.

Well, she left. But now her family believed she was dead.

"What do you mean?" Jamison asked.

Here comes a big whopper of a lie. "My mom," she said.

"That's rough. That's the one person you're supposed to be able to depend on."

"Exactly. And that's why you struggle with yours."

"My mother and I were always very close until this happened. I did feel betrayed. Much like I did when Cheryl cheated on me."

"That makes sense. But now, let's take this one step further. What your parents did was to protect you from something that shamed them and something you couldn't understand as a child. Your mom didn't want to break up her family, even though she risked it all when she had the affair. Your dad didn't want to hurt your brothers, even though he left a few times. Steve had his own shit to deal with, and while doing that, he tried to respect everyone's wishes. But because he didn't take responsibility for his actions early on, he was the easy one to blame. But aren't you also feeling like something was stolen from you?"

"That's the rub. I've always been proud of who I am. I'm not sure I know how to be a part of Steve's world and be proud of it."

"You won't know until you spend a little more time getting to know him, but don't do it at the expense of losing yourself. You, my friend, have not changed. Your circumstances have, but you have not."

That was something she wished had been true of herself. Unfortunately, everything about who she thought she was had changed the second Timothy had taken control of her life with his fists.

She was still trying to find her way back to her old self. But, sadly, that person was probably gone forever. Timothy had beaten her to death. Maybe that was a good thing, considering Bryn Tinsley needed to be stronger and fiercely independent.

"I'm ready for a nap after that," he said. "So, how do I move past all this?"

"By spending time with each of your family members separately. Get to know them again. Reconnect."

"I don't know. Steve told me he's going to propose to my mom. She's going to move into this house if she hasn't already, and I just can't see her living like this. The only one in my family that would really like this lavish lifestyle besides my ex-wife is my private investigator brother, Rhett, and even he would have to scale it back."

"Is there another reason you're angry with your

mom besides her affair and lying to you about who your birth father is?" Bryn relaxed into Jamison's arms.

Birds chirped overhead. The sun beat down, warming her face. It had been years since she'd felt comfortable in a man's embrace, and that scared the shit out of her for a variety of reasons. This shouldn't feel normal. She shouldn't want to be here like this with Jamison.

She should be sitting in her own space, but she wasn't, and she wasn't doing anything to get there, either.

"You're a smart woman," he said.

"Why are you so angry with your mom?"

Jamison pressed his lips against her temple. They were warm, soft, and she felt safe. Maybe too safe.

It was a set of emotions that she wasn't sure what to do with. On the one hand, she wanted to stand up and run. Being in a man's arms wasn't smart. Yet, it seemed benign. As if nothing would ever come from this moment. Only she knew if this continued, something would indeed happen and she couldn't afford to be entangled with anyone, especially someone like Jamison.

It was difficult to get a read on him, and because he could be controlling, she needed to put an end to this insane thinking.

And hugging.

But she didn't move.

So, there was that.

He took her chin with his thumb and forefinger, tilting her head toward him.

She blinked, catching his gaze. She swallowed as she stared into his intense eyes.

There was no doubt about it. He was going to kiss her, and she wasn't going to stop him, and that was a mistake. One she'd have a hard time recovering from. And then there was the fact that she worked for him and would have to see him on a regular basis.

She needed to stop the kiss before it happened.

Too late.

His lips brushed over her mouth. They were soft and tender and felt like silk.

"Are you kidding?" a female voice said.

Bryn sat up and wiped her lips. Heat rose to her cheeks. Not so much because they'd gotten caught kissing by someone, but because she'd enjoyed it so much.

She turned and saw Cheryl standing with her hand shielding her eyes from the sun.

"You're unbelievable," Cheryl whispered.

"What are you doing out here?" Jamison asked.

"Your mom said you were out here and asked if I would come and check on you. She thought you might be upset."

"You can go tell my mother that I'm fine." He jumped to his feet, pulling Bryn with him. "Now, if you will excuse us, we were kind of in the middle of something."

"So I saw," Cheryl said with a heavy dose of sarcasm. She folded her arms. "Your mom is worried about you. So is Steve. You really need—"

"You lost the right to tell me anything when you slept with one of my best friends."

Bryn tried to tug her hand free, but Jamison held it tightly.

"You left me for nearly two months. I had no idea what was going on with you or when you were coming back. I was scared and alone."

"Why do you always try to blame your cheating on me?" Jamison ran a hand across the top of his head. "You were the only person who knew where I was, and I asked you to come with me. No. I *begged* you to. You chose to get to know Steve, listen to my mother, and sleep with Troy. So don't give me the sob story that you tell everyone else while leaving out the key truths." He turned his attention to Bryn. "I'm sorry you have to hear this crap this way."

Bryn squeezed his hand. "It's okay." She didn't know what else to say. While she didn't believe there was any unfinished business between Jamison and his ex-wife, at least when it came to Jamison, there was a shit ton of conflict in the poor man's heart, and everyone wanted to tell him how he was supposed to feel.

That was the problem.

Something Bryn understood.

Cheryl pursed her lips. "I came out here as a favor to your mom. She just wants you to—"

"Cheryl, stop," Jamison said in a calm voice. "You're not my wife anymore. It's not your responsibility to try to make things right between my family and me. So, please, I beg of you, leave me and my relationships alone."

"Excuse me for trying to help." Cheryl turned and practically ran toward the house.

"Fuck," Jamison mumbled. He released Bryn's hand and inched toward the water. "Every single time I'm around her I end up feeling like the bad guy."

Bryn twisted her hair as she joined him at the edge of the ocean. She stared at the birds swooping down at the waves, looking for their lunch. She shouldn't get involved, not even as a person who lent an ear. But she couldn't let him torment himself.

"I'm going to say some things that might not be very popular."

He turned his head and caught her gaze.

She reached out and squeezed his biceps. "Ultimately, Cheryl betrayed you and broke a trust that, for some, can't ever be mended. You have every right to walk away from that relationship and not look back. Nor should you be made to feel guilty about it."

"Thank you," he said. "However, I get the feeling there's a *but* to that statement."

"You've mentioned there were other problems,

and I don't pretend to comprehend what they were, but from the two interactions I've seen so far, from what you've told me, and from what I know about you, sometimes you can be controlling, stubborn, and things have to be done your way. I can tell it's a struggle for you to let someone else be in the driver's seat."

He nodded.

It was a good sign that he at least had self-awareness about his shortcomings. However, that didn't mean she would cave to her desires by kissing him. That could never happen again.

Ever.

"She's younger than you, correct?"

"Eight years. She was only twenty-two and I was thirty when we got married. I always worried about that. I actually fought my feelings for her when we first met, which was when she was twenty. Well, it was before that, but that's when things changed. We started dating when she turned twenty-one. I took her out on her birthday. There were moments she acted like a kid, and other times, she was so worldly I was amazed."

"But I suspect you had somewhat of a parent-child relationship." Bryn's training as a therapist bubbled to the surface. She'd only practiced for a short period of time before her husband had flexed his muscles and made the statement that no wife of his was going to work, especially as some counselor that weak people blabbered their stupid problems to.

"You sound like the psychologist I go see off and on."

She tried to contain her smile. It felt good to know that he had sought help for his problems and that she was on the right path in her thinking. "While I'm not suggesting that you are at fault for her actions by any means, deep down, you know there are things that you've done that led to the demise of your marriage. That perhaps it was over even before the affair happened."

He planted his hands on his hips and stared at the sky. "I could have done a lot of things differently when it came to Cheryl. About six months before I found out that Steve was my father; she and I had a huge fight. I thought for sure that was the end. We said some nasty things to each other. But when we made up, we decided that we both needed to make some changes. I needed to treat her like a capable adult, and she needed to let me be who I was. I really thought we were on the right track. We'd even started working on the house again."

"Were you in marriage therapy?"

"No. And that was probably a mistake because I thought we were getting back to where we were when we first got married. But when Steve made his big announcement, she got the dollar signs in her eyes again, and I was having an identity crisis and things went south real fast."

"That's a hard thing to go through."

"Don't I know it," he said. "The thing that hurt the most with Cheryl wasn't her cheating or the fact that it was with Troy, but that I had started to fall in love with her all over again. I get that she loves me, as much as she can love anyone because she has her own set of issues, but she cheated on me when I had the potential of giving her the one thing she wanted more than me. Money. And that's something I don't understand."

"Maybe it's not for you to understand."

He laughed. "Isn't it ironic, though?" He waved his hand toward the house. "My mom has loved Steve since she met him, which was about two years before I was born. She risked losing her family to have an affair with him because she loved my dad, too, at one point. Doesn't matter that they had a tough marriage. That's bound to happen when a cop is married to a defense attorney."

"That does have conflict written all over it."

"It sure does," he said. "But they stayed together because they wanted us boys to be a family." He tapped his heart. "Looking back, I think that might have been a mistake. But if they hadn't stayed together, where would that have left me?" He dropped his hands to his sides and stared into her eyes. "I hate feeling this way. I sound like a pathetic child having a pity party."

"No. You don't." She stretched out her arm and palmed his cheek. "You've been through so much in the last two years. But if you're ever going to get past these emotions, you need to let go of some things."

"I'm working on it." He took her hand and kissed it. "Steve and I had a good conversation, but then my mom sent Cheryl out here when she likely knew you were with me. You think I have control issues? My mom is the worst. Us boys always called her the puppet master. She was not happy that I became a firefighter, but man, you should have seen the look on her face when Miles decided to become a mechanic."

"Are you sure they sent Cheryl out here?"

"Well no. but my mom has been wanting me to give Cheryl a second chance."

"I don't have an answer for that, but one of the reasons I don't get along with my mother-in-law is that when my husband and I first got married, I always planned on working if and when we had kids. She told me that no way would the mother of her grandbabies be in the workforce. She actually said, '*Over my dead body will that ever happen.*'"

He looped his arm around her waist. "If I were to ever get married again, which is highly unlikely, or have kids, my wife would probably have to work because it's really hard for more than one person to survive on my salary."

"I bet you make at least triple what I do."

He kissed her temple. "After today, I wouldn't be surprised if you sell out of all your current inventory. I overheard five people talking about your pieces and looking at your website on their cell phones."

Without thinking, she wrapped her arms around him and patted his chest. "Don't joke with me about stuff like that."

"I wouldn't dare." He smiled. "Let's get back to the party so you can hear all the compliments firsthand."

Her stomach flipped and flopped as they strolled, arm and arm, toward the massive house on the beach. She should pull from his protective embrace, but she couldn't. Or maybe wouldn't. She couldn't tell the difference anymore.

11

*I*t had been a couple of days since Bryn had seen the man in the hoodie hiding in the bushes in her yard, but she still couldn't go outside after the sun set, and that pissed her off.

She'd never be free of fear.

Her phone buzzed, and she damn near jumped right off the sofa. She clutched her chest as she fumbled for the phone that had fallen between the cushions.

Jamison.

Ever since that kiss on the beach, he'd found his way into her dreams. It was the only thing that got her through the darkness, and she resented that. She hated relying on a man, even if he had no idea about her dependence.

"Hello," she said as calmly as possible.

"Hey, what are you up to this evening?"

"I just finished working, why?"

"I'm with Chip and his wife, Erica. She's dying to meet you and see some of your jewelry. Do you think maybe we could stop by?"

Jamison had been talking her up left and right. All her referrals had come from him, mostly, outside of a few random calls, but those had actually either come from friends of his mother's or people who'd found her website.

But she couldn't complain. Her jewelry was selling. People were talking about it and recommending her. That's all she could ask for.

Who was she to turn away business?

"Sure. What time?"

"We're ten minutes away," Jamison said.

Shit. "I don't have any food, really. And no wine or anything."

"No worries. We'll stop and pick something up. You just worry about setting up a few stellar pieces for Erica to look at. Chip owes her a birthday gift, and they are both looking for something to get her mom. Something classic. Those are her words, not mine."

Bryn laughed. "Yeah. Because I don't ever see you using that descriptor."

"See you soon." The line went dead.

She jumped off the couch and raced into her bedroom. Quietly, she checked on Zadie. The precious little thing was sound asleep. Hopefully, she'd stay that way as she had the night before until about nine. Bryn checked her watch. It was seven. That was two hours. Normally, she'd be putting her feet up and dozing because Zadie could be up from nine to midnight or later. Every day was a new schedule and a new adventure.

Next, Bryn went into the spare room and went through all her best pieces.

What in the hell had Chip's wife meant by *classic*? Was that like 1950s classic or something else?

Bryn filled a display case with twenty pieces. If Erica didn't like them, she had thirty more. But that was it.

She'd sold out of a lot of pieces and even had inventory on backorder. She should see that as a good thing. Lifting the case, she carried it into the family room and set it on the coffee table. She stood back and stared at her work. A sense of pride filled her gut. She'd come a long way since her days of having to hide her jewelry making from her family.

Headlights flashed in the picture window. Butter-flies filled her stomach. She'd done private showings twice before. Both times, they'd gone great. Jamison's mother had even suggested she do parties.

It was an excellent idea.

One she planned on figuring out. Even Willa offered to babysit. As long as it was worth the money, she'd do it.

She pulled open the door before they had a

chance to ring the bell. "Hi. Welcome," she said. "Oh. That's weird. This is your home."

"No. It's yours for as long as you're renting it from us," Chip said as he took her into a slightly awkward hug. "I'd like you to meet my wife, Erica."

"I've heard so much about you." A petite woman with short, red hair stepped into the family room. "It's nice to finally put a face to the name."

"I can't thank you and your husband enough for all you've done for me," Bryn said.

"My Chip is a good man." Erica looped her arm around Chip's waist. "But I'm sure it was all Jamison."

"Hey. I'm insulted," Chip said.

"No, you're not." Erica laughed. "And tell me I'm wrong about Jamison doing most of the work on this place."

"You're not wrong, dear." Chip held up a six-pack of beer. "Can I put this in your fridge?"

"Yes you can."

"We also brought some cheese and crackers and some seltzer for you." Jamison leaned in and kissed her cheek. He held a bag in his right hand. "I'll go set up a tray while you ladies discuss stuff I know nothing about. Sound good?"

"Perfect," she said, trying to ignore the butterflies that filled her gut.

"You've really made this place your own." Erica

smiled. "I'm so glad. It felt like such a dungeon after Chip's mom passed, and the last tenants never did anything."

"I can't say I did anything." Heat rose to Bryn's cheeks. She owed Jamison so much, and while she'd gotten to know him well enough that she knew he didn't do anything unless he wanted to, she still didn't like the sensation of owing anyone. "I'm sure you heard the story about my arrival in town."

"Everyone has."

"Shit. I keep forgetting to ask Jamison about Jon Kaplan. He wants to interview me for a local magazine for my jewelry line."

"It depends on his angle," Jamison said as he strolled back into the family room, carrying a tray of tasty treats. "If it's just a spread about you, it's fine. But if he wants to talk about me and the baby delivery, cut him off at the pass."

"You really don't like to be a hero, do you?" Erica took the beverage her husband handed her and bent over to look at the display.

"No. I don't," Jamison said. "But it's more than that, and you know it."

"Yeah. I do. And I'm sorry. However, I'll always believe you're being a bit unreasonable." Erica lifted a necklace from the case. "My God. This is beautiful. Can I try it on?"

"Please. I insist." One thing Bryn had learned

during her years as the wife of a rich man was that she hated it when salespeople were insanely pushy. Especially when she was standing right there. So, in that vein, she took a step back, taking a seat on the sofa with Jamison at her side.

He took her hand and squeezed.

She couldn't help it; she laced her fingers through his and glanced in his direction, smiling. "So, I shouldn't give this Jon Kaplan guy an interview?"

"I didn't say that." Jamison took a sip of his beer. "He's a decent sort of fellow. He's actually the one I was talking about when I said I knew a guy. But he recently did a piece on Steve, and I worry he might try to tie all the pieces of the puzzle together in one story about me and my family using you so he can make a shit ton of money and a bigger name for himself."

"Jamison is paranoid that way," Erica said. "He thinks if someone can make a buck off someone else's heartache, they will."

"And reporters like that prove me right all the time." Jamison leaned forward, tugging his hand free and snagging some cheese.

Her fingers felt cold.

He had a valid point. Bryn had known a lot of people like that back when she was married to Timothy. Someone always wanted to bring their family down. If she'd had the courage, she would have given one of them the story of their careers, but she hadn't been brave enough back then.

Still wasn't.

"But if he were to stick to my business, would it be worth it for me?" Bryn asked.

"Hell, yes," Jamison said. "Why?"

"He approached me on the beach at Nancy's party." She stared into his deep, intense eyes. She wanted to look away but couldn't. "But if he's going to turn this into something else, I don't want to do it."

"The one thing I know about Jon is that if you set the ground rules, he's pretty good about following them. But he can be sneaky, so you just have to watch out for the trick questions," Jamison said. "If you want, I can go with you to the interview."

"No," she said, probably a little too quickly as Jamison jerked his head back.

"Why not?" Jamison asked.

"Because you'd control the conversation," she said bluntly.

Erica burst out laughing. "She's got your number."

For some reason, that made Bryn feel really good.

"I'll take these four." Erica held up two necklaces, a bracelet, and a pair of earrings. "Jamison's mom told me you do custom work and showed me a picture of something you did with a wedding dress. I have a lot of beadwork on mine, and I'd like to do something with it for my kids. Would you be interested in that?"

"I love doing stuff like that." Once again, Bryn was indebted to Jamison. However, he was bringing her paying customers. How could she argue with that?

"Great. Maybe we can go to lunch next week to talk about it." Erica set the pieces she'd picked out on the table.

"Would you mind just coming here? It would be easier for me with my little girl and all." Bryn gathered up the jewelry and stood.

"I can do that," Erica said.

"Wonderful. I'll just go wrap these up for you." Bryn tried to contain her excitement, but it was pretty hard.

"I'll go with you," Jamison said.

Bryn wanted to tell him not to. She would prefer if he stayed with his friends, but she figured that would be rude, so she said nothing.

Once in the spare bedroom, she found small boxes to wrap the pieces in and she went about the task as if he weren't even standing there staring at her. Only, after about five minutes, she couldn't take it. She paused and glanced in his direction. "What?" she asked.

"You're amazing."

"Excuse me?"

"You heard me," he said quietly. "You put together a showing of some of your best pieces in a few minutes. You held your own with Erica, who has a sharp tongue. You're calm. You're collected. And you put up with me."

"It's that last one that I should be given a medal for."

He tossed his head back and burst out laughing. "That's the damn truth."

"I was kidding."

"I'm not." He cleared his throat as he closed the gap. He took the box from her hands and set it on the desk. "I'm meeting with my mom tomorrow. And if it weren't for you and all the encouragement you've given me, I'm not sure I'd be doing it."

She smiled. "I'm glad you're moving forward with all that."

He rested his hands on her hips. She wanted to step back, but she didn't. Especially when he inched even closer. His lips were so dangerously close to hers, she felt his warm breath on her skin. "I know I need to work on things with her. It's not going to be easy, and I'm sure I'll make mistakes, but it's a start, and I want to thank you for being there for me and listening."

"Anytime."

He leaned in and brushed his mouth over hers in a tender but passionate kiss. It was short, but it was powerful.

Too powerful because when it ended, she stood there staring at him, hoping he did it again.

Instead, he curled his fingers around her forearm

and tugged her into the hallway. "We should probably head back to the family room."

"That's a good idea," she whispered but then moved back to grab Erica's purchases. "We don't want to give them the wrong impression."

"It's a little late for that."

12

---

*J*amison sat on the outdoor patio of his
mom's favorite diner and sipped a soda
while he waited as patiently as he could
for the chief. His cell vibrated on the table.

Chip: *Don't shoot the messenger but check out Jon
Kaplan's article.*

Fuck. He quickly pulled up the local magazine
and cringed. It was all about Steve and his family, and
it mentioned the local police chief and her son.

Or *their* son.

Well, shit.

It wasn't the first article that Jon had written, and
it wouldn't be the last, but Jamison was tired of it. He
set his phone, screen down. He wasn't going to deal
with it now. At least this article hadn't been an
interview.

Egrets ran about the seaside restaurant. Kids

laughed and cried while their parents tugged them toward the beach access.

He loved the Lazy Turtle Diner but didn't come often because it was his mother's spot, and he ran into her almost any time he came lately, which was the last thing he wanted.

She'd called this meeting, and since it was a week after the scheduled biopsy that he wasn't supposed to know about, he hoped that was the reason for their lunch.

If it were something else, he would polish off the roll of Tums burning a hole in his back pocket.

"Sorry to have kept you waiting," his mother's voice called over all the tropical sounds.

"No worries," he said. "But I do have to get back to a contracted project, so I don't have much time. I'm sorry. I really am."

"It's okay. Seth tells me that your side business is starting to take off and that your website looks really nice. He mentioned that Bryn did it for you."

"She did. She's also working for me, taking leads when I'm at the station. It's really paying off."

"Seth mentioned that." His mother waved at the waitress and mouthed something. The waitress smiled and nodded. "I'm glad that's working out for you."

"It's all coming together, and I wouldn't have been able to do it without Bryn."

"She's quite the talented young woman," his

mother said as the waitress placed a Diet Coke with lemon in front of her. "I'll have my usual."

"Sure thing," the waitress said. "And for you?"

"Bacon cheeseburger, loaded, and fries."

"How do you want that cooked?" the waitress asked.

"Medium."

The waitress tucked her notepad into her pocket and headed back inside.

"Everyone raves about Bryn's jewelry and the quality of her work. I have a second appointment with her later today to discuss some custom pieces for Nancy, Farrah, and your nieces."

"She does amazing work. You won't regret it," he said. "But can you do me a favor and not let her give you the friends-and-family discount? Or the you're-Jamison's-mom discount or whatever she'll try to call it. She does that way too much."

"She did that with the first few pieces I bought, so I'll make sure I put my foot down." His mother pushed her sunglasses up on her head and sipped her soda. She stared out at the ocean. A strong breeze sent the waves crashing against the shore with an angry slam. "I wanted to thank you for staying so long last week at Nancy's party and for talking with Steve. That meant a lot to the both of us."

"You're welcome." He wasn't sure that was the right response. The party wasn't about him, his mother, or Steve. Besides, he'd had a really good time with Bryn. The only real negative that'd come out of it was that he was now fielding a lot of questions about his relationship with Bryn and what she meant to him, and that wasn't easy to define.

Because he didn't know.

He didn't understand his feelings.

They didn't make much sense to him, and the more he tried to sort them out, the more they became jumbled in his mind and heart.

"You and Bryn looked as though you were having a lot of fun together."

"We did," he admitted.

"Are you dating her?"

"Is this why you called me here today? To find out about my love life. Are you going to report back to Cheryl?"

"I guess I deserve that."

He wished it was six, and he was done working for the day because he could use a beer. "I'm sorry. I shouldn't have come in so hot, but you're always so ready to set me up with my ex."

"For the record, I'm not giving your ex-wife a detailed report."

He wasn't sure if he believed his mother or not. Maybe it would be a good idea if she did run back to Cheryl with the details of this conversation. Perhaps that would get his ex-wife off his back.

"But I am curious about you and Bryn, so are you going to answer my question?"

"Why do you care?"

She narrowed her stare. "You're my son. I care about you, and who you're seeing matters to me. And there are things that concern me about Bryn."

Fuck. This was the last thing he needed. He shouldn't ask, but curiosity killed the cat. "Like what?"

"I know the father of her baby died in a car crash. But have you looked into that crash?"

"Please, tell me you haven't."

"Not yet," his mother said. "But I'm starting to get suspicious. She has no family. No friends. No one from her past comes to visit. It makes me wonder if she's running from something."

Jamison was sick and tired of people meddling in his fucking life. "Has she given you any reason to believe she's anything other than the person she says she is?"

"Well, no."

"Then drop this."

"I can't. I love you. I want what's best for you."

"Oh, and Cheryl is?"

His mother shook her head. "No. I can see that now. But I don't think Bryn is right for you, either."

"Mom. Stop. I spoke with Steve. It was a good conversation. We're on the right track. Why are you trying to go and screw that up?"

"Because things with Bryn don't make sense. I'm a cop, and I see things differently than other people. It's my job, and there's something off with that young woman."

"I've heard enough. If you can't back off Bryn, then you and I are done for good. I mean it, Mom. If you start poking around in her background or start asking her weird questions and making her feel uncomfortable, I will do what I said I would do two years ago and just haven't had the balls to do."

"You won't cut me out of your life. Not over this."

"Watch me." He suddenly lost his appetite. He stood and dropped forty dollars onto the table. "Have a nice day." He stomped off toward his Jeep in the parking lot.

"Jamison. Wait," his mother called. "That wasn't fair."

He paused mid-step and glanced over his shoulder. "A lot of things in my life lately haven't been fair."

"Before you leave, there's something else I need to tell you."

He took in a deep, cleansing breath and blinked. "Is this about your biopsy?"

"Who told you?"

"Doesn't matter," he said. "Did you get the results back?"

"Do you care?"

"Of course, I fucking care," he mumbled. "But you didn't give a flying rat's ass to tell me." He planted his hands on his hips. "And then you summoned me to this lunch, and I thought we were going to talk about whether or not you have cancer and hopefully mend our relationship, but you had to go and pull this bullshit about whether or not I'm dating Bryn. Only to make that worse by being a cop about it and not a mother."

"So, what you're saying is if I had cancer, you'd be willing to—?"

"Oh, my God. This is so fucked up I can't stand it. I take it the results were negative?"

"They were."

He leaned in and kissed his mother's cheek. "I'm truly grateful for that news. And whether it was positive or negative has nothing to do with our relationship. That's a fact. It's your actions that dictate our inability to have one. Don't go poking into Bryn's life. There's no reason to. We can try lunch again when I've calmed down. Okay?"

"All right," she said.

Sometimes, his family drove him batshit crazy.

"Be safe out there," he said. "I love you. I do mean that."

"I love you, too, kiddo."

His chest tightened. It had been years since she'd called him *kiddo*, and it reminded him of when he'd been six years old and had broken his arm. She'd sat with him for hours in the hospital waiting room.

"I understand that you and Cheryl are over. I

accept that," his mother said. "I'll do what I can to help her move on. I mean that."

"You can stop acting like her mother-in-law for a start."

"That's a fair point."

"Can I trust you not to ask Bryn a million questions this afternoon?"

"How about I keep it to twenty?" His mother smiled. "I can't help it. I'm a cop. It's my nature to be suspicious of everything. And I don't think she's a bad person, I just can't help but wonder what her story is. Don't you?"

"Haven't you considered that maybe I already know and have decided that it's no one else's business?" That should quench his mother's thirst but did nothing for his.

"Fair enough," his mother said. "Now, will you come back and eat lunch with me?"

His stomach growled. He nodded. He could only hope that his mother wouldn't bring up any other hot topics.

They returned to the table. Out of the corner of his eye, he noticed Jon Kaplan.

"I can feel your anger all the way over here," his mother said. "What about Jon Kaplan has you tied up in knots?"

Jamison tilted his head. "You're fucking kidding, right? Jon just did a second piece about Steve, and in the article, he mentioned you and me and all of this shit again. And now, Jon wants to interview Bryn about her business. I'm calling bullshit. It's going to be all about coming at me again."

"Jon's not a bad guy. Maybe he wants to talk about how you delivered her baby."

"Right. That's total bullshit. That article would be a paragraph long. I can see it now. *Local firefighter does his fucking job*. Big damn deal."

"Bryn's baby nearly died. And don't tell me that's not true."

Jamison still had nightmares about Zadie and how blue she'd been when she was born. Or how tightly the cord had been wrapped around her neck. So, yeah, he knew how close to death that precious little girl had been, but that didn't change the fact that Jon wanted to turn the article into something else, and Jamison didn't want his life in print for all of Lighthouse Cove and the surrounding towns to judge.

"That's not the point, Mom."

The waitress showed up with their food, and even though his stomach growled, indicating that he was hungry, his mind told him a different story. Jon Kaplan standing and strolling from his table to theirs made it all worse.

"Well, hello there," Jon said. "And how are you two this lovely afternoon in south Florida?"

Jamison wanted to burst out laughing. Who the hell greeted people with a location?

"We're doing well. And you?" his mother asked.

"I'd be better if this young man would agree to do a sit-down with me."

"About what?" Jamison asked. "There's no story worth telling. Besides, it's old news," Jamison said.

"I agree. We missed the boat on your heroic act. But not about your—"

"Jon. This isn't the time," his mother said. "My son and I are enjoying a nice lunch, and neither of us has much time."

Jon furrowed his brow. He glanced between Jamison and his mother.

Jamison got the impression something was going on between Jon and his mom. His heart dropped to his stomach, and it pitched left and right and rolled around like a tiny boat lost at sea in a storm.

"Rebecca, are you going back on your word?" Jon asked.

"Mother. Are you giving Jon an interview? About us? About Steve?"

"Not about Steve and me or any of that. It's all about being a female Chief of Police, and what's that's like in a male-dominated profession."

Jamison shook his head. "I can see where this is headed, though. A three-part series, tying it all back to the bastard son." He decided to scarf down his lunch as quickly as possible. All he wanted to do was finish his project and then get a good night's sleep because he started a three-day shift tomorrow. That would be a nice break from everyone.

"That's not how I'd do it," Jon said. "I take it you read the piece I did about Steve."

"Not the point," Jamison said.

"Jon. This really isn't the time or place," his mother interjected.

"I can take a hint." Jon raised his hands. "I'll talk with you both later."

"Not me, you won't." Jamison raised his soda and nodded. "Have a nice life." He stared at his mom and glared.

"It's not what you think."

Thankfully, he'd already left his money on the table. He pushed it toward his mom. "You're putting a spin on what you did. I get that. You're a public figure, and you have an image. I'm sure it hurt your popularity. But I'm not going to take part in this. I was serious when I said you've all got to stop pushing me. If you want me in your lives, you need to do so on my terms and respect my boundaries." He took one last fry. "Remember what I said about Bryn. If I find out you're doing any digging, we're done."

"I hear you loud and clear."

He certainly hoped so, but he wasn't holding his breath.

Jamison knew showing up at anyone's home, especially a woman's, unannounced was a big no-no.

The few girlfriends outside of his ex-wife that he'd had over the years had never once appreciated it and he suspected Bryn wouldn't either.

So, he decided it was best if he pulled off the road and called.

It rang twice before she picked up.

"Hi Jamison," she said in that sweet voice that got him all hot and bothered under the collar. "Is everything okay?"

He glanced at the clock on the dashboard. Shit. He should have checked the time before he called. "I'm sorry,. I didn't realize how late it was. I was over at my grandmothers."

"How's she doing?"

"Good." He chuckled. "She took twenty bucks from in me blackjack."

"I think you need to stop betting that woman."

"Agreed," he said. "Hey listen. I'm in the neighborhood and thought maybe I could stop by and we could watch a movie or something."

"Yeah. Zadie is zonked out for the night, so that might work."

"I'll be there in five."

"Don't you have to work in the morning?" she asked.

"I do, so I'll be leaving right after whatever we watch. See you in a few." He slammed the gear shift into drive and punched the gas. She was only a couple of blocks away, but he couldn't get there fast enough.

He knew his feelings for her were growing and he wasn't sure what to do about that.

They were friends.

Good friends.

And she'd just had a baby.

One that he'd fallen madly in love with.

He wasn't sure if he could have a relationship with a woman who had a child. Hell, he wasn't sure he could ever be in a serious committed relationship with someone ever again. The idea of long term tended to make him want to jump out of his skin. Trust didn't come easily. Not after what happened with Cheryl.

And with his mother and Steve.

However, Bryn made him question why he had so many hang ups.

He pulled into her driveway and practically raced to her front door. He rang the bell and waited for what seemed like forever but was probably only one minute.

"That was quick," she said as she pulled back the door. "I made some popcorn."

"Perfect." He wanted to pull her into his arms and kiss her, but then what? So he opted to press his lips against her cheek. "You look comfy."

She smiled. "I look like I've been dealing with an infant who didn't want to sleep all day." She waved her hand toward the family room. "For all I know our night could be cut short by a screaming kid, so I took the liberty of picking the movie."

"Sounds good to me." He could have cared less what they watched. All he wanted was to be in her presence. He sat on the sofa, hoping she'd join him, and she didn't disappoint. "Why don't you put your feet up." Though he didn't really give her a choice. He lifted her feet off the floor and placed them on his lap. "So, what are we watching?" he asked quickly in hopes of taking her mind off the fact that his hands were rubbing her bare feet.

It seemed to be working.

"It's about the royal family."

He laughed.

"Sorry. It's late and I live alone. Thrillers and anything remotely scary is not going to happen."

"I'm okay with that," he said. "So, how did things go with my mom today?" He wasn't sure he really wanted to know the answer.

"Wonderful. We had a great time and she's having five custom pieces made. I'm really excited about it."

"Good. I hope she was on her best behavior."

"She told me you'd ask about that."

He cocked his head. That took him by surprise. "What else did she say?"

"Nothing that I'm going to tell you." Bryn lifted the remote and pointed it toward the television. "Let's enjoy the show."

The last thing he wanted to do was be entertained

by the royals, but he sat back and rubbed her feet while staring at the TV. Only, about a half hour in, he found himself trying not to nod off. It certainly wasn't the company that bored him to tears.

He leaned sideways on the sofa, closer to her, snuggling into her body.

She didn't protest, so he tucked himself behind her, wrapping his arms around her, holding her close to his chest. His kness were tucked up right behind hers and he rested his chin on her shoulder.

He couldn't remember anything feeling this good in a long time. They fit together like the last two pieces of a puzzle. He closed his eyes and breathed deeply. She smelled like honeydew. He knew nothing could happen and he was okay with that. This was all he needed.

"Jamison?"

"Huh?" He blinked, realizing he might have dozed off.

"The movie's over."

"Oh," he whispered. "I guess it's time for me to go."

"It is midnight and Zadie will be getting up one last time to nurse."

He pushed himself to a sitting position. He stared into her loving eyes. "Thanks for letting me come over."

"It was nice to have the company."

He leaned over and kissed her forehead. Then her

cheek. He took her hand and helped her to her feet before he ravished her lips on the sofa.

That wouldn't have been a good idea.

"I better go." He took her chin with his thumb and forefinger. "Lock the doors behind me."

"I will."

He caved to his desired and took her mouth in a tender kiss. Her tongue greeted his tentatively at first, but soon the kiss grew more passionate and wild.

She took a step back.

"Good night, Bryn." He turned and walked out the front door. It was going to be impossible for him to control his desire.

13

---

*B*ryn bolted upright from a deep sleep. She gasped for air, unable to fill her lungs, which burned as if she'd swallowed flames. Blinking frantically, she tried to adjust to the darkness. She reached for the light on the nightstand, hoping she didn't wake her little princess.

She found the dimming switch. Ripping back the covers, she swung her legs to the side of the bed. The fuzzy rug felt warm against her bare feet. Taking in a deep, cleansing breath, she let it out slowly through her nose. The digital clock showed that it was four in the morning.

Her heart beat so fast, she was sure she would have a heart attack. Ever since she'd seen the man in the hoodie hiding in her bushes, along with the reporter who thought she looked like someone else, she'd been having nightmares.

Of course, she never remembered anything about the dreams. Only the terrifying emotions that woke her, and the inability to calm down after. She'd rescheduled the interview with Jon Kaplan, citing that she needed a little more time to recover after having a baby. It wasn't an unreasonable request, and he'd had no problem whatsoever giving her a few more weeks.

She wasn't concerned about being in the magazine since he didn't get any coverage outside of a fifty-or-so-mile radius. But after reading the latest article he'd written, she had some doubts.

However, since he'd agreed not to use her picture and only focus on her jewelry, she and Jamison both thought it would be good for her business.

Still, she couldn't shake the idea that someone could recognize her. Didn't matter if she'd gone from a blond to a brunette. Or that she'd grown her very short hair too long and no longer had bangs. Or that she was a good thirty pounds heavier, even without the baby fat.

None of that mattered.

Someone could still look at her and see the similarities and start questioning whether Brenda Thompson Perish really died in a fiery crash as her car plummeted into a ravine.

She took in a few more breaths, grateful they came more naturally. Quickly, she peeked at Zadie.

Sound asleep.

Bryn snagged her robe, her eReader, her cell, and

made her way to the kitchen. There was no way she would get back to sleep now, so she might as well get a jump-start on the day, and that meant a nice, big mug of fresh decaf coffee.

She'd never thought she'd get used to drinking unleaded, but it was certainly better than nothing. She found her favorite blend and put it in the machine before settling down in the family room with her device. What she loved about digital books was that she didn't have to turn on all the lights. She could sit in the dark and read. It made her feel safe because she could see out the windows, but people couldn't necessarily see in.

Or, at least, that's how she felt.

It would be another hour before the sky would start lightening, and Zadie usually started to fuss around that time.

She nearly laughed out loud at that thought. Her baby girl was only three weeks old. Every day they experienced was a new normal.

Like bottles of breast milk.

At first, Zadie wouldn't have anything to do with them. Now, she tolerated the one that Bryn forced her to take every day, though Zadie did better when Willa gave it to her. At least that had been the case the last two days.

Bryn stared out the picture window and twirled her hair. Thoughts of Jamison popped into her mind. She hadn't seen him in a couple of days, and she resented that she missed his company and that she'd formed an attachment to him so quickly. Maybe if she'd met more people outside of Willa, things would be different. But she struggled with becoming close to his two sisters-in-law, only because they were related to him, not because they weren't nice. Nancy had been incredibly gracious during her party. And Seth's wife, Farrah, had offered to have a jewelry party next week, which Bryn had thought a brilliant idea.

However, as far as girlfriends went, so far, Willa, her eighty-year-old neighbor, was it. Perhaps that was for the best, because Bryn couldn't afford to get too close to anyone.

A shadow appeared from behind the big palm tree on the left side of the carport.

Her heart lurched to the back of her throat.

She tried to swallow, but it proved too painful. She folded her eReader case closed and leaned forward, squinting.

The shadow moved. Though not much. Maybe it was the leaves rustling in the wind.

She held her breath for a long moment and waited.

More movement.

No wind that she could discern.

Someone was out there. Watching. Waiting. She could pack up and run in the middle of the night. But where would she go? And that was only if the person out there knew that she was Brenda and not Bryn.

Or she could do nothing and wait it out.

But that was stupid.

Or, she could call the police.

She lifted her cell and dialed 9-1-1. If anyone knew that she was alive and had been lurking in the shadows even for a day, she wouldn't be sitting in the comforts of her home.

"Nine-one-one. What's your emergency?"

"I think there's someone in my yard, watching me."

"Who am I speaking with, and what is your address?"

"Bryn Tinsley," she said before rattling off her address. She gasped as whoever was out there darted across the yard. "The person is now hiding in my side bushes."

"Are all your doors and windows locked, ma'am?"

"Yes," Bryn said. She thought about checking on Zadie, but then she wouldn't know what this asshole was doing. But what they were after her little girl?

"A patrol car is five minutes away. Stay on the line with me, okay?"

"I can do that." Bryn shifted in her seat so she wasn't a sitting duck by the window, but she also wanted a bird's-eye view. "I can't see them anymore." Oh, God. What if they'd dropped to the ground like a snake and slithered across the ground toward the backyard? On shaky legs, she stood.

"Stay inside, ma'am. The police will be there

shortly. Don't open the door for anyone but an officer or another first responder. We've had two other calls from your neighborhood in the last five minutes, and one a half hour ago when someone broke into a car."

She blew out a puff of air. Not that she was relieved, because she wasn't. It still creeped her out and concerned her that someone was out there, wandering the neighborhood, casing out her house, along with others, even if they had no idea who she had been in her past life.

Or maybe that was all some sort of distraction so the culprit could get their hands on her precious little girl.

"I see headlights," she whispered as if whoever was outside might be able to hear her. No sooner did she say that than the lights cut out. "Wait. Maybe not." She swallowed. Maybe Timothy's family had found her, after all.

"The police don't want to scare him away. Please, stay put and stay on the line with me."

"Okay." Bryn stood on the side of the sofa and peered out the window. Whoever was in the bushes popped up and took off running. Away from the house. But what if they ran into the backyard and came in through the sliding glass doors?

Red lights flashed from the vehicle that had parked on the corner. Another police car came barreling down the street and stopped right in front of her house. A man jumped from the driver's side, weapon at the ready, and hauled ass.

Bryn clutched her chest. Her heart pounded. "Two police officers are chasing whoever was hiding in my bushes." She needed to check on Zadie, so she padded back to her bedroom as fast as she could and let out a sigh of relief when she saw her precious little girl sleeping blissfully in her bassinet. She scooped her up into her arms, not caring if she woke her up or not and cradled her against her chest.

"Let's wait until one of them comes knocking on your door before we hang up. Does that sound good to you?"

Bryn breathed deeply, letting oxygen fill her lungs until there was no room left. She hurried back to the front of the house and peered out the window. She blinked, doing a double-take and making sure her eyes weren't deceiving her and that what she saw was indeed a man wearing a police uniform headed toward her front door. "I see an officer walking up my path."

"You're sure it's one of ours?"

"Yes," she said.

"Okay, then. Take care, Bryn."

Bryn tapped her screen, yanked open her door, and gasped. She held her daughter tightly.

"Are you okay?" Nathan asked.

She'd met him briefly at Nancy's party since he'd been on duty that day. She nodded. "I guess I should have expected to see someone with the last name of Kirby when calling the police."

"It's a pretty good chance that one of us will be on duty."

"Did you catch whoever was out there?"

"Another officer is cuffing him and getting ready to take him to the station," Nathan said. "But I need to ask you a few questions."

She bounced up and down. "Why don't you come inside?"

"This will only take a couple of minutes," he said. "Did you get a look at him?"

"No. He was just a shadow. Actually, I couldn't tell you if it was a male or a female."

"Have you seen anyone sneaking around in the bushes before?"

She swallowed. "No." Lying had become her new normal.

"Would you mind stepping outside and telling me if you've ever seen this man before? There have been a couple of break-ins tonight, and a few last week."

"I'd rather him not see my daughter."

"I understand," Nathan said. "How about I come back later today with a picture? Would that be okay?"

"Sure."

"Thanks. And I'll need to take a formal statement, but we can do that when I come back, too."

"I appreciate that."

"Thanks to you and a couple of other neighbors,

we caught the guy." Nathan reached out and squeezed her shoulder. "This is a safe town. But I do recommend keeping your doors and windows locked when you're gone and at night. Most of our crime is that of opportunity."

"I always do. Thanks, Nathan." Her phone vibrated in her hand. She jumped.

It startled Zadie.

Bryn glanced at the caller ID. "It's your brother," she said softly.

"They listen to the police scanner at the station, so I'm sure he heard what was going on." Nathan nodded. "I'll be in touch. Call if you need anything at all."

She secured the door and plopped herself on the rocking chair before tapping the green button on her cell and setting it to speaker mode. "Hey, Jamison."

"I just heard what happened. Are you okay?"

"Yeah. Shaken up, but fine." Zadie let out a wail.

Bryn adjusted her top. It was sooner than Zadie would normally wake and start her day, but shit happened.

"Is Zadie okay?"

"She slept through it all until I panicked and woke her up."

"I think I would have done the same thing."

"I can't picture you panicking." Bryn stared down at her daughter and patted her bottom. Zadie changed every day. It was all so mesmerizing, and

JEN TALTY

right now, the way Zadie held her mother's gaze seemed to stop feeding every few seconds to crack a slight smile brought tears to Bryn's eyes.

"That part, maybe not. But I would have picked her up and given her a good squeeze just because," he said. "I'm glad you called the police. So many people think they see a shadow but don't do anything about it."

"I was honestly really scared." The entire thing replayed in her mind, and her pulse picked up. "I was sitting in the front room reading when I noticed someone hiding behind the tree. Nathan said there were a couple of robberies in the neighborhood already tonight." She shivered.

"Don't worry. You live in a really safe place. It was probably some teenager or random person looking for open doors. It happens every once in a while. It's not something you need to stress over."

"But I am," she admitted. "I know Chip has that doorbell camera system installed, but that wouldn't have helped me. What if the guy managed to come inside?"

"He wasn't there to hurt you."

"That's not making me feel any better."

"How about if I pick up a security system when I get off work tomorrow morning? There are some decent, inexpensive ones that are easy to install. I can do it first thing."

"I can't afford it right now," she said.

"You can't afford to have sleepless nights. It's not good for you. It could affect your breast milk, and that wouldn't be good for Zadie. I won't buy anything that's outrageous, and I will insist on you paying me back."

She bit back a sob. She knew he was nothing like Timothy. Jamison was a good man. Flawed, but decent.

However, she couldn't rely on anyone, especially a man. If she became too entangled with Jamison, he could use it against her. She didn't want to believe he'd be that way, but she knew from experience that it was entirely possible.

"Jamison. I appreciate you and everything you've—"

"Bryn. We're friends, right?"

"Yes," she said, but how else would she answer that question. If she said no, she was a total bitch. If she hesitated, she might give him the wrong impression. She couldn't afford to do that. "But even best friends don't go out and buy this kind of gift—"

"It's not a gift. You're paying me back for it, remember? I'll take money out of your paycheck and lead commissions."

She could live with that. "Okay. It's a deal."

"Good. I'm sorry. There's a call coming in. I've got to run. Text or call if you need anything at all. Promise?"

"Promise." She ended the call and dropped her

head back, rocking slowly. She wanted to believe that Jamison was a kind man. A true gentleman.

But it was hard when her late husband had started off much the same way.

Jamison sat in the station's break room on the final night of a seventy-two-hour shift. He picked at a muffin and sipped some tea. He generally didn't like pulling anything longer than forty-eight hours, and it wasn't often granted, but the flu had been going through the house, and they'd needed bodies. Other than pestering Bryn, Jamison hadn't much else to do.

Well, that was a lie. He had quoted a deck and building a new dock on the canal. Both had accepted his bid, and he would start work on one tomorrow and the other next week. Plus, he still had to put the finishing touches on Bryn's built-ins.

Taking on this extra shift was more about avoiding his family after Nancy's party. He'd even stayed for another two hours after sulking on the beach, which had shocked everyone so much, they'd had no clue what to say to him. That had been kind of fun to see, his brothers approaching him all tongued-tied. That didn't happen often.

Of course, then there had been his lunch with his mom. That still disturbed him, especially knowing that she planned to do an interview with Jon Kaplan.

The subject matter might be about being a woman in what some considered a man's job, but her life choices would be brought into it. There was no doubt about that.

He stared at his cell. He'd contemplated calling Bryn at least five times, but after the last text, she'd made it clear that she was fine. That she was no longer shaken from the morning's events, and that Nathan had taken her statement. While she'd never seen the boy they had arrested, Nathan had told her that he worked at the local discount store and had been stealing from open cars and houses in the neighborhood for weeks.

But checking on her wasn't the only reason he wanted to call her. He wanted to hear her voice, and that was a thought that terrified him on many levels. He hadn't felt this way since he'd first started developing deep emotional ties to his ex-wife, and look where that'd landed him.

Not that Bryn was anything like Cheryl. Far from it. But that wasn't the point.

The sound of feet shuffling across the floor pulled him from his thoughts. He glanced over his cell.

Troy.

Another relationship he was trying to mend. Only this one should be a lot easier. His family was complicated. You couldn't choose family. He had no control over who he was blood-related to.

But his friends and brothers by choice? Those, he could pick to his heart's content.

Troy had fucked up. There was no doubt about that. He'd shit on their friendship and broke the bro-code.

Worse, they worked together, and that had put the entire station on edge. The first few months after Jamison had separated from Cheryl, his captain had made sure that he and Troy were on opposite shifts. But that wasn't fair to ask that to continue, and both he and Troy could set aside their differences. It never interfered with their job performance.

"Hey, man," Troy said.

"What's going on?" Jamison asked. He pretended that he was interested in the news program on the television that hung in the corner of the kitchen. The volume had been turned down, but he could still hear it.

"I'm starving all of a sudden. Do you know if there is any of that lasagna left?"

"I believe so," Jamison said. "You can heat me up some while you're at it. This muffin isn't doing anything for me."

"Sure thing." Troy set his phone screen up on the table as he moved about the kitchen.

It dinged.

Jamison wished he hadn't looked since it was a text from his ex-wife. Not that it mattered. It didn't bother him. Not anymore. He had to admit that when he'd found out, not only was jealousy one of the emotions that'd flowed through his body, but he'd also wanted to beat the crap out of his friend.

"Are you still dating my ex-wife?" It was rare that he and Troy ever spoke about Cheryl and their relationship. When the affair happened, Jamison had been so wrapped up in his problems with his family that he literally hadn't had the chance to process his wife's infidelity or his friend's betrayal. He'd asked Cheryl to leave, which she had, and then he told Troy they were no longer friends.

Troy had respected that boundary and, other than work, they didn't speak until about three months ago. Jamison just didn't pay attention to Troy and Cheryl's relationship. He'd found out later that they didn't have one at first. That Cheryl had told Troy she wanted to try to work things out with Jamison, and that Troy and Cheryl didn't become a thing until about six months ago.

"Nope. She wants you back and she says she's going to do whatever it takes to get you." Troy put a plate in front of Jamison. "And I'm tired of being second best."

"I'm sorry." Jamison took the fork and cut into his after-dinner dinner. "But I'm never going to get back with Cheryl, so you are free to pursue her all you want."

"I'm honestly done with her," Troy said, lifting his cell and shaking his head. "However, the last thing you need is to hear me bitch about your ex-wife."

Jamison laughed. "I'm over it. Really." He shoveled food into his mouth and chewed. It tasted so damn good. Or maybe it was being able to have this kind of conversation with an old friend that he missed. "If you care about her, and she's who you want to be with, I support it."

"I don't want to have a relationship with someone who'd rather be with someone else," Troy said. "Although, I'm not sure she has any clue who or what she really wants."

"You might have a good point there." That had been one of Jamison's concerns about getting married. He'd even thought about having a much longer engagement, but his mother—and Cheryl's—took over. The next thing he knew, he was walking down the aisle.

But he had loved her, so there was that. And for a while, things were good. However, he'd always worried that they'd rushed into things—and he'd been right about that.

"Don't take this the wrong way, but I think she only wants you back because Steve is rich and she thinks you have a new girlfriend." Troy set his fork down and pushed his plate to the side. "Do you?"

"I'm not dating Bryn," Jamison said.

"That's not what people are saying." Troy leaned back and folded his arms. "Not to be a gossip, and I'm only repeating what I heard since I was at the party, but the talk is that you and she might as well have been swapping spit poolside."

"I didn't kiss her anywhere near the pool." Jamison couldn't contain his smile if he tried. He'd had many romantic moments in his lifetime, but none held a candle to the few minutes he'd held Bryn on the beach.

"But you *did* kiss her."

"I can't confirm or deny."

Troy laughed. "Didn't she just have a baby? And didn't you deliver it? How do you feel about getting involved with a woman who has a kid?"

"I honestly don't know." It wasn't that he had a problem with dating a woman with children. He loved babies. But he wasn't prepared to deal with families. And hers was a complicated situation because he still didn't agree with her choice to keep her daughter from her late husband's mother. Granted, it wasn't his business.

But if he dated her, he felt it would become his business, and that was an issue.

"Not to bring up another sore subject, but is that because of your personal situation with your dad and Steve?"

"A little," Jamison admitted.

"I didn't get any details about the baby's father, so I'm sorry if I'm asking questions about things you don't want to talk about."

"He was killed in a car crash."

"Wow. That sucks."

Jamison nodded. "It has less to do with dating a woman with kids and is more that I'm not sure I can be completely present in any relationship with anyone while things are still so fucked up with my family. I mean, Steve plans to propose to my mom, and that just makes me want to run back to the Bahamas. And not because my mother wants to be married to someone other than my dad, but because it's Steve, and because they keep pushing me to accept him as my biological father. I can't do that. I might be able to get on board with this if they just back off—"

"I'm going to stop you right there because we've been friends for a long time."

Jamison arched his brow. "Minus a little betrayal."

"That's fair," Troy said. "However, you can't change what your mom and Steve did, and you can't change DNA. All you can do is change how you respond to it all. That's up to you."

"That's true. But I don't think it's too much to ask for them to respect my boundaries, and they don't. They expect me to sit around the campfire, holding hands and singing Kumbaya. It doesn't work that way. And every time they say they are going to give me a little space, it lasts all of a week."

"Your family has always been insanely tight. Maybe you could find it in your heart to meet them halfway."

Jamison knew Troy was right, and it wasn't like he wasn't trying. Only, every time he gave his family a little slack, they came at him aggressively. Well, his mother did, anyway.

Maybe he just needed to deal with her differently.

"I agree."

"And maybe you should go for it with Bryn because when you talk about her you grin from ear to ear."

Once again, Jamison tried not to smile, but it proved impossible.

"That's what I'm talking about," Troy said.

"It's complicated. And not just because of Zadie."

"I know," Troy said, pointing to the television as the programming changed from the news to true crime. "Do you ever watch this shit?"

Jamison glanced at the TV. "No. Never. Why?"

"It's fascinating. Tonight, they are talking about the Perishes, a crime family out of California. They have never been caught, but the son, who died a little over a year ago, was thought to have been involved in money laundering and Ponzi schemes. I don't understand it all. A month after he died, his wife was killed in a car crash. Some believe that one or both of them are still alive. It's totally crazy."

Jamison blinked. A picture of Brenda Perish flashed across the screen. She had incredibly short, blond—no, it was almost white—hair that was spiked on top. If it weren't for her eyes, Jamison wouldn't have seen the resemblance.

Or maybe it was because he'd become so sensitive to these things that he recognized how close they were to Bryn's eyes. So close, they could have been sisters.

Before he could say anything, the radio went off.

Duty called.

14

*B*ryn didn't like leaving Zadie for any length of time with anyone, not even Jamison. It wasn't that she didn't think Jamison wasn't capable of handling Zadie because Jamison handled babies like he'd been doing it his entire life.

It was just that Bryn still looked over her shoulder as if someone were watching and lurking in her bushes.

And not some kid wanting to steal her television or laptop.

She parked her car as close to the main doors of the post office as she could. She had twenty packages to mail, all thanks to Jamison. Well, she assumed it was from him and his great salesmanship. He'd told everyone about her jewelry, and his sisters-in-law had raved about the pieces he'd given them. Hell, even his mother talked her up, which shocked Bryn because she still seemed to think that he was getting back together with his ex-wife.

Not that it affected her, because as much as she was attracted to Jamison, she wasn't going to pursue a relationship with him. She couldn't. She needed to be prepared to get up and move when the hairs on the back of her neck stood even taller. It was bad enough that she was sure she reminded that Jon Kaplan guy of someone else.

The last time she'd run into him, he'd brought it up again, but Zadie had been so fussy that Bryn hadn't had the opportunity to find out who. Now, she really wanted to know. Because if he said Brenda Thompson Perish, Bryn would be packing her bags in the middle of the night and taking off for Alaska.

No one would look for her there.

She opened her trunk and lifted her tote bags. She had all the packages labeled and ready to go. All she needed to do was pay for the shipping and send them on their way. She lifted one tote onto her shoulder and then the other before closing her trunk and turning toward the door.

A woman with her head down as she stared at her phone raced past her, nearly hitting Bryn's tote as she pulled open the door. It wasn't until the lady was inside the post office that Bryn realized it was Cheryl.

"Come on. Pick up the phone," Cheryl said.

Bryn didn't want to have any conversation with Cheryl because she didn't think it would end well.

Besides, what would she say? Unless Cheryl wanted to buy jewelry, the two women had nothing to say to each other.

"I'm not leaving a damn message." Cheryl took her phone from her ear and tapped at the screen. She pounded on it like she was beating the damn thing. "Now. Answer." She let out a long sigh.

Bryn did her best to mind her own business, but that was cut short when Cheryl mumbled something under her breath, stuffed her cell into her back pocket, and glanced over her shoulder.

"Oh. Hi," Cheryl said. "Aren't you Bryn?"

"Yes. That's me." She smiled. Like this woman didn't know who she was. "How are you?"

"Not great," Cheryl said. "I'm trying to reach my husband. I take it he's not answering because he's doing some favor for you. He's always doing something for you."

"Isn't he your *ex*-husband?" Shit. Why the hell did she have to go and say something so antagonistic? The last thing she needed was to make a bigger enemy out of Cheryl. Or out of anyone, for that matter.

"Not the point."

"Well, I'm not his keeper, so I have no idea why he's not answering his phone." Hopefully, he was busy taking care of Zadie and finishing the built-in shelves and cabinets. He didn't have much left to do, and she wanted to take a few more pictures of her jewelry displayed on the shelves. The lighting next to the window was perfect.

"It's important that I talk to him right away." Cheryl moved closer to the service desk as they called the next person to be helped.

"I'm not sure what you want me to do about it."

"Call him for me."

Shit. Bryn was not getting in the middle of this one.

"I'm sorry. I'm not comfortable doing that."

"He's at your house, right? Watching your kid and doing whatever else for you." Cheryl adjusted her purse strap. "You know, you're not the first damsel in distress he's been Prince Charming for. That's kind of his thing. He likes to be needed. But once you're on your feet, or someone comes along who is in a worse state than you, he'll drop you like a hot potato. Just ask Gina."

"Who's Gina?" Bryn found herself asking a question she shouldn't care about because she wasn't *that* kind of woman. And she wasn't involved with Jamison in that way. They were friends. She kept her attraction to him under lock and key. Especially now that she was going on six weeks from giving birth, and the doctor had told her that sex wasn't out of the question.

It wasn't until after that she had explained to her new physician that the father had passed, and she had no boyfriend. Perhaps the good doctor would have refrained from mentioning it at all if she had said something sooner. And then she wouldn't be fantasizing about the sexy firefighter who was constantly coming around and occasionally taking off his shirt as he worked.

That thought sent a warm shiver to all her erogenous zones.

"I'm surprised you haven't met her yet. She lives in Jamison's neighborhood, and her husband was in the military. Special forces, actually. He died while on a mission. He was constantly doing things for her, and she fell for him. Hard. I swear, she was madly in love with him, but the more she got her shit together, the more he pulled away. And now he has you. She's pretty heartbroken over the whole thing."

Bryn would not give Cheryl the satisfaction of getting into any kind of discussion about her and Jamison. All Cheryl wanted to know was if Jamison and Bryn were more than friends.

Even if they were, it was none of Cheryl's business.

"That's between Jamison and Gina and has nothing to do with me."

Cheryl jerked her head back as she moved closer to the counter. "Are you kidding? He's going to do the same thing all because he's still in love with me."

Oh, dear Lord. It took all the energy Bryn had not to bust out laughing.

"I don't know what he's told you, but he's been through a lot and—"

"I'm sorry, but this isn't my business, and you're up." She pointed toward the postal person waving at Cheryl.

"Oh. Well. Consider yourself warned. And tell Jamison to call me as soon as possible. It's urgent."

"Will do." Bryn would wait to text Jamison until after she'd mailed her packages.

Cheryl finished her business and glanced over her shoulder.

Bryn did her best to ignore the woman while she piled her packages on the counter.

"Don't forget to do what I asked," Cheryl called.

"I'll tell him." Bryn waved and went about her business. Maybe she'd wait until she got home.

As carefully as he could, Jamison set Zadie in the bassinet inside the crib. He turned the monitor on and tiptoed out of her room, tugging the door closed. Once in the hallway, he exhaled.

He hadn't realized that he'd been holding his breath.

He hadn't babysat his nieces and nephews when they were this young, so he hadn't realized how exhausting it could be.

However, he'd enjoyed every moment with Zadie. She was so sweet, even when she was screaming.

Only, he felt guilty that he'd been peering into her eyes to see if she looked like this Brenda Perish. He felt even worse for asking his private investigator brother to look into Bryn's past and check into the possibility that she might be related to Brenda. That maybe Brenda was the sister she'd left behind.

But she'd said that her sister was alive.

Brenda was dead.

Had she not known about her sister's passing?

That didn't make sense. Or maybe it did. He had no idea. But he wanted to find out.

The sound of a vehicle pulling into the driveway tickled his ears. He hadn't expected Bryn back this soon, but since she had planned to go to the grocery store, he'd better haul ass and help her with the heavy stuff.

He found himself practically skipping toward the front door. The spring in his step faded when he looked outside and found his ex-wife strolling up the walkway. "What the hell are you doing here?"

"I've been trying to reach you all day, but you don't answer my calls or texts."

"I've been busy." Before stepping outside, he snagged the receiver for the baby monitor and set it on the railing. He tugged the door closed, knowing Bryn would not appreciate anyone in her home.

"You're babysitting?"

"What I'm doing is none of your business." He was so tired of this bullshit, and he couldn't be nice about it anymore. His patience had beyond thinned. It was completely gone now. Especially now that Cheryl was messing with other people. "You can't keep showing up in my life, and you certainly don't have the right to show your face here unannounced. I know that Bryn wouldn't appreciate it, and I can't imagine what kind of business you have with her unless it's to buy jewelry."

"I'm not here to see her," Cheryl said. "I'm here because I need to talk to you."

"About what?"

"Bryn and the fact that she doesn't have a digital footprint except for this jewelry-making stuff. Don't you think that's strange? And even weirder, there is nothing on the internet about her until she moved here. Nothing. Nada. Not one thing."

Jamison leaned against the railing and rubbed his temple. "You're seriously spending your free time googling Bryn?"

"The next step is to hire your brother Rhett to—"

"He won't take the case." But only because Jamison had already beaten her to the punch.

Cheryl waved her hand in front of her face as if she were batting away a fly. "I'll find someone if I need to, but you should really be concerned about this."

"Why?" Actually, the bigger question was why he even entertained this conversation, but he had to admit, he wanted to know what'd put a bug up Cheryl's ass. Had she seen the story, too? Who else was making this connection? And should he say something to Bryn?

"What did she do before she moved here? Why doesn't she have any social media accounts before that? There is no record of her anywhere. That's weird because even you have a digital footprint, and you hate that shit."

He chuckled. "Yeah. But I only have it because you created it for me."

"Not true. There was stuff out there on you before me. Old high school records because of sports. Your firefighter picture. Just stuff. But not one single thing comes up about Bryn Tinsley outside of her Etsy shop and now her website, which lists a post office box in Lighthouse Cove as her address."

Jamison had to admit that it did seem weird. And he *was* having his brother look into it, but he wouldn't tell Cheryl that.

"She's hiding something."

"You're jealous," Jamison said. "And we're not getting back together." He arched a brow. "Troy told me you broke things off with him."

She opened her mouth but snapped it shut quickly.

"We're never getting back together, Cheryl, and

trying to dig up non-existent craziness about Bryn isn't going to change that fact."

She narrowed her eyes. "This isn't about you and me."

"Are you sure about that?"

"I can't believe you would even think that." She breathed in and out so hard that her nose flared like a bull's. "I'm here because I care about you, and I would hate to see you get taken for a ride."

"No. You're here because you still have dollar signs in your eyes, and you're jealous just like you were when you thought there was something going on with me and Gina—which was the craziest thing in the world."

"She wanted you even before her husband passed, and don't go trying to tell me otherwise."

Sometimes, Jamison wondered what he'd ever seen in Cheryl. The older she got, the worse she became. Instead of growing up and becoming a reasonable adult, she seemed to move backward. He wished he knew what the hell had happened that'd caused her to become so insecure. Or how he'd missed it when they'd first gotten together.

The only thing he could think of was that he'd been focused solely on her and no one else when they were dating. When they got married, that remained true. There was no reason for her to be jealous. It wasn't until she started wanting to spend more than they had and pushed harder for him to leave his job that things had become difficult.

And then the shit really hit the fan when Steve showed up.

"Now you're being delusional," he said. "I'm not going to listen to this crap on Bryn's doorstep. You said your piece, now it's time for you to go."

"I'll leave, but I want you to look into this."

"And I want you to stop meddling in my life. We're not married anymore," he said. "You know, Troy really cares about you, and you fucked that up by becoming obsessed with me again. And it's not even me you want. If it were, you wouldn't have cheated on me in the first place."

"I made a mistake. I apologized to you for that. I don't know what I have to do in order to get your forgiveness."

"Nothing," he said. "I forgive you. I really do. But that doesn't mean there is an us to come back to. Because there isn't. That ship has sailed. Now, if you'll excuse me, I have work to do."

"You're babysitting, and it's sleeping."

He laughed. "I'm actually working on a cabinetry project for Bryn, but that's none of your business." He gently curled his fingers around her biceps and guided her toward her car. "For the record, and just so we're clear, I'm being paid." Well, he and Bryn had bartered services, but he wasn't about to tell his ex-wife that.

"Her daughter was sleeping, and Bryn had an errand to run. Since I was here, I said I'd watch Zadie. But Bryn will be back any minute, and I want to finish this project today. I have other ones lined up."

"I can't believe you're finally getting this business off the ground. Why couldn't you do that when we were married?" She pressed her key fob, and the lights on her car flashed.

That was a loaded question, and one he wasn't going to answer because he'd have to be honest, and that would start another fight. "Patch things up with Troy."

She tilted her head. "You punched him when you found out about us."

"That was a different time," he said. "He's a good man, and if you care about him, you'll figure your shit out and let all this stuff with my family and me go." For good measure, Jamison leaned in and kissed her cheek. "I'll see you around." He pulled open the driver's side door.

She slipped behind the steering wheel, obviously unsure of what to say. It was rare that Cheryl was at a loss for words, but when she was, it meant that she might actually be contemplating the current topic.

Jamison could only hope.

Stuffing his hands into his pockets, he waited until her car disappeared down the street before heading back inside. Thankfully, Zadie was still sound asleep. He glanced at his watch. All this paranoia over Bryn's past was too much. He was tired of not trusting people. Bryn was the most real person in his life. So what if she had a past? He understood not wanting people in your life who had wronged you, he could respect that. His only concern was that maybe Bryn would want to know about Brenda's death. But maybe she already knew. It wasn't for him to judge.

He decided it was time to sweep Bryn off her feet with some of his grandmother's awesome cooking. Actually, he decided it was time to show Bryn his place. She might enjoy the view and maybe a nice hot tub soak after dinner.

Maybe even a little snuggling under the moon and stars.

15

"That was an amazing dinner." Bryn eased into the lounge chair next to the hot tub and dropped a blanket over Zadie so she could breastfeed.

"It's my grandmother's recipe. She used to make Alfredo every Sunday, but now, since we're all older and we don't get together every week, it's more like once a month."

"You're a surprising man," she said. "Oh. I keep forgetting to tell you. I ran into Cheryl at the post office, and she wants you to call her. Said it's urgent." Bryn should feel bad that it had taken her about four or so hours to tell him that, but she really didn't. She doubted Cheryl's message was all that important.

"I spoke with her, and it was far from important. But thanks for the message." He stretched out his arms on the sides of the Jacuzzi. "Mind if I ask you a kind of personal question?"

"No. Go ahead," she said.

"Where were you before you came here?"

Her heart plummeted to the center of her stomach and sloshed around like a fish out of water. "What do you mean?"

"You mentioned that you didn't tell your mother-in-law about the baby, so I assume you weren't living in Colorado for the last nine months." He took a quick sip of his beer. "I was just curious as to where you were."

"I went to visit a friend. I wasn't sure where or what I wanted to do. She helped me figure out a lot of things." That wasn't a total lie. But close to it. However, the real mystery was why the hell Jamison had asked her that in the first place. Did he suddenly question who she was or her backstory?

Shit. She was insanely paranoid.

"Did your sister know where you were?"

"No," she said. "We haven't spoken in years."

"I'm sorry. I shouldn't pry. I was just curious because you seem so alone, and that makes me sad for you."

She wasn't sure if she believed that. "That's sweet," she said with a weak smile. "I have always kept a small, tight circle. Most of my friends when I was married were my husband's."

He chuckled. "I know how that goes. Cheryl was

so much more extroverted than me. I preferred to stay at home and watch a movie, stream a series, or go sit by the fire pit with another couple, where she wanted to go out to dinner and bars every weekend. All part of our age difference, I guess."

"Not necessarily. Because Timothy." She coughed. She hadn't meant to say her husband's name out loud. She'd never given him a name before. Fuck. First major slipup. "He loved going out to listen to live music, and he had to do something at least one night a week. It drove me nuts because he expected me to go, and I'm the kind of person who would rather order in and eat from a paper plate."

"Now that's my kind of date night," he said. "When you're done feeding, why don't you join me? I set the bassinet up in the guest room over there. You can leave the door open. I also hooked up the monitor."

"I guess I'm lucky I remembered to pack my suit," she said.

"It's private here, so naked works." He winked.

She laughed. "I'll be back in a few minutes." She lifted Zadie over her shoulder and stood. "It will be a few minutes before she's asleep."

Most nights, she sat and rocked Zadie long after she'd fallen asleep. Not only did she enjoy holding her little girl during the stillness and quiet of the night, but sometimes, Bryn didn't want to drift off into dreamland. Her nightmares still lurked in the corners of her mind, waiting to torment her during her peaceful rest.

However, she found herself wanting to put Zadie in her bassinet as soon as she finished nursing tonight.

So, that's exactly what she did.

Luckily, Zadie didn't seem to mind. She stretched and squirmed a little bit when Bryn set her down, but a few little strokes on her belly, and she settled right back into a deep sleep.

Bryn quickly changed into her suit. It was a modest one-piece. She stared at herself in the mirror. She felt like she was twice the size she used to be when she was married to Timothy. Of course, she'd barely eaten back then and might have been one hundred pounds soaking wet at one point. Now, she had to be closer to one hundred and sixty pounds.

She looked healthy.

Her cheeks heated because, all of a sudden, she wanted to be sexy for herself.

And for Jamison.

She sucked in a deep breath and headed back out to the patio.

"That was quick," Jamison said.

Butterflies filled her gut as she eased into the warm water.

He smiled. "I can't believe you just had a baby six weeks ago. You look amazing."

Her stomach flipped and flopped. Her heart squeezed. She wanted to be close to him. She wanted his arms wrapped around her body, holding her tightly. Everything she feared melted away when she was in his presence.

It was best if she didn't snuggle. That would only lead to kissing. And that would send her down a path she knew would only lead to her hurting him in the worst way.

Sneaking out in the middle of the night and disappearing for good.

"Thank you. I feel like a marshmallow."

"You don't look like one."

She laughed, wrapping her arms around her belly. It shook.

He leaned over and pushed her hands away, planting his on her stomach. "Nope. Definitely not mushy like a marshmallow."

"Oh, my God. You are so weird."

"And you're so sexy," he whispered. His hot breath made her shiver. He rested his arm around her shoulders and pulled her closer. His lips were so close to hers, she could feel the heat they generated. "I want to kiss you."

She blinked.

It wasn't as if they hadn't done that before, but it'd been a few weeks and she'd decided that he'd realized she came with a lot of extra baggage.

Of course, so did he.

And that was the last thing she needed.

Her thoughts were cut short when he took her mouth in a wet and wild kiss full of intent, and her body felt it to its core. A burning sensation crawled across her skin from her head to her toes. It started slow and built, and by the time it reached her belly, every inch of her was on fire.

She found herself lost in a passion she'd never thought to experience again. The last time she'd felt this way had been after her honeymoon. That was when things had changed. Life had been truly horrifying from that point on. There had been times when she thought she'd was going to die.

And times she prayed she would.

Straddling Jamison, she felt desperate to be the woman she'd once been, or at the very least, a whole person. She gripped his shoulders, digging her nails into his skin. She'd forgotten what it was like to desire a man.

Or what it was like to feel wanted by one.

And, right now, every erogenous zone in her body exploded like the Fourth of July. Even when she'd enjoyed sex, which she could barely remember, she didn't initiate, and she didn't allow herself to be wild and out of control like right now.

She wanted Jamison like she wanted the air that filled her lungs.

He cupped her face and pried their mouths apart. "Hey," he whispered.

A chill crept into her heart. Fear filled her soul.

Rejection was not something she could deal with. Not from Jamison.

"I'm sorry." She tried to climb off his lap.

"Oh. Trust me. There is nothing to be sorry about." He wrapped his arms around her waist, heaving her toward his chest. "I'm worried about going too fast."

She raised both brows. "You're a man, so forgive me, but that's shocking."

He laughed. "I'm a little gun shy for a few reasons."

"About sex?" She nearly choked on the words.

"Not just that," he said. "But since you brought it up, we can discuss that first."

"First?" She swallowed. "What's to talk about?"

"You just had a baby. Is it okay? I don't want to hurt you."

"Oh. That," she said. "The doctor told me after six weeks it's safe. As for whether or not it will hurt, there's only one way to find out."

He dropped his head to her shoulder and groaned. "You have to promise me if I'm hurting you in any way, you'll tell me to stop."

"Deal. But now I'm scared that there's more to discuss." She had to admit, chatting with him while his hands roamed up and down her back, cupped her ass, and then repeated the motion was incredibly sexy. A total turn-on. She'd never met anyone like him, and she worried about what would happen when it all came to an end.

"I'm sure I don't have to say this to you; however, I need to for my sanity."

"Sounds serious."

"I care about you and Zadie."

She swallowed. She was crazy to get involved with any man. Especially one like Jamison. It wasn't his complicated life, because when one really examined it closely, his life was pretty simple. It was the people in it that made it difficult. And Jamison was only trying to navigate the changes on his terms, not theirs.

He had boundaries, and they weren't being respected. She respected *him* for not cutting everyone out of his life, even though he all but had when she'd first met him. The reality was that he worked hard to keep his mother and all his siblings close. Hell, he was even trying to find room for Steve and his children. He just didn't want to define those relationships as *family*.

Not yet, anyway. And that was his call.

Jamison was everything Bryn had thought she was getting in Timothy and more.

"I care about you, too," she admitted. "I didn't expect this."

"Neither did I. And one of the things I'm always being accused of, and it's true, is that I can be pretty intense."

"You mean controlling."

"That, too." He laughed. "I still have trust issues."

She leaned in and kissed the side of his neck under his ear. "Are you asking me to go steady?"

He burst out laughing. "That is one way to cut the tension."

"I'm sorry, but I had to. You really are way too serious for your own good." She brushed her lips over his. "I'm thirty-three years old. I got married at twenty-three."

"That's young."

"It is. But other than him, I was only with one other person, and we were together from seventeen to twenty. So, I'm nothing like your ex-wife."

He brushed her hair from her face. "I never said you were."

"But that's part of your issue."

"It's not just me needing to say that when I date a woman, I only date her and expect the same. But there's a lot we don't know about each other. I want you to feel safe with me. I want you to be able to tell me about your past. About the things that put a wedge between you and your sister."

Tears burned the corners of her eyes.

"Oh, shit. I'm sorry. I didn't mean to upset you."

She palmed his cheeks and kissed him. Hard. She'd find something to tell him about Anna—or Arleen as she'd decided to call her sister—later. Maybe she'd tell him that her sister had been in an abusive relationship and she couldn't stand to watch her ruin her life. That she knew how to reach her, and if she wanted help getting out, then she'd be there for her.

Yes.

That would work.

Jamison lifted her out of the hot tub and set her feet gently on the patio. He wrapped a towel around her body. With careful attention to detail, he dried her exposed skin before doing the same to himself. He took the baby monitor in one hand and pressed his other one to the small of her back, guiding her to the master bedroom.

"You're a beautiful woman," he said.

She smiled. It was hard not to. "You're not so bad yourself."

He toyed with the straps on her bathing suit. He pushed the one strap off her shoulder. And then the right.

She resisted the urge to cover her exposed breasts with her hands as he lowered her suit to her midriff.

He dabbled her body with sweet kisses, not letting even an inch of her skin go without attention until she stood before him, completely exposed. He traced a path with his index finger from her chin, down the center of her chest, around her puckered nipples, then circled her belly button and continued lower and lower.

She closed her eyes and enjoyed every sensation.

He laid her on the bed and continued spoiling her

with tender touches. Her body responded in earnest. Needing to feel more of him, she reached for his suit, curling her fingers in the elastic waist.

It had been a long time since she'd considered touching a man without being forced to, and her hand shook.

"You don't have to if you don't want to." He shifted to his side and removed his shorts.

She stared into his eyes, getting lost in his gentle kindness. She had no idea what to say. She opened her mouth in hopes that the words would find her, but all she did was gasp.

"It's okay." He kissed her shoulder and massaged her breast, fanning his thumb over her nipple.

She arched her back. "Oh, God." The way he touched her, it was as if he knew exactly what her body needed. It made her want to scream. She gripped his shoulders and leaned into him, nearly begging him to take her. He must have gotten the hint since he rolled on top, easing himself inside her, slowly. Almost as if to torture her.

A sudden need to be in control came over her. She flipped him onto his back.

"Whoa," he said, squeezing her hips. Hard. As if to slow her down.

But she wasn't having any of that. She needed him. And she needed him now. Years of pent-up frustration and desire had been unleashed, thanks to him.

Or maybe it was because of him. Or perhaps it was all for him. It didn't matter.

Her orgasm tore through her body like a tornado ripping a house right from the land and tossing it miles away. As soon as she thought she might catch her breath, another one gripped her insides.

He sat, rolling her onto her back and thrusting into her, matching her desperation. He groaned and whispered sweet words into her ear before collapsing on top of her as he kissed her tenderly.

This was like nothing she'd ever experienced before with any man.

She suspected it would be a once-in-a-lifetime encounter.

He pulled the covers over their bodies and held her tightly. "There's no point in you leaving," he said. "Please stay all night."

She snuggled in, resting her head on his chest. She should pack up her little girl and leave, but she wasn't going to. She would enjoy this for as long as she could.

Eventually, she'd have to find a reason to move from Lighthouse Cove and, hopefully, Jamison would be able to forgive her.

16

*B*ryn blinked her eyes open. The smell of fresh soap assaulted her nostrils.

"Mommy's awake," Jamison said.

She shifted in the bed, painfully aware that she was naked, and her breasts were completely full of breast milk. She tugged the sheet over her body and pulled herself to a sitting position. "What time is it?"

"Six." Jamison held Zadie between his legs. He wore nothing but his boxers, and it was obvious he'd just gotten out of the shower. "This little angel just woke up about ten minutes ago. We have a clean diaper, and we're all ready for breakfast." He pointed to her boobs. "Looks like you're ready, too."

She glanced down, mortified that she'd started leaking. Her cheeks flushed.

He leaned in and kissed her temple. "Do you want me to leave?"

"Um. No. This is just all kind of new to me."

"You and me both." He took an extra pillow and placed it on her lap for Zadie to rest on. "I made some decaf coffee. I'll go grab you a mug while you get situated. Can I get you anything else?"

"I'm kind of hungry."

"Do you like chocolate chip muffins?"

"That might get you a little treat this morning."

He jumped from the bed and raced out of the room like a kid on Christmas morning.

"Oh, Zadie. What have I gotten myself into?" She pulled down the sheet and brought her baby girl to her breast. Zadie latched on immediately. The little bundle of joy glanced up, and Bryn could have sworn she paused and smiled. "You're the most precious thing in the world."

"I have to agree." Jamison set a mug on the night-stand next to Bryn. He climbed back into bed, broke off a small piece of the muffin, and placed it in her mouth.

She forgot all about the fact that she was completely naked. She nearly moaned when the chocolate melted in her mouth. "I'll take more of that."

He plopped a piece into his mouth and then kissed her, swirling his tongue in her mouth. "I shouldn't have done that while you're nursing."

"No. It's fine, and it tastes better when it comes from you."

271

He chuckled. "I feel like an asshole, but sitting here watching you nurse like this has to be the sexiest thing in the world."

She glanced down and blushed. The sheet had fallen to her waist, and she was completely exposed. She should be utterly embarrassed, but she wasn't. If anything, she felt totally at ease. "I don't know about it being sexy, but it's not weird."

He fed her another bite of muffin. "It's not like I want to ravish your body or anything, but this is beautiful, and being a mom is amazing."

"Yeah, it is." She adjusted Zadie before shifting and locking gazes with Jamison. "When I first found out that I was pregnant, Timothy had only been dead for a few days. I wasn't sure how I felt about it all."

"I'm not sure how to approach this subject, and I can't do it while you're sitting here like this." He pulled the covers over her bare breast and put his arm around her, tugging her a little closer. "I recently saw something on television, and I couldn't help but notice how much you looked like this woman who had been beaten by her husband."

Bryn tried like hell not to tense up and panic.

"This crime documentary," he continued. "It talked about how this man had died in a crash and then, a few weeks later, his wife died the same way. I know you don't like to talk about it, but I wondered if maybe she could be your sister. Her name was Brenda Perish."

Bryn gasped.

Zadie arched her back and let out a cry.

"Shhhhh, baby girl." Bryn patted her daughter's back and did her best to calm her. "No. That's not my sister. Her name is Arleen. Why would you even think that?" she said with a combination of fear and anger.

"I'm sorry. I didn't mean to upset you. I really didn't." He pressed his lips against her temple.

She closed her eyes. She should have known that her past would catch up with her and that she couldn't hide. There was no place on this Earth where she could run and escape her husband's family. Deep down, she knew that someone, if not the Perishes themselves, would put it all together, and she'd be outed. Then they'd come and find her and take her precious daughter from her for good.

Well, she couldn't let that happen.

No way.

Tonight, she'd gather up what she could, take all her savings, and sneak off into the night, never to be heard from again.

She knew it would be hard. But what choice did she have?

"This woman just looked so much like you, and I know you're hiding something." He hugged her tighter. "It's okay. I, of all people, understand. You can tell me anything, though. You can trust me."

"You don't believe me?" She stared at him with wide eyes.

"Of course, I believe you," he said. "It's just that she looked so much like you."

"That's not my sister."

He took her chin with his thumb and forefinger and kissed her lips softly. "Tell me about your sister, Arleen. What happened between the two of you? I want to know, and only because I care so much about you and Zadie."

She dropped her head back. Her heart hurt. She absolutely believed Jamison, and that broke her soul. She knew he cared. His feelings were so strong that he wanted to know what'd torn her family apart. Just like she wanted to know about him and his family.

This was genuine.

She knew that to be true. But, sometimes, truths didn't matter.

Especially when they were lies.

"I really don't want to talk about this right now."

"Okay." He kissed her shoulder. "I won't push, but I'm here when you're ready to talk."

"And if I never want to tell you about her or why we don't speak anymore?"

"It's probably too soon to say something like this, but I'm falling for you."

She opened her mouth to protest his declaration, but he pressed his finger against her lips.

"I can see in your eyes how painful this is for you, and I'm kicking myself for bringing it up. However, I know it's not me who put that hurt in your heart. Just like if you were to start asking me about Steve, his children, and my mom. And those are all issues I need to come to terms with. That's something you and Zadie have helped me see. I need to resolve my conflict with the people in my life. Especially my mom. I love her dearly, and I'd hate for something to happen to her and for me not to have put all this craziness in the past."

"What about Steve, his children, and your brothers?"

"All of them, too. I know I need to find room in my life for them all. And I will. That's why, when I saw that story and thought if maybe she, or someone like her, could be your sister, I wondered if there was some way you could mend fences."

She nodded. "While that woman isn't related to me, my sister is involved in a relationship I can't stand behind. That's part of why we don't speak."

"Enough said." He kissed her temple. "I have that deck and dock I need to work on today. You and Zadie are welcome to hang out here all day if you want."

"I have to get working on some jewelry, so I do need to get back to my place. But not until after her morning nap and my use of your big soaking tub."

"I have to work a twenty-four-hour shift tomorrow. If you want, you and Zadie can sleep here. Hell,

JEN TALTY

you can bring all your jewelry-making stuff and sit out by the pool and enjoy the sun."

She let out a long breath and ran her hand over the top of her daughter's head. "I don't want to take advantage."

"I'd like to consider myself your boyfriend. And if that's the case, you wouldn't be doing that at all."

She turned and caught Jamison's gaze. "I'm not sure I'm ready for all of this."

"Neither am I."

"We've lost our minds."

"Probably." He kissed her lips. It was soft and tender and reminded her of warm cider. "Is she done yet? I was hoping to get that morning treat you mentioned."

Jamison gently laid Zadie in her bassinet. "Are you going to stay asleep so Mommy and I can have a little romantic time this morning?" He rubbed Zadie's belly for a long moment, just to make sure the little girl stayed passed out.

Sure enough, Zadie's eyes remained closed.

He raced back to the master bedroom and was happy to find Bryn still in bed.

Naked.

Waiting for him with open arms.

Never in a million years had he expected to find someone so perfectly matched to him, and he didn't even know everything there was to know. Still, he understood the basics.

Her favorite foods. The music she liked. How she enjoyed watching the sun rise on the beach. She loved reading mysteries but preferred listening to non-fiction in audiobooks. However, it all seemed a bit superficial. He wanted to know the things that really excited her on a deeper level. The things that made her tick. What riled her up and made her heart beat a little faster.

"Did you turn the monitor back on?" she asked.

He double-checked the receiver after climbing between the sheets. "Yup." He pulled her body tight against his, enjoying her silky skin.

He'd enjoyed the company of a few beautiful women over the years, but no one had ever been as amazingly sexy and sweet as Bryn. She was, in his humble opinion, the perfect woman. Sure, she probably had a flaw or two, though for the life of him he couldn't think of a single one.

And he wasn't going to try to find any.

He would enjoy being blissfully unaware.

"Are you sure you don't mind me hanging out here tonight?"

"Um. Why would I mind? I'm going to be here." He chuckled.

JEN TALTY

"What about tomorrow when you're not here?"

He kissed her sweet lips. "You and Zadie are welcome to stay here. I want you to. Actually, I'd feel better if you did."

She jerked her head back. "Why? Is there something wrong with my place?"

"No." He dropped his head to her shoulder. "That didn't come out right. I just mean that I want you to have the pool, the hot tub, the soaking bath where you can enjoy bubbles while you watch television after putting Zadie down."

"You're spoiling me."

"Isn't that what boyfriends are for?"

She curled her fingers around his length and squeezed.

He hissed.

She pressed her lips against the center of his chest.

His breathing became labored. He ran his fingers through her hair and relaxed into the bed. "Are you going to have your way with me this morning?"

"That's the plan." She licked his nipple, rolling her tongue over the tight nub.

He fisted her hair, tugging slightly.

She squeezed harder.

He groaned.

"You don't have to do this."

"I want to," she said.

"I'm not going to stop you," he whispered in a raspy voice.

278

She kissed her way down his torso until her hands and mouth found his manhood.

He gripped the sheets. No woman had ever touched him the way she did, and it wasn't about the execution but connection.

She glanced up at him as she brought her lips over the tip, easing down on the shaft, slowly but firmly.

His fingers dug into her scalp, massaging wildly. He hoped it wasn't too aggressive, and he tried like hell not to press her head down on him. The last thing he wanted was to force anything on her, and he wanted this to be about what she wanted. But, damn, he enjoyed this more than any other time in his life.

If he could make this last forever, he would. This was exactly the way men and women were supposed to be together.

Fear gripped his heart like a magnet hitting metal.

He'd fallen in love with Bryn. Totally and completely. Without reservation, he loved her.

"Babe, I need you to stop," Jamison said. He rolled her onto her back and took her mouth in a hot, hard kiss. It was the kind that claimed a woman. It was wild and animalistic. His tongue swirled around in her mouth like a beast in search of its meal.

He nestled himself between her legs, entering her in a long, slow stroke.

She gripped his shoulders, digging her nails into his back. She moved her body with his, grinding her hips against his, begging him to bring her the kind of pleasure only he could give.

He hoped he didn't disappoint because he could no longer contain himself.

Her climax came fast and hard.

His followed seconds later.

They lay together, panting, desperate to catch their breaths, holding each other and practically laughing at their inability to make it last longer than a couple of horny teenagers. But he didn't care, and neither did she, it seemed.

He was so thoroughly satisfied.

"Oh, shit," she said, her body stiffening. "I can't believe I totally forgot."

"What's the matter?" He cupped her face and gazed into her eyes. "Are you okay? Are you hurt or something?"

"No. It's not that, but we forgot something very important."

"What's that?"

"I never went back on birth control, and while breastfeeding might make it harder for me to get pregnant, it's not out of the realm of possibility."

He waited for a second for the panic to set in, but it didn't.

Adding a second child to the mix wouldn't be the worst thing in the world.

Suddenly, his entire world made sense.

She glanced up at him with wide eyes.

"It's okay," he kissed her forehead. "If you're pregnant, we'll deal with it."

"How can you be so calm about this?"

"Because as crazy as this sounds, I love you and Zadie."

17

"*I*'ll see you tonight."

"Okay," Bryn said.

Jamison stood behind her in the master bathroom and squeezed her shoulders. "Feel free to stay for as long as you like. Just lock up when you leave."

She turned and kissed him on the lips. Hard.

"Hmm. That was nice." He patted her bottom. "Have a good day." He turned and disappeared into the other room.

Bryn felt bad that she couldn't bring herself to repeat the sweet words that Jamison had said to her earlier, but he kept telling her that it was okay. That if she didn't feel the same way or wasn't ready to say it, he understood.

But how could that be?

He had to be hurt that she'd just sat there and

stared at him and then got out of bed to take a shower.

However, the reality was, she felt exactly the same way. Yet fear prevented her from telling him that she loved him. She wasn't afraid of him but her past. She needed to tell him the truth. If he could handle that and still love her, then they had a future.

She raced from his bedroom to the kitchen. "Jamison?" she called. "Where are you?"

No answer.

She opened the door to the garage and found he'd already climbed behind the steering wheel of his Jeep.

He jumped from his vehicle. "What's wrong?" He took her into his arms. "Are you okay? Is Zadie okay?"

"Yes. We're both fine," she managed between ragged breaths. "We need to talk."

"About?"

"My past," she said. "I don't want to keep things from you. I love you."

He cupped her face and smiled. "I love you, too." He kissed her lips.

"You're not listening to me."

"I heard you," he said. "You want to tell me something about your past. We can talk about it when I get back tonight."

"It's not going to be easy for you to hear."

"We can handle anything." He pressed his lips against her forehead. "As long as we're honest."

She nodded.

He winked. "It's going to be okay." He climbed back into his Jeep and turned the key. He backed out of the garage and waved as he drove off, leaving her standing there.

She wasn't so sure that being honest would make everything okay, but she was willing to give it a try.

Jamison sat in front of the computer in his brother's office and stared at the Facebook page for a Brenda Thompson Perish. Despite her white, spiky hair and anorexic figure, he could have sworn she was Bryn Tinsley.

Not her sister. But Bryn.

Fuck.

He did another quick search on the internet and found that she had a sister named Anna and her father, Herold, was alive and well and living in California. They'd both posted angry rants about her late husband and his family and how they blamed them for their beloved Brenda's death.

"Jamison? Where the hell are you?" his brother Rhett called.

"In your office." He scrolled through articles, pictures, and other information, and his stomach soured.

He'd poked the bear, and he didn't like what he'd found.

And it pissed him off that his mother had been right.

Of course, this could be what Bryn wanted to talk to him about tonight, and he had to give her the benefit of the doubt.

He had to. Because he loved her, and he couldn't change that fact if he tried.

Rhett crossed the threshold and tossed a folder onto the desk. "You really don't want to read that."

"What is it, exactly?" He opened the file and let out an audible gasp. "Jesus."

"That's the only hospital record I found, by the way. But I bet there are more."

"Her husband did that to her?"

"That's not what the report says, but yeah, I'd say that man was quite the bastard."

Jamison swallowed as he turned a few pages and scanned what his brother had uncovered.

"The night Timothy Perish died, he got into a wicked fight with his wife. There aren't any pictures or anything that I could find, but there are reports from those that worked at the club. One person said she was out of control. Another person said it was him that was over the top. Lots of conflicting stories, actually. But everyone can agree that when Timothy left the club, he was drunk and possibly high on coke. His parents wholeheartedly blame Brenda for his death. They even threatened a wrongful death suit against her when the authorities didn't see any reason to bring charges against her."

"There would be no reason since she wasn't in the car," Jamison said as he continued looking at images and stories that didn't make any sense.

Bryn had lied to him.

About everything.

Part of him understood. Deep down, he knew that he'd do the same thing. One hundred fucking percent he'd lie.

The question then became: Was she going to tell him the truth?

"What else have you found out?" Jamison asked.

"The Perishes have spent a fair amount of money looking into Brenda's death. There was an investigation, and they were adamant at one point that she wasn't dead. They have people watching Brenda's sister and her dad."

"Jesus. I wish I could bring them to Bryn. This is just so fucking unfair."

"I agree. But to tell you the truth, Bryn did the right thing by disappearing. That family is horrible. What he did to her for ten damn years—"

"I don't need a recap," Jamison said. His heart beat so fast it hurt. If the Perish family knew about Zadie, they would come after her, and they wouldn't give a shit who they stepped on in order to take her from her mother.

There was no fucking way Jamison would let

anything happen to Zadie, much less allow mother and child to be separated.

From him.

As angry as he was that she hadn't yet trusted him enough to tell him the truth, based on what he'd learned about her in-laws, he didn't blame her. Hopefully, he'd be able to get her to do that tonight.

"A friend of mine is poking around the family. I should know more by tomorrow."

Jamison picked up his cell and texted a couple of buddies, asking them if they could take his shift.

Immediately, one of his friends responded with a yes.

Wonderful. He could spend tonight with Bryn, and he wouldn't have to get up at five in the morning to go to work. He could stay and take care of her, and they could work on a plan for what to do next.

"Stay on this," he said. "And promise me you won't tell Mom yet."

"I won't, but we might need her help. And Dad's. And not to bring up a sore subject, but Steve's money might help with—"

"I get it," Jamison said. "I'm willing to do whatever it takes to help Bryn and Zadie, so if it comes to that, I'll do it."

"Wow. You must really care about this girl."

"I do," Jamison said. "I love her. But that's not the only reason I'd be willing to ask Mom and Steve for help."

Rhett cocked his head. "Excuse me?"

"I'll never accept Steve as my dad. I have one of those. But I can accept the biology, and he does have four kids who are my half-siblings. Besides, I can't deny that he loves our mom. I'm tired of being angry and hurt. I'm sick of harboring resentment over shit that I can't control." He waved his hand in front of the computer. "All this shit, and my love for Bryn and her daughter, has taught me that holding on to shit from the past does nothing but keep you there. Mom and Dad made mistakes. Steve made them, too. They have all said they're sorry, and I know they mean it. It's time for me to grow the fuck up and be a man."

"It took you falling in love with a woman and her baby to figure that out?"

Jamison chuckled. "I guess so."

Rhett slapped him on the back. "Why don't you get the fuck out of my house and get back to your new woman? Let me do the private investigative work."

"Sounds good to me."

18

*B*ryn raced around her house like a giddy schoolgirl. Being in love was like being on cloud nine. It didn't negate that she needed to come clean about who she really was, and while she was absolutely prepared to do that, and tonight, it didn't change the fact that she'd finally met a man who was genuine and cared about her for who she was and not what he wanted her to be.

Her heart paused for a moment. There was still a chance that he'd hate her for lying, but something told her that he had a good idea she'd kept some big secrets from him, and that once he got over the initial shock, he'd be okay. The only real concern she had was for her sister and father. They could never be brought into this. They had to believe she was dead. That was the only way they would be safe.

And she would be able to live her current life.

She found herself in her bedroom, standing in front of the dresser, frozen, unable to finish packing her overnight bag.

She plopped down on her bed and clutched her pillow. This was the biggest mistake of her life. What the hell had made her think she could love Jamison and tell him the truth?

Shit. She would have to come up with some great lie or run.

She squeezed her eyes shut. Her life sucked, and it had been hell since the moment she'd met Timothy Perish.

A door slammed.

She jumped to her feet.

"Hello?" she called. "Who's there?"

No answer.

Holding the pillow, she slowly made her way toward the front of the house.

"Hello, Brenda," a familiar voice said. "Surprised to see me?"

She dropped the pillow. She stared at Mark Perish. Her heart dropped to her gut. Her veins went cold. She tried to swallow, but her muscles didn't work properly.

"I heard you had a baby," Mark said. "Where is my grandchild?"

"I don't know what you're talking about." Thank goodness Jamison's sister-in-law, Nancy, had stopped by with her two little girls to use the pool and had offered to look after Zadie.

"Where's the baby?" Mark asked again, a little louder this time, showing his weapon. "Don't make me hurt you."

Phone. Where was her cell? Her purse in the kitchen, she hoped. "She's not here."

"You had a girl?"

Bryn backed up slowly, slightly surprised that Mark hadn't known what she'd had. She could use that. "She's at the 'sitter's." Think. Think all this through. Bryn breathed slowly and methodically. She needed to be strong and brave. Not just for Zadie but also for herself.

"I want my grandchild," Mark said.

"My babysitter can bring her home. Let me text her."

"Okay. Let me get my cell," Bryn said.

Mark pointed his gun at her face. "No funny shit, or you're dead. For real this time."

She held up her hands. "Okay. My purse is in the kitchen." Slowly, she turned and inched into the other room. She dug into her pocketbook and found her phone.

"Give it to me," Mark said. "What's your 'sitter's name."

"Rebecca Kirby. Tell her that plans have changed and that I need her to bring Jamie here." She didn't want to use her daughter's real name, but more importantly, she wanted something cryptic to send to Rebecca without giving away Jamison's name, just in case.

He tapped away on her cell. "You might as well take a load off. But don't get too comfortable. As soon as my granddaughter gets here, we're taking off. And then you will meet your maker once and for all."

"Jamison!"

His mother came barreling into the kitchen.

"Where are you?"

He cradled Zadie in the crook of his arm and rocked her back and forth. She was close to a full wail, and Bryn had not answered her cell, which wasn't like her. "What's the matter?"

"Something is terribly wrong." She skidded to a stop at the end of the island. "Is Bryn here?

"No. Why?"

His mother shoved her cell in front of his face. "I got these cryptic texts from her. They don't make any sense to me, and other than responding that I'd do it, I didn't think I should say anything else. Oh, I sent your brothers over to her place, but they are under strict orders to do nothing except report back to me."

"Nancy is here with the kids." Jamison traded Zadie for the phone. "I don't understand this," he mumbled as he read the texts. "But there are some things about Bryn's past that Rhett and I just found out."

"Like what?"

"Do you know who the Perish family is?"

"I don't know. Should I?"

"Long story short, Bryn was married to a man who used to beat the shit out of her. He's dead, thankfully, but his parents are bad people, and if they knew she was alive and had a kid, they'd come after her."

"Looks like they found her." His mother bounced up and down, pressing her lips against Zadie's pudgy little cheek as the baby cried.

"Who's Jamie?" Jamison asked.

"I'm guessing that's you. But Bryn texted me, the chief of police, so we're doing this my way." She kissed Zadie. "You be a good little girl for your Auntie Nancy while Jamison and I go save your mommy."

"Relax? You want me to fucking relax?" Jamison paced two blocks from Bryn's house as he ran his hand over the top of his head. "Some crazy lunatic is holding her at gunpoint and that's your best advice?"

"Let me do my job," his mother said as she strapped on her bulletproof best.

His brothers Nathan, Emmett, Seth, and Emmerson all did the same thing.

Jamison leaned against his Jeep and folded his

arms across his chest. He'd never felt so helpless in all his life. "I'm going in with you."

Seth held his weapon at the ready. "No. You're not. You're going to stay right here."

"They know what they're doing, so let them do it," his father said.

"I concur." Steve handed him a bottled water.

Fucking wonderful. His dad and biological father were ganging up on him, and there wasn't a damn thing he could do because he knew they were right.

"It's going to be okay. She's a smart girl. What she had him do by texting me was genius," his mother said. "Let's roll, boys."

His father put an arm around him and gave it a good squeeze. "Your mom knows what she's doing."

"I agree with your dad," Steve said.

"Do either of you have any idea how fucked up it is to hear the two of you talking like this?"

"Wait until we start in on who Zadie is going to call Grandpa or Pappy or whatever," his father said.

Steve laughed. "I'll just be happy to be included."

Jamison couldn't help it. He chuckled as he watched his mother and brothers jog off down the street. But that sound was cut short the moment they disappeared.

"It's really going to be okay," Steve said. "According to your dad, your mom and your brothers are the best at what they do."

"He's right about that."

Bryn sat in the rocking chair and stared out the picture window.

Mark stood by the sofa and did the same thing. "How far away does this chick live?"

"About twenty minutes." Bryn lied. "But it takes a few minutes to pack up all Jamie's things." It felt so weird to call her daughter by a different name, but she needed to go along with the fib for as long as she could. She hoped Rebecca understood that something was wrong. Considering that she'd texted back saying she'd be along shortly, it seemed like she'd gotten the hint.

But she had no idea what she was walking into, and Bryn had no way of telling her that.

She could only assume that Rebecca had contacted Jamison, but that didn't mean he'd been able to shed any light on the situation because she hadn't been honest with him. That could end up costing her or someone else their life.

No. That couldn't happen.

Hers. Yes. She could live with that. But not anyone else's.

"How did you find me?"

"It was a combination of things. A reporter named Jon Kaplan and a private investigator looking into your death. The fact that they were both from this area made me want to take a look, and it wasn't hard to find you after that. I got on the first plane I could this morning, and here I am. I have to admit, you faked your death damn well."

She sucked in a deep breath.

He laughed. "Don't worry. They don't know I'm here, and they still think you're dead. We'll keep it that way since, in a few hours, that will be the—"

The front door flew open.

Rebecca jumped into the family room with her gun drawn. "Drop your weapon and put your hands where I can see them."

Emmerson stood two feet behind her with his weapon pointed right at Mark.

Boots stomping across the kitchen caught Bryn's attention. She turned her head.

Nathan and Seth appeared in the hallway.

"I'd do what my mother says," Seth said. "Or I'll shoot."

"What the fuck?" Mark dropped his gun and raised his hands over his head. "I'm going to get you for this, you little bitch."

"Is that a threat?" Rebecca said. "Because my other son, the one pacing in the street outside, won't take too kindly to you talking to his girlfriend that way." She smiled. "Will one of you cuff this piece of shit and get him out of my sight?"

"Gladly, Ma," Emmerson said.

Rebecca holstered her weapon. She stretched out her hand and helped Bryn to a standing position.

"Jamison is freaking out. Why don't we go find him and let him know that you're okay?"

"Zadie? How is she?"

"Fine," Rebecca said, palming Bryn's cheek. "She's still at Jamison's place with Nancy. We'll get you home to your little girl as quickly as we can. But I am going to need a statement from you. Oh. And your father and sister have been notified. Yes, we know the whole story. They will be here tomorrow."

Just then, Jamison came barreling through the door.

"Bryn," he said. "Are you okay?"

She leapt into his arms and couldn't contain the tears. "You called my sister and dad?"

"We did. I didn't think you'd want them to believe you were dead for a second longer."

"I love you," she whispered. "Thank you. I have no idea how I'm going to repay—"

He pressed his finger to her lips. "Allowing me to love you is repayment enough."

EPILOGUE

*J*amison gripped the counter and took in a deep breath. He glanced outside at all the people, and his heart pounded against his chest like a jackhammer.

"Hey, Jamison," Henry said as he leisurely strolled into the kitchen. It had been nice for both Bryn and Zadie to have Henry and Anna move to Lighthouse Cove. Unexpected, not necessary, and, honestly, a little crowded since three out of four of Steve's kids had moved into town, too, and Jamison had been doing his best to have a relationship with all of them.

"You look pale." Henry laughed as he slapped him on the back. "You're not getting cold feet, are you?"

That was the rub. He couldn't get cold feet because he and Bryn had run off and eloped over the weekend. While they loved their families, all of them

298

in one place could be overwhelming. His mother was still trying to tell him how to run his life, including his romantic one. However, she realized that Bryn was the perfect woman for her son. At least, that part was good.

But there was still the meddling, and now she would harp on his parenting skills—or lack thereof.

And she still pushed the Steve agenda.

Jamison would never accept him as a father. Not even a stepfather. But as a friend and confidant…he could do that. Steve wasn't a bad guy. Actually, once Jamison gave him half a chance, he'd learned that he kind of liked the man.

Jamison also enjoyed his two half-sisters and brothers.

He struggled less to accept them, but they still had their reservations, and he completely understood.

"I assume since you're having this party that today is the day you're finally going to pop the question? I mean, you went to all that trouble to tell me you love Bren—I mean, Bryn." Henry patted his chest. "I know how much it means to my daughter to keep her new identity, and I want to honor that. But it's hard sometimes."

"She doesn't care that you call her Brenda occasionally. She just doesn't want to confuse Zadie as she gets older and starts talking. Eventually, we'll have to tell Zadie about her past and where she came from. We don't want her to go through what I did, but Bryn doesn't want Zadie to be tied to her past."

"Trust me. I respect that." Henry pointed to the pool patio. "You have quite an interesting family. They too are trying not to hold to past mistakes. It takes a lot of love to do that. You're a lucky man."

Jamison's chest tightened.

"Just relax. breathe. You know she's going to say yes. So, ignore the rest of us." Henry snagged a beer from the fridge. "See you outside."

Jamison groaned. The last thing he wanted to do was displease his future—no, *present*—father-in-law. He and Bryn hadn't gone away for a romantic weekend with the idea of getting married. They'd done so because she'd stopped nursing and Steve and his mom had agreed to take Zadie for a night.

It was a win-win in his book.

The sight of his beautiful wife padding across the tile floor made his pounding heart slow just a tad.

"What's wrong, honey?" She set the baby monitor on the counter.

He wrapped his arms around her waist and pulled her tightly to his body. It still terrified him that he could have lost her. Mark Perish had every intention of killing Bryn and taking Zadie. From prison, Mark and his wife still rambled on about how he'd make sure that Bryn paid for what she'd done.

Bryn and Jamison took the necessary precautions simply because the Perish family had connections, and Jamison being part of a family filled with cops helped. However, they didn't spend their lives looking over their shoulders. Nope. There was enough evidence regarding Mark and Barb's businesses to send them away for eighty years.

And people were turning on them left and right.

It was over.

"Your dad thinks I'm going to propose to you today."

"Well, he is going to get some great news." She glanced up at him, and her eyes sparkled with mischief.

He laughed. "I'm still in shock over that one."

"You and me both."

"Shock over what?" Jamison's father said as he entered through the big sliders.

"All part of the big announcement we'll make in a bit." Jamison kissed Bryn's temple before leaning against the counter, keeping an arm around her waist. "What's in your hand?"

His father waved a folder and set it on the kitchen table. "That there, my friend, are the official adoption papers for Zadie.

"What about Mark and Barb?" Bryn asked with a shaky voice. "Can they contest the adoption?"

"They can ask to be heard," his father said. "But no one will listen. Not only has Mark been charged with kidnapping and attempted murder, but a plethora of charges are being brought against them both for their businesses now, too."

"But what you're saying is they could always be part of our lives, and they *could* try to stop this," Jamison said. As much as he wanted to officially be Zadie's dad, he knew, in his heart, that he'd always be the one who loved her the most. The one who would be there for every skinned knee. For every runny nose. Jamison would be the one who scared off all the wrong boys, and he'd be the one who walked her down the aisle—that was if she didn't run off and elope, stealing that honor from him. Inwardly, he groaned.

Of course, he and Bryn wouldn't have done a wedding anyway. They'd both done it before and weren't interested in doing it again. They didn't need the ceremony.

They only wanted the marriage.

The partnership.

"Let's remember I generally defend people like Mark and Barb. If I were their attorney, I'd recommend that we do whatever it took to reduce the number of years they serve. And dealing with this" —he tapped the folder on the table—"would not be something I would want my clients focusing on. Still, the short answer is, yes. But from behind bars, there isn't much they can do. And as parents, you're going to want to do what's best for your child, and that's not bringing grandparents into the mix that have a criminal record, especially when it includes holding Zadie's mother at gunpoint." His father tilted his head. "You don't have anything to worry about. And I'm sure the adoption will go through." His father inched closer and pressed his hand on the center of Jamison's chest. "But never forget. The parent-child bond starts here. Not with a piece of paper."

"Thanks, Dad."

His father smiled. "Don't forget, Steve's not a bad guy. And I, for one, am grateful that his biology made you."

Jamison rolled his eyes. "You know, when you put shit that way, it's kind of hard to keep pushing all of them away."

His father chuckled. "Come on. Let's get outside and enjoy this party." His dad stepped through the sliding glass doors and moved back into the crowd of family.

"We might as well get this over with." Bryn laced her fingers through his and tugged. "Zadie's afternoon naps are only lasting about forty minutes lately, and with all these people, I doubt she'll last even that long."

"Let's do this." His entire family expected him to get on bended knee, declare his love, and ask Bryn to marry him. Well, he'd done that a week ago when he'd asked his father to draw up the adoption papers, and he and Bryn had filed for a marriage license. It wasn't a great proposal. He hadn't even bought a ring yet.

But it had been well thought out, and he knew without a doubt that Bryn and Zadie belonged in his life.

"Can I have everyone's attention for a moment?" He stood by the pool with Bryn at his side.

She leaned into him, holding his forearm tightly, digging her fingernails into his skin.

Everyone they loved stared at them with bright smiles, clutching their drinks by their chests, waiting for the big moment.

He almost busted out laughing.

Boy, would they be surprised.

"Bryn and I have something to share with everyone." He lifted her left hand.

She wiggled her fingers.

There was a collective gasp from the crowd.

"You already proposed?" his mother exclaimed. "When?"

"Last week," he said.

"When do you plan on getting married?" Steve asked.

Bryn glanced up at him with a beaming smile. "Four days ago," she said, taking his left hand and showing off his wedding band.

"Oh, my," his mother said in a faint whisper.

Everyone shouted, "Congratulations," and clapped.

Needing to get it all out there before their siblings stormed them with hugs, he raised his fingers to his mouth and whistled. It was the only way to shut the crowd up. "There's more."

Silence.

He cleared his throat. "Honey, would you like the honors with this one?"

She took his hand and rested it on her belly. "Zadie is going to be a big sister."

"I love you," Jamison whispered over the screams and shouts of their loved ones. For the last couple of years, he'd felt lost and alone. As if he didn't belong anywhere.

And now he had his family back, along with four new brothers and sisters.

Not to mention, he had his own little family that was his to keep. His to love. His to protect.

He was right where he belonged.

Thank you for taking the time to read *Mine To Keep*.
Please feel free to leave an HONEST review.

Sign up for my Newsletter (https://dl.bookfunnel.com/ 82gm8b9k4y) where I often give away free books before publication.

Join my private Facebook group (https://www.facebook. com/groups/191706547909047/) where I post exclusive excerpts and discuss all things murder and love!

ABOUT THE AUTHOR

Jen Talty is the *USA Today* Bestselling Author of Contemporary Romance, Romantic Suspense, and Paranormal Romance. In the fall of 2020, her short story was selected and featured in a 1001 Dark Nights Anthology.

Regardless of the genre, her goal is to take you on a ride that will leave you floating under the sun with warmth in your heart. She writes stories about broken heroes and heroines who aren't necessarily looking for romance, but in the end, they find the kind of love books are written about :).

She first started writing while carting her kids to one hockey rink after the other, averaging 170 games per year between 3 kids in 2 countries and 5 states. Her first book, IN TWO WEEKS was originally published in 2007. In 2010 she helped form a publishing company (Cool Gus Publishing) with *NY Times* Bestselling Author Bob Mayer where she ran the technical side of the business through 2016.

Jen is currently enjoying the next phase of her life… the empty nester! She and her husband reside in Jupiter, Florida.

Grab a glass of vino, kick back, relax, and let the romance roll in…

Sign up for my Newsletter (https://dl.bookfunnel.com/ 82gm8b9k4y) where I often give away free books before publication.

Join my private Facebook group (https://www.facebook.com/ groups/191706547909047/) where I post exclusive excerpts and discuss all things murder and love!

Never miss a new release. Follow me on Amazon:amazon.com/author/jentalty

And on Bookbub: bookbub.com/authors/jen-talty

ALSO BY JEN TALTY

Brand new series: SAFE HARBOR!

MINE TO KEEP

MINE TO SAVE

MINE TO PROTECT

Check out LOVE IN THE ADIRONDACKS!

SHATTERED DREAMS

AN INCONVENIENT FLAME

THE WEDDING DRIVER

NY STATE TROOPER SERIES (also set in the Adirondacks!)

In Two Weeks

Dark Water

Deadly Secrets

Murder in Paradise Bay

To Protect His own

Deadly Seduction

When A Stranger Calls

His Deadly Past

The Corkscrew Killer

Brand New Novella for the First Responders series

A spin-off from the NY State Troopers series

PLAYING WITH FIRE

PRIVATE CONVERSATION

THE RIGHT GROOM

AFTER THE FIRE

CAUGHT IN THE FLAMES

CHASING THE FIRE

Legacy Series

Dark Legacy

Legacy of Lies

Secret Legacy

Emerald City

INVESTIGATE AWAY

Colorado Brotherhood Protectors

Fighting For Esme

Defending Raven

Fay's Six

Yellowstone Brotherhood Protectors

Guarding Payton

Candlewood Falls

RIVERS EDGE
THE BURIED SECRET
ITS IN HIS KISS
LIPS OF AN ANGEL

It's all in the Whiskey
JOHNNIE WALKER
GEORGIA MOON
JACK DANIELS
JIM BEAM
WHISKEY SOUR
WHISKEY COBBLER
WHISKEY SMASH
IRISH WHISKEY

The Monroes
COLOR ME YOURS
COLOR ME SMART
COLOR ME FREE
COLOR ME LUCKY
COLOR ME ICE
COLOR ME HOME

Search and Rescue
PROTECTING AINSLEY

PROTECTING CLOVER

PROTECTING OLYMPIA

PROTECTING FREEDOM

PROTECTING PRINCESS

PROTECTING MARLOWE

DELTA FORCE-NEXT GENERATION

SHIELDING JOLENE

SHIELDING AALYIAH

SHIELDING LAINE

SHIELDING TALULLAH

SHIELDING MARIBEL

The Men of Thief Lake

REKINDLED

DESTINY'S DREAM

Federal Investigators

JANE DOE'S RETURN

THE BUTTERFLY MURDERS

THE AEGIS NETWORK

The Sarich Brother

THE LIGHTHOUSE

HER LAST HOPE

THE LAST FLIGHT

THE RETURN HOME

THE MATRIARCH

More Aegis Network

MAX & MILIAN

A CHRISTMAS MIRACLE

SPINNING WHEELS

HOLIDAY'S VACATION

Special Forces Operation Alpha

BURNING DESIRE

BURNING KISS

BURNING SKIES

BURNING LIES

BURNING HEART

BURNING BED

REMEMBER ME ALWAYS

The Brotherhood Protectors

Out of the Wild

ROUGH JUSTICE

ROUGH AROUND THE EDGES

ROUGH RIDE

ROUGH EDGE

ROUGH BEAUTY

The Brotherhood Protectors

The Saving Series

SAVING LOVE

SAVING MAGNOLIA

SAVING LEATHER

Hot Hunks

Cove's Blind Date Blows Up

My Everyday Hero – Ledger

Tempting Tavor

Malachi's Mystic Assignment

Needing Neor

Holiday Romances

A CHRISTMAS GETAWAY

ALASKAN CHRISTMAS

WHISPERS

CHRISTMAS IN THE SAND

Heroes & Heroines on the Field

TAKING A RISK

TEE TIME

A New Dawn